Nell Grant

Easy Live and Quiet Die

This paperback edition published in 2024
© Nell Grant, 2024

Nell Grant has asserted her right under the Copyright, Designs and Patents Act, 1988, to be identified as the Author of this work.

Cover design by Dave Sneddon, Firehouse Design

All rights reserved. No part of this publication may be reproduced or transmitted in any form or by any means, electronic or mechanical, including photocopying, recording, or any information storage or retrieval system, without prior permission in writing from the author.

ISBN: 9798320248998

The author would like to express her sincere thanks to Rod Grant, Stewart Anderson, and my dear friend 'Get Fit with Mags' for all their help and expertise.

Chapter 1

Lockhart watched closely as the flight attendant acted out the safety demonstration to the voice-over playing through the speakers. It was clear that the girl's mind was elsewhere as she robotically clicked the replica seatbelt open, then shut, before pulling on the excess grey fabric to show the tightening process. Lockhart wondered how often she had performed the same routine to a captive audience. The girl then used hand gestures to indicate the exits to the left, right, and the lights down the gangway. Would Lockhart even remember a word of these instructions if the aircraft began nose diving towards the ocean; it was doubtful. The plane crashing was not something that she gave much thought to. The issue that had been gnawing away like a beaver on a log was her decision to be on the flight in the first place.

A fellow stewardess walked past each row of travellers, checking that all seatbelts were firmly fastened and that all electronic devices switched off.

Lost in her own reflective, torturous thoughts, Lockhart physically jumped when a light tap drummed on her shoulder.

'Excuse me, madam, I must ask you to place your bag under the seat in front of you for take-off.'

Until that moment, Lockhart was oblivious to the fact that the holdall was still on her knee, let alone the vicelike grip she had on it.

'Here, let me help you,' the kindly attendant suggested, reaching for the bag in Lockhart's hands. 'Come on, madam, let go. I am just going to push it under the seat for safety. You'll still be able to see it,' she coaxed.

The bag contained nothing of great importance, but to Lockhart, it took the form of an unlikely security blanket. She became embarrassed as the girl unfurled her fingers from the handles. Her holiday companions, either side of her were staring. Lockhart apologised as the stewardess took possession of the bag, tucking it up snugly under the seat.

'Well done,' the flight attendant said, flashing her adorable dimples. 'Now, let's get this seat belt on.'

The girl stood at the end of the aisle for a moment, just smiling. Lockhart presumed it was to make sure she didn't make a grab for her bag the moment she walked away. Whatever her motive was, Lockhart found it somewhat unnerving.

When the stewardess left, presumably to seek out another difficult passenger, Lockhart rested her head back in the seat and shut her eyes. Her spirits felt low, lower than they had ever been. The future for her was a bleak place that she had no desire to visit.

What the hell am I doing on this plane with girls I barely know, heading to a place geared up for young partygoers?

They didn't expect me to take them up on their offer.

So, why did I say yes?

Because I'm nothing but a sad, old fool.

Oh God, what am I going to do in Turkey for two weeks with girls less than half my age?

I just want to go home, put on my pyjamas, and read a book.

Her mind drifted back to the day she entered the staffroom at work, shell-shocked from the blow that had befallen her the previous evening. Functioning solely on autopilot, she had stood in front of the girls, dazed and broken. Her youthful colleagues had been excitedly planning their summer holiday to a resort in Turkey. The room had fallen silent as she walked through the door. The details were sketchy in her memory, but she could recall one of the girls shouting across the room, 'OMG, look at Lockhart!'

'Lockhart! You've buttoned up your coat wrongly. What's happened to your hair?' another one shouted.

Lockhart couldn't remember who said what, only their looks of astonishment.

Someone in the room stood up to guide her into a plastic moulded seat at the table. The pain she was suffering on that day was unbearable, it hurt even to think about it. It was difficult to remember exactly what she had told them, but it was just a one-line explanation of the facts.

If her recollections served her accurately, there had been a long pause after she had shared her news with the girls. Within this period of heavy silence, Tracy, a bubbly girl in her early twenties, took the executive decision to invite her to join them on their holiday. Lockhart couldn't be sure, but there was a vague memory tormenting her where two other girls had flashed a look of anger at Tracy, one of whom may even have given her head a shake. Of course, Lockhart couldn't be sure of any of this. The part that followed was, however, cringingly clear in her mind.

'Yes!' she remembered announcing to the girls, 'I think I will join you on your holiday.'

'Great,' was Tracy's joyless response. The others said nothing.

Why did I do that?

I think it was a distraction from the pain, a quick fix. Maybe my feelings of rejection were soothed by the fact that someone actually wanted me to join them.

That's a joke. Of course, young girls didn't want some old thing of almost fifty tagging along on their holiday. It would be like taking their mother with them. I'm not even a youthful, fun older lady. I'm an annoyance to all who know me, and I hardly know anyone.

Lockhart was seated in the middle of a row of three. Two of her five travelling companions were on either side of her. The girls leaned over her to discuss their plans for when they reached the resort. Lockhart decided to refrain from joining the conversation, partly because she didn't know what they were talking about. That said, she could hazard a good guess at the meanings behind the talk of indulging in a shagathon and downing Jagerbombs, but the rest of the banter back and forth was like another language from a different world. From what she could understand, this was not like any holiday she had ever been on before. In short, she was entering a nightmare that would last two full weeks unless she could get an early flight home.

The girls on either side of her shrieked with laughter. For Lockhart, there was no escape from the talk of lashes, spray tans and nails. Could she go to the toilet again, she wondered. It was only an hour into the journey and she had already been twice, just to get away. Her friends had

pegged her as an old lady, now she'd be seen as an old lady with a weak bladder. She didn't care.
'Excuse me,' she said, squeezing past to get to the aisle.
Without stopping her conversation, Mel moved her legs to one side.
'Thanks.'
Lockhart walked slowly to allow other passengers to enter the queue in front of her. How much time could she waste on this trip? Perhaps she could strike up a conversation with one of the other passengers. That would certainly burn valuable minutes, but she wasn't very adept at speaking to strangers.
'After you,' she told a gentleman who was waiting to leave his seat.
'Oh, it's alright,' he replied. 'Go on.'
'No, please, I insist.'
On her return from the toilet, she noticed that Tracy, who had been on her left, was sitting in her seat. This was a good move. Why hadn't she thought of it before? Now settled in at the window, she could relax and just stare down at the ocean below. Memories preceding the holiday, once again, met her head-on, forcing her to relive them and catalogue them in some kind of chronological order.
The day after it happened, she went to work as usual. In hindsight, this was a mistake as she was barely functioning but desperately fighting to keep a sense of normality before she came unstitched at the seams.
It was her husband, George, who had encouraged her to take a Saturday job at the supermarket. He said it would get her out of the house and give her something to talk

about. Looking back, it was probably a polite way of saying she was boring. Since the day they married, back in their twenties, her life had been mainly committed to being a good housewife. Her thinking had been that if George was the one putting in long hours at the office to give them a better life, then it was up to her to prepare special meals and keep a tidy, comfortable home. The hours of her day had become a routine of shopping, cooking, and cleaning.

Every Sunday night, Lockhart selected recipes for the week ahead. She made a lengthy list of all the ingredients she would need. The food for the evening meal was bought fresh each day from the greengrocer's, the butcher's, the fishmonger and the baker's.

Preparation for the evening meal started at around three-thirty in the afternoon, a little later if she had to pick up George's suits from the dry cleaners or if he had given her a list of items he wanted her to buy for him. On list days, things could be fairly hectic, but she tried to make allowances timewise for these diversions.

After her shopping trips, she liked nothing more than drinking a frothy latte while listening to Classic FM on the radio. Next on her agenda was to lay out the freshly purchased ingredients on the granite worktop, ready to be prepped. It saddened her that over the years George had stopped complimenting her cooking skills. No matter how varied the dishes were, he made no comment on the presentation or flavours that she had worked so hard to get just right. She was a good cook, and she knew it, yet she had yearned for his praise after a meal. In the early days, they sat down in the dining room to eat together, they would often still be there after nine in evening. It was difficult to pinpoint an exact time when things became different between them, but they did. It was small changes to their routine which led to noticeable changes in their relationship. Latterly, George would come in from work, sit in his old leather armchair, and drink whisky until his dinner was brought to him. The television was switched on and remained so until bedtime. If there were any high-profile court cases on the news, chances were that George would be involved. He enjoyed seeing himself giving a statement to the media on the court's front steps. Lockhart knew nothing of the cases that everyone seemed to be talking about. Whenever she asked him about his work at the law firm, he gave a brief answer, explaining that he came home to relax, not to talk shop.

Yes, things had definitely cooled down in their marriage over the years, but George's job had also evolved, demanding more of him. Being promoted to partner in the firm meant his workload had really cranked up several levels, leaving him exhausted. There was no lovemaking anymore; in fact, they rarely went to bed at the same time. She had accepted that they were now fast approaching their fifties so perhaps it was normal for sexual activity to slow down. Sadly, she had no friends in her life to exchange notes on this.

On a Saturday, she worked in the local supermarket which was situated on the main street of her hometown. The day was spent passing shopping items over a machine until it bleeped. It was monotonous but it gave her a chance to speak to people when they came to her checkout. After work, she picked up pizzas for dinner from the takeaway place on the corner. George always appeared happier to see the pizza than he was to see her. When he sat in his leather chair, he oohed and aahed over every cheesy bite. How she yearned for him to make the same sounds of approval over her food. It was irrational to harbour resentment towards a pizza, but she did.

Lockhart began to feel the familiar sensation of pressure within her eardrums; the plane was beginning its descent.

Oh no, I'm about to arrive at my holiday destination.

The passengers queued in the plane gangway as the heavy doors opened. The flight attendants thanked each and every one of the passengers for choosing their airline. Lockhart wished with all of her heart that she hadn't.

After climbing down the moveable, metal staircase, they were herded onto a rickety bus on the runway, which took them to the airport terminal building. The crowds then flowed out toward the conveyor belt, to wait for their luggage. Lockhart's small red suitcase was the first to appear. She snatched it off as it passed, then stepped back from the crowds to wait for her friends. The air in the baggage claim room was oppressively humid. Lockhart could feel sweat forming under her arms. Holding her blouse by the hem, she wafted it back and forth to cool things down a little. Once again, she asked herself, *Why am I here?*

Just over forty minutes later, the last of Lockhart's companions received their second large suitcase from the carousel. The heat in the airport brought out the worst in her as she felt a prickling irritation and resentment towards the girls. Taking the lead, Lockhart led the party towards the main exit, where she hoped the bus would still be waiting to take them to their resort. The girls trundled along after her, wearing high-heeled slingbacks, dragging their heavy cases behind them.

No one would believe that we're all part of the same group, Lockhart thought, as she strolled ahead in her flat, comfortable shoes.

The scowl of disappointment on Kelly-Ann's face did not go unnoticed when she realised that she had to sit next to Lockhart on the bus.

Tough luck, Kelly-Ann, Lockhart thought. *It looks like you are the one stuck with the oldie this time.*

Lockhart stared out the window while Kelly-Ann knelt on her seat, leaning over to the others behind her. Lockhart heard them talking about borrowing each other's clothes and shoes when they went to the clubs.

'I've got a blue, sequinned dress that is completely backless. I think you'd look great in that, Mel,' Tracy offered.

'Sounds gorgeous,' Mel said. 'I've got a dress with me that takes a hell of a lot of balls to wear. It's black mesh!'

'I'm totally up for that if you don't mind lending it to me.'

I wonder if this would be a good time to throw a few of my clothes items in the mix, Lockhart thought with a smirk. *They would go crazy for my M&S flowery blouse and my linen trousers with the drawstring waist.*

Shutting out the discussion of bra tops and six-inch wedges, Lockhart stared out of the bus window at the passing dry landscape. She knew she had no right to be irritated by the girls' unsophisticated tastes or shallow conversation. They were young, without a care in the world. The grown up life with all of its trials would come to them soon enough. She was annoyed with herself for thinking she could be a part of this youthful venture and actually fit in. The truth was that it was the closest she had ever felt to having her very own cloak of invisibility. They couldn't possibly regret inviting her because they didn't even notice that she was there. She had been neither spoken to nor looked at since arriving at the airport. They had completely forgotten she existed, and, on this occasion, she was glad. Invisibility beat pretending to be young any day.

What would I have been doing when I was the same age as the girls?

Hazarding a guess that the girls were all in their early twenties, she would have been on her honeymoon. The images she managed to conjure up of that time were sharp. She was sitting laughing with George in the outdoor restaurant of their small hotel in Italy. After dinner, they drank champagne whilst staring out at the distant lights across Lake Garda. The memory brought with it the real, physical pain of loss. It had been such a wonderful time, full of new love where they could not keep their hands off each other. George had made her laugh every day with his sarcastic humour and witty observations of people. He mimicked everyone with exaggerated voices and mannerisms. He was hilarious.

She remembered lying awake, just leaning her head on her hand, staring at him sleeping.

Thinking back to such a happy time was not helpful for her, especially when she was embarking on this dreaded trip with young strangers. Tears of regret rolled down her cheeks onto her lap.

Please, God, let this be over soon. Fourteen days and nights, I can't do it. I just can't do it.

The bus turned into a remote village. The driver took them to the end of the long straight road, lined with bars and restaurants, before grinding to a halt outside several blocks of newly built apartments. The driver shouted the resort's name, and Tracy stopped talking long enough to listen.

'That's us!'

The girls clip-clopped off the bus, out into the intense Turkish heat whilst the driver reached into the luggage area to find their many suitcases. The girls dragged their luggage across the dry dirt ground that had still to be cultivated for tourists. Kelly-Ann caught her heel on an embedded rock, falling face down on the ground. Her friends laughed. Lockhart came to the rescue, helping her to her feet before relieving her of one of her suitcases.

'I could have broken my ruddy neck there,' she shouted at the hysterical females standing around her watching.

'I'll drag this case for you if you think you can manage the other one,' Lockhart offered.

Kelly-Ann limped on her way with only one suitcase to worry about. She appeared to have accepted Lockhart's offer although she said nothing to confirm it.

I'm starting to believe that I really don't exist. Maybe I died or something. Can they see me? Carrying her lightweight case in one hand, she dragged the dead weight of Kelly-Ann's luggage behind her.

Chapter 2

The five girls and Lockhart were sharing two rooms. The best thing Lockhart could say about the basic accommodation was that it appeared to be clean. She took the bed that remained after her new roommates, Valerie and Mel, had chosen theirs. Unpacking her beautifully ironed summer clothes, she arranged them in the drawers beside her bed. No matter the outcome of the holiday, she had decided that she would make the best of a very bad situation. She watched as the girls dragged out various dresses from their cases to show one another. Within a matter of minutes, the floor of the room was strewn with clothes, shoes and toiletries.

For Lockhart, this was a glimpse of things to come. A gnawing feeling of dread scraped away at her insides.

Help me, someone, I can't do this. I want to go home.

A raised voice from the room next door shouted, 'Hey! Are you guys coming through or what? Bring that see-through dress you were talking about.'

Mel reached into the side compartment of her suitcase, pulling out an object wrapped in a pillowcase. Unwinding the brushed cotton fabric used for protection, she revealed a bottle of vodka. Holding it up in the air, she shouted, 'Here's a little something to get us in the party mood!'

Mel and Valerie left the trashed room as was and headed through to see their friends. As Valerie reached the door, she looked back to say, 'Lockhart, do you want to come through?'

Lockhart really appreciated the gesture but smiled, shaking her head. Happy to be left out of the party, it suddenly dawned on her that she couldn't be invisible after all.

The basic but clean room fell silent. Only the screeching whoops from the girls next door could be heard. Lockhart had never felt so old and alone.

Is this all the future holds for me? Why do I feel like the expression 'there's no fool like an old fool' applies perfectly to me?

She quickly wiped the tears from her eyes when she saw Valerie come running into the room to grab her sunglasses.

Valerie explained that they were going out to explore with a view to having a few drinks. 'You are more than welcome to come,' she told her.

Lockhart knew that phrase only too well. It really meant, 'You are not wanted, but I am going to be a nice person and invite you, but hopefully, you will pick up the real message and not come.'

Lockhart said no to the invite but told her it had been nice of her to ask.

I think I followed the protocol very well there, Lockhart congratulated herself. *Valerie will feel like a good person without having to be lumbered with the dead wood on the trip.*

In the last few years with George, he regularly went out to evening events with his law firm, or to functions where he had been invited to speak on legal matters. She would be told not to prepare a meal that evening because he was going out. He would request his dinner suit to be pressed and white shirt to be ironed. Whether it was guilt or a sense of always having to do the right thing, he would then throw in, as he was leaving the room, 'You are more than welcome to come.'

She never did.

The laughter from the girls faded away as they left the building. Lockhart was completely alone. Not quite knowing whether to laugh or cry, a thought entered her head.

If only George could see me now. He'd be so jealous!

This thought made her smile and left her wondering if, subconsciously, that had been her motivation for booking the holiday. Did she want George to think she was independent and adventurous? Who knows what her thinking had been back then. She was here now. That was the problem.

Giving herself a shake, she decided to search for her holiday representative. Maybe there was a flight home within the next day or two. The idea of it really excited her, and she quickened her step.

Would the girls even notice I was gone? she wondered. *Of course, they would. They would be raising the flags, popping the bubbly, and singing at the top of their voices, ding dong, the witch is dead, which old witch? The Lockhart witch.*

Feeling hopeful, she ventured out of the apartment into the heat of the outdoors to search for a travel agent or rep. The walk to the shops was not long, but the stifling humidity weighed heavily on Lockhart's shoulders. Her feet began to resemble a pig's trotters as they swelled within her sandals. Looking at the unimaginative buildings around her, she suspected that the town had been newly built for the sole purpose of accommodating holidaymakers. A picture of a green-clad leprechaun smiled at her from the Irish bar across the street whilst loud music pulsated out the door of a cocktail bar as she passed. Behind the row of souvenir shops and restaurants, she could see apartment blocks identical to the one she was staying in, only they were still in various stages of construction. She had been informed that the resort had a beach, but it was certainly not visible from where she stood. The town was in no way picturesque, but it didn't have to be, as its short-term residents came to sleep all day and party all night. In the distance, she saw an outdoor bar with tables and chairs arranged strategically in the shade.

If I stop there for a latte, I can slip off these damnable sandals for a while. That's if I can dislodge them from my puffy flesh.

The waiter almost ran over to serve her before she had even sat down. A look of disappointment showed through his smile when he discovered that she only wanted coffee. Lockhart chose a table near the pavement.

People-watching had always made her feel less conspicuous when she sat anywhere alone. Perhaps she did it in order to create the illusion of sitting and waiting patiently for a friend to arrive.

The hot frothy coffee was set down on the table before her, with an offer from the waiter to call if she needed anything else. Thanking him, she agreed that she would do just that. Lifting the spoon from the saucer, she formed an ornate L for Lockhart on top of the froth. A memory flitted through her mind of the early days when she would write a G for George on her coffees. Thoughts of the last holiday they had taken together returned to her. They had gone to Madeira, to stay in a villa which stood in an elevated position overlooking the whole panoramic view of Funchal Town. They had spent their days visiting the tourist attractions and enjoying ice cream with strawberries in the main square. It had been such fun riding in a cable car to the top of the mountain before using the traditional method of coming down the hill in a Madeiran basket. The evenings had been romantic, walking hand in hand along the promenade after dinner. On one occasion, she had taken out a pack of playing cards from her handbag whilst they sat at a table with drinks in a pavement café. They hadn't played cards in years, so she thought it might be an entertaining pursuit for them on holiday when they had all the time in the world. Using the change in their pockets, they had gambled in games of pontoon and gin rummy. George had insulted her, pretending to be angry when she cleaned him out of coins. It had been just like old times. Lockhart willed it not to end. As far as Lockhart was concerned, the sense of loving closeness between them was as strong, if not stronger, than ever.

The memory that followed made her sit upright, wincing. She clutched her stomach, attempting to relieve the physical pain she was experiencing. They had arrived back home sunned and refreshed. George had carried their suitcases up the front steps to the door. Once inside the hallway, she turned around to look at him, ready to thank him for a wonderful, unforgettable time.

He spoke before she could say the words. 'Well, at least we know that we won't go back there again. That holiday really dragged. If we ever go away again, we need somewhere that can offer more things to do. I thought it would never end.'

A whack in the face from a sledgehammer would have hurt her less. She couldn't reply. Madeira, and their time together there, were never mentioned again. It was their final holiday together.

Lockhart drained the last of her coffee and left the outdoor bar. Her thoughts had pulled her down into a dark place. Now, she needed a distraction to enable her to climb back out.

Further down the dusty road, she carried on with her quest to find a way out of the nightmare she had foolishly put herself in. Two shops down, she spotted an open-fronted unit that appeared to have an air of travel agency about it.

Could my ticket home be waiting for me right now? Imagine if there were a flight tonight, and I didn't need to go back to that dreadful apartment. I would drop everything, leave my clothes, and go to the airport this very minute. Hold on, Lockhart, she warned herself, *you are building up your hopes, setting yourself up for disappointment.*

Entering the doorless office space, she saw only one rep sitting at a desk with a phone and computer at her disposal. Her pleasant face lifted into a smile as Lockhart walked towards her. The oversized bow holding her blonde hair back was visible in the mirror on the wall behind her. She gestured with her hand, instructing Lockhart to sit in the seat across from her.

'Hello, my name's Judy Bailey. How can I help you today?'

'I was hoping to get an early flight home as soon as possible. Ideally today. I will take any airport in Scotland, or England for that matter.'

She shook her head doubtfully, dropping her brow. 'Well, as I said, I'm Judy Bailey, and I will do everything in my power to help you, but I am making no promises.'

Judy Bailey pressed a speed dial button on her phone, which began to ring immediately. Whilst waiting for the caller to pick up, she clicked away frantically on the buttons of her computer with her lacquered nails. A woman answered the phone, quoting the company she worked for, but Lockhart could not quite make out the name.

'Hello, Judy Bailey here. I have a customer here who is looking for a flight...'

Lockhart, being Scottish, could not pinpoint the region of England that Judy Bailey came from. However, she marvelled at the number of times she said her own name and how she slackened her jaw, showing her tongue at the end of Bailey.

'No... no... I thought not, but if anything turns up, just call back on this number and ask for Judy Bailey.'

She won't need to ask for Judy Bailey because Judy Bailey is the only one working here.

Looking around the small office, there were no other desks, chairs, or sales assistants.

The clicking on the computer keys continued, as did the calls on the landline. It was becoming more and more apparent that not even the remarkable Judy Bailey could help her now. She was going to be stuck there for a two-week duration.

When the search was exhausted, Lockhart rose from her seat despondently.

'I'm sorry,' Judy Bailey told her. 'Were you returning home for an emergency?'

'No, I made a mistake booking this holiday on impulse with girls half my age in a resort that only comes alive when I'm ready for bed.'

'I see,' Judy said, with a smile that told Lockhart she had an ace up her short-sleeved uniform blouse. 'Why don't you leave the girls and the resort behind? We'll get you booked into the five-star hotel and spa outside of town. It's called The Blue Lagoon. I think it is far more suited to your needs.'

Judy Bailey, you might be on to something, Lockhart thought to herself, sitting back down in her seat.

'Yes, I think that would be great. Thank you.'

Judy's demeanour showed signs of excitement as she dialled The Blue Lagoon's number.

'Hello, Judy Bailey here...'

Judy Bailey came up trumps, organising a room in The Blue Lagoon five-star hotel and spa for two weeks commencing that very day. She gave Lockhart the phone number of a local taxi firm and told her to have a wonderful time.

Lockhart experienced a tiny flutter from the wings of exhilaration within her stomach. The flight home was still two weeks away, but she had bought herself a ticket to freedom meantime. She thanked Judy Bailey very much for all her hard work and headed to the open front of the shop, which would lead her back onto the street.

As she walked away, Judy shouted after her, 'When you get to the hotel, just say Judy Bailey sent you.'

Leaving the comfort of the air-conditioned office, Lockhart returned once again into the baking heat.

Okay, she analysed, *I would rather be going home, but a five-star hotel and spa certainly takes the sting out of the situation. Who knows, I might even have a nice time.*

She made her way back along the street in the direction of the apartment building that she would no longer be staying in.

No more drunk girls, no more mess on the floor, no more sharing a bathroom, no more being ignored, and no more single beds in basic accommodation.

Fortunately, the girls had not returned from their exploration trip to the local bars. Lockhart removed her folded clothes from the chest of drawers and packed them back into her suitcase. After rummaging around for some time, she finally found an old shopping list and a pen at the bottom of her bag. Turning the list over to the blank side, she wrote:

Dear Girls,

I have checked into a hotel nearby which is more suited to oldies like me. I am sorry that I wasn't good company for you. I think I made a mistake coming. Thank you for inviting me, as it made me feel wanted.

Have a wonderful time and enjoy the shagathons and Jagerbombs, although if I am being honest, I don't really know what they are exactly!

Have a wonderful holiday

See you soon.

L xxxx

P.S. Have a drink on me.

With the note, she left 100 euros.

The phone number for the taxicab was written on a piece of paper which she had squirrelled into the pocket of her M&S linen trousers. Using her mobile phone, she dialled the number asking for a taxi as soon as possible to The Blue Lagoon. After a quick check that she had everything, she grabbed her case and left, shutting the door behind her. A sense of great relief washed over her knowing that this part of the doomed holiday was over.

Chapter 3

The taxi drove clear of the town, which made Lockhart happy. The resort had made her feel like an ageing misfit, so the further away she moved, the better. The driver took her along a main thoroughfare before

slowing down to turn onto a private road. Seeing from the cab window the manicured lawns around them, Lockhart realised they were now on the hotel's driveway. The narrow, winding road climbed higher and higher. From the back window of the taxi, she saw the full panoramic view of the diamond-encrusted ocean.
Ah, she thought, *so we really were near the sea.*
The taxi ascended until it reached a modern glass-fronted building with marble steps leading to the foyer. A bellboy stood at the front door with his legs astride, his arms folded behind his back. He waited eagerly to greet all the guests. With his white gloved hands, he opened the car door for Lockhart. He then collected her small red suitcase from the boot, which the driver had already opened. Indicating for her to follow him, he led her into the hotel's cool, air-conditioned reception area. Standing at the check-in desk, she looked around at the marbled floors, chandeliers, and exotic flower displays.
Now, this is much more like it.
Lockhart relished her decision to switch accommodations.
The receptionist took her details and gave her all the information she needed to know about the hotel. Lockhart booked herself a table in the restaurant for every evening at 7pm with, ideally, a sea view. The receptionist gave her some literature about the hotel and the services available. She then nodded to one of the smartly dressed porters to show her to her room.

The porter opened the bedroom door with the key card and led her in. Slipping five euros into his hand, she thanked him for his help. This was something she had never done before but she had witnessed George doing so on many occasions. *Maybe I should have made it 10 euros due to inflation.*

When he left, she visually wallowed in the sumptuous surroundings. Her eyes were drawn to the glass door leading out to the balcony. She threw off her sandals, then ran to unlock it, and, oh joy, it had the most incredible sea view. Sitting down on one of the wicker patio seats provided, she stared out across the mesmerising, slow pulse of the ocean, inhaling the warm Turkish air. For the first time since it all happened, she believed that things would be okay for her.

Wounds heal, hearts mend, and pain lessens. Now, who once said that? No one. I think I just made it up. Let's hope it comes true.

When only a fan of orange rays remained where the sun had once been, Lockhart left her viewing point on the balcony and headed to the comfort of her room. Although she had not eaten all day, she experienced no feelings of hunger. The table in the dining room had been booked for seven o'clock, but it was way past that time now. She couldn't quite believe how long she had sat, staring out across the sea.

I'm sure I read that the ocean can be instrumental in the healing process. I don't think I made that up.

The leather-bound book on the dresser contained a menu for room service. It was a good idea to eat something, she decided, lifting the phone to call reception. After offering an apology for not honouring her table booking, she asked for sandwiches and fruit to be brought up to her room.

Whilst she lounged on the king-sized bed with its overstuffed pillows, she flicked through the leaflets that the receptionist had presented her with on arrival. Sea Salt Spa was the heading on the first brochure she looked at. The cover showed a woman lying face down on a massage table with smooth black rocks lying on her bare back. The rocks weren't quite Lockhart's thing, but she examined the list of other available treatments. When she had decided exactly what she was looking for, she called the number given and arranged a massage for the following morning.

Next, she ran a deep, hot bubble bath using the products supplied by the hotel. As she rummaged in her suitcase for her pyjamas, she spotted the glass door of the minibar. From the well-stocked contents, she selected a small bottle of Moet champagne.

The bath water was almost at the rim on the top of bath, turning the place into a steam room. Lockhart searched through the basket of toiletries on offer. A shower cap was not an item that she used at home, but hey, it was there, and it was free, so she pulled it on over her brown wavy hair. The hotel slippers and white towelling robe were laid on the floor, and the glass of Moet was placed on the side of the bath. She removed the crumpled clothes that she had travelled in before climbing into the deep, relaxing water.

This is wonderful.

Life, up to now, had never been about spoiling herself.

*

After a night of restful sleep, she awoke with a stretch. She found herself in the middle of the large bed with the pillows tucked around her. Her first thought was of the massage she had booked for herself. Her second thought was of George.

There now, I must be getting better because George has always been the first thought that enters my head.

A growl came from her stomach as she glanced at the almost untouched food on the tray that she had ordered from room service.

It's been a long time since I have felt hunger pangs.

Wearing her navy linen trousers with a white top, she ran her fingers through her hair before heading downstairs for the buffet breakfast.

The smell of bacon, sausage and sweet waffles met Lockhart in the foyer before she entered the dining room. The hotel guests were helping themselves to the extensive selection of food on display which was geared towards suiting all tastes. Plumping for the chopped-up, ripe melon and some scrambled egg, she carried her breakfast outside to a table directly in the morning sun. Leaving her food behind, she returned to the dining room for Columbian ground coffee and a glass of freshly squeezed orange juice. The view was incredible, and Lockhart just had to position herself in front of it. With the heat of the sun on her face, a gentle breeze from the ocean brushed her cheeks. Her face was upward and her eyes were shut as she ate everything on her plate.

Life is filled with surprises, good and bad. Just when I thought I couldn't get any lower, life reached out a hand to pull me up.

Never could she have predicted that she would be sitting alone in a hotel in Turkey. At that present moment in time, there was nowhere she would rather have been.

When she had finished breakfast, she entered the lift, pressing the button for the top floor. The overwhelming smell of the spa's fragrances hung heavily in the air before the lift door opened. Lockhart strolled into the spacious salon with its calming music playing in the background. Scented candles had been placed on glass shelves throughout the open area. Several tunic-clad beauticians stood smiling, ready to greet her.

A receptionist took her name and details and then led her through to the massage room. Lockhart was rather taken aback when she saw an attractive male masseur standing by the table. For a fleeting moment, awkwardness took over, and she dearly wished she had put her make-up on. He welcomed her in, then left the room, giving her some privacy to undress. Scrambling up on the table, she lay on her stomach, placing her face through the hole. Feeling around behind her, she reached for the sheet to pull over her lower half. She placed her hands by her sides, then moved them to above her head. Lying almost naked on a table, waiting for a young man to come in, was a new experience for her, and it was making her feel embarrassed. With one hand at her side, she decided to put the other above her head. She switched them around at the last minute, then switched them back.

All she could see through the hole in the table was a small area of polished floor. Her heart began to thud when she heard the man entering the room. He said nothing as he worked skilfully on her back and shoulders. Slowly and deliberately, he gouged his thumbs roughly into the taut areas in her body. It felt good. Just as it became almost painful, he stopped. Then ever so gently, he ran his fingertips over the whole area of her back. Involuntary shivers crawled down her spine. It felt like a breath blowing on her naked flesh. Using only the tips of his fingers, he brushed gently along her inner arms, then up to her shoulders. He then lingered his fingers around her lower back in a circular motion, laying the palms of his hands flat on the top of her buttock area. His hands remained in that area, gently squeezing and kneading at her flesh, moving further and further under the modesty sheet. After a period of tender treatment, he returned to the almost unbearable roughness of his thumbs and fingers.

Glancing furtively sideways, she caught sight of his strong, muscular, brown hands. This was the most unexpected experience for her, and she felt quite overcome by it all. Thinking back, she had not felt the touch of a man in years, not even her husband's.

Her breathing was becoming heavier, but there was not a damned thing she could do about it. All she could hope was that the masseur did not notice that her body was trembling. The climax of the treatment was rounded off with a massage to her scalp. Suddenly, he grabbed her hair back, tightening his grip for a fraction of a second in a dominant manner. It was unexpected and incredibly erotic, and it only lasted for seconds.

When the session came to an end, Lockhart thanked the young man, avoiding his gaze. Then, walking to the lift with her unsteady legs, she couldn't help but feel that she resembled a lame woman walking for the first time.

I hope no one's watching me. I'm afraid my legs are going to buckle.

The incredible massage experience made her realise how dried up and closed off she had become. The memory of those skilled hands pounding on her flesh and the tightened tug of her hair stayed with her for the rest of the day. She relived the experience over and over in her mind.

Headline: Middle-aged, single lady cannot get over being touched by a stranger!

I am so incredibly sad.

Lockhart spent the remainder of her day under a sun umbrella by the pool. Thoughts of her experience in the spa flitted through her thoughts. The good-looking young man, his strong hands, his gentle, then rough technique; it was thrilling.

By ten to seven, she was showered, changed and heading down the marble stairs to the dining room. An ageing but elegant waitress led her to the window. The woman drew out Lockhart's chair from the table, instructing her to sit down. She then skilfully flicked the cloth napkin and laid it on her knee.

'What would madam like to drink tonight?' the waitress enquired.

'I'll have a glass of red wine, please.'

'May I recommend a wine made from locally grown grapes?'

Lockhart liked that idea. 'Yes, that would be lovely.'

'May I also suggest that you order a bottle, especially if you fancy having a drink on the terrace after dinner?'

What a saleswoman.

'Yes, that sounds perfect.'

The waitress then bowed, giving an almost unnoticeable click of her heels. Lockhart smiled at the woman's gesture after she left, as it seemed to say, '*Excellent decision.*'

Lockhart pictured the scene.

The manager lines up the staff before the restaurant opens. He warns them that they have an overabundance of wine made from locally grown grapes. Whatever you do, get rid of that bloody wine. Talk them into buying the whole damned bottle!

The wine arrived at her table, and the waitress asked if she would like to taste it first.

'No, just fill it right up,' Lockhart told her.

The woman did as she was told, then left.

Lifting the glass to her lips, Lockhart sipped on the rich, garnet wine.

What a pleasant surprise. This is wonderful.

Lockhart took several more gulps.

The power of the alcohol alleviated any feeling of awkwardness she had been feeling about eating alone. The meal was excellent, the service was perfect. When she finished, she put her knife and fork on the plate and dabbed her mouth with the napkin.

Now I will do exactly as the waitress suggested and finish my wine on the terrace.

The dining room was almost full by now, but Lockhart felt no sense of embarrassment walking past the other guests with her glass in one hand and bottle in the other.

On the terrace, Lockhart chose a table that was set far from the hotel. Placing the wine and her glass down, she sat in a seat that maximised the ocean setting with its fading pink light. This was going to be a holiday where she would please herself, answering to no one.

George crept into her mind like an unwelcome visitor. Hurtful memories began to torture her. She could not allow this to happen. Cursing the intrusive thoughts, she vowed to let nothing spoil her two weeks in Turkey.

How can I banish that man from my head? He doesn't deserve a place here on the terrace with me.

Tears stung her eyes.

Her sad reverie was broken into by a voice from behind.

'Hello.'

She turned around, startled, 'Hello.'

'Are you on holiday alone?'

'Well, I didn't start out that way, but yes, I am now.'

'Do you mind if I join you for a while?'

Something about him was familiar. 'Have we met?' she asked.

'Wow, you have a short memory. Yes, I gave you a massage earlier today,' he said, laughing.

At this point, she was grateful for the dim, pinkish evening light as her face, ears, and neck turned burning hot.

'Oh yes,' she said, laughing nervously. 'I didn't recognise you without your white tunic on and the relaxing background music!'

This comment made him laugh, which pleased her. She noticed that he had a great smile, which turned his face handsome. He asked her what her name was, and she replied, 'Lockhart.'

He laughed again, saying that it was a strange but pretty name. 'I won't forget that name.'

'And you are?' she asked, pretending to be a bit insulted.

'Aslan.'

It was her turn to laugh. 'Do you know that Aslan is a character in a famous book, and it is a lion?'

'Do you know you are about the 199th person to tell me that?'

She wished that she hadn't made that comment. She wanted to be witty and clever, not predictable.

Aslan sat down in the seat opposite her. Lockhart caught the eye of a passing waiter, asking him to bring another wine glass. When the waiter returned, she poured two glasses of wine from the heavily depleted bottle.

'Cheers, he said, raising the glass in the air. 'Here's to an unforgettable holiday for you.'

'I'll drink to that.'

His company was easy, which gave her confidence to be herself. He furthered everything she said as though it were the most interesting topic he had ever heard. They had a similar humour, and oh how he laughed when she told him about how her holiday began. The compliments he paid her were like a soothing balm to her critically wounded ego. Never had she connected in such a way with another human being. On several occasions, she caught herself staring at his muscle hugging white shirt which highlighted his golden-brown tan. *He is sexy*, she decided. *I've only ever seen sexy men in the movies, never in real life.*

The hour was very late, the hotel bar had closed. Lockhart reluctantly made the first move to end the evening. Aslan took hold of her wrist, saying, 'I have a special birthday tomorrow. Would you like to go somewhere with me to celebrate?'

'Oh, I also have a big birthday coming up in a couple of weeks. What's *your* big birthday?' she asked, enjoying the shared coincidence, which seemed to give them even more in common.

'I will be thirty,' he said.

All the 'coincidence' enthusiasm melted away when she heard this. What was she thinking, of course he was just a young man. Did she really think he was going to turn around and say that he was also fifty? *There's no fool like an old fool*, she thought for the second time on the holiday.

'And you?' he probed.

'Fifty.' The reply came as an apology. How could she have misread this situation so badly?

'Fifty,' he repeated with a laugh. 'Man, you look great for fifty!' He looked her up and down approvingly. 'I would never have imagined that you were fifty.'

She gobbled up the compliment hungrily but could not shake off the feeling that she had made a bit of a fool of herself… again.

'So, what time will I pick you up tomorrow?' he asked in a manner that meant nothing had changed.

'Is eleven too early?' she replied, unable to let go of a good thing.

'Eleven is fine. I will wait here for you.'

Chapter 4

The elevator delivered Lockhart up to the floor where her room was situated. Her stomach was knotted with excitement yet tinged with dread. The undistracted attention Aslan had shown her made her feel so visible. This feeling was addictive, the very idea of another fix was more than she could resist.

Am I really going out on a date with a gorgeous young man of thirty?

She shook her head in disbelief.

Maybe not. He may see me as a mother-type figure. The problem is though, I am not feeling motherly towards him. I mustn't get carried away with this. I am inexperienced and vulnerable and the last thing I want is to get hurt again. Aslan and I are just friends, I mustn't forget that, we are just friends.

A hideous thought occurred to her as she exited the elevator. This realisation made her run along the corridor to her room. Once inside, she knelt down at the chest of drawers and began dragging out every item of clothing she possessed.

Why did I bring all of these dated linen trousers and flowery blouses? What the hell was I thinking?

This was one time that she did not want to look like an old frump. Throwing herself onto the bed, she reached for the phone to call reception.

'Hi, could you tell me if there is a market nearby and when it opens in the morning?'

She listened to the response.

'Great, could you arrange a taxi to pick me up at eight tomorrow morning?'

*

Aslan stood on the terrace, talking to another member of staff. His colleague wondered why he was at the hotel on his day off. When Aslan explained that he was taking a lady out for the day because he was celebrating his special birthday, his workmate laughed heartily.

Aslan walked away.

It was a hot, humid morning, and Aslan could feel himself perspiring through his shirt while he waited outside the hotel. Checking his watch, he saw that it was seven minutes past eleven; she was late. This was surprising to him; women didn't often keep him waiting. He had planned a great day for them, and he was really looking forward to it. When Lockhart had turned up for a massage the previous day, he had been instantly attracted to her. She was exactly his type. Spending the evening on the terrace talking and laughing with her had really sealed the deal for him

Maybe she has decided against the trip?

Thinking back, he realised she had seemed quite shocked by their age difference.

I hope she hasn't changed her mind. It's not my fault that I'm young.

As he stood wrestling with his doubts, there was a tap on his shoulder. With a start, he turned around to see Lockhart smiling at him. She seemed so different, younger. He unashamedly admired her up and down in her vibrant red, peasant-style dress, with her hair loosely over her shoulders.

He really liked what he saw.

*

Lockhart stood for a moment enjoying Aslan's reaction. It was exactly what she had been hoping for. As he stepped forward to kiss her cheek, she was pleasantly overcome by the smell of fresh sweat mixed with the herbal aroma of his shiny, black hair.
I could eat this man alive.
Aslan led her by the hand to the car park. On the hotel steps, his work colleagues stood laughing, shouting comments to him in Turkish. Lockhart noticed that Aslan looked embarrassed. She presumed they were mocking him for taking an older lady out for the day. Ignoring the heckles, she could feel him quicken his pace to the end of the row of parked cars. To her surprise, he stopped when he approached the motorbike, which rested on its stand. From the back of the bike, he took the two helmets, handing one over to her. At this point, Lockhart realised that the dress did not seem like such a good idea. Mixed emotions stirred within her as she stared at the two wheeled vehicle. Yes, she couldn't deny that she felt a fleeting thrill at the prospect of having something large and powerful between her legs. But this initial thrill was soon doused by the sheer terror she felt about mounting the thing. Taking a deep breath, she told herself to be strong, that this was a once-in-a-lifetime opportunity. Pulling the helmet over her head, she climbed on the back, hitching her dress up as she went. She screwed her eyes tight shut, clung like a limpet to a rock and waited for the bike to roar into action beneath her.

They drove at full speed along the coastal road. The wind smelt of the hot, earthy ground as it blew relentlessly in her face and hair. It was truly invigorating.

Images of an old James Dean movie came to her mind while she held tightly around Aslan's waist. Hysterical giggling rose up in her throat, but she did her best to stifle it.

Hey, Lockhart. You weren't expecting this on your trip to Turkey, were you? she asked herself with a smile.

The volume of noise from the gears shifting was most welcome to drown out the uncontrollable nervous laughter that was now escaping from her throat.

Calm down. This gorgeous young man will think you're deranged.

After passing the most wonderful scenery by the sea, they arrived at a quaint village. Seeing a parking space outside a restaurant, Aslan veered the bike in and switched off the engine. The silence was deafening. Several locals stared at the arrival of the noisy visitors. Lockhart swung her leg awkwardly over the motorbike in an effort to dismount. Her legs were positively bowed when she tried to walk.

Oh, my joints have completely seized up. I don't want him to be reminded of my age.

Pretending to tighten the strap on her sandal, she tarried behind Aslan to hide her painful limp.

Aslan walked ahead to arrange a table in the somewhat empty restaurant. The menu was limited, but there was enough on it that suited their needs.

The waiter took an order for ice cream, then coffee, as he cleared the plates and cutlery from the rather rustic-looking table.

'Was that your first time on a motorbike?' Aslan asked her while they waited for dessert.

'Yes,' she laughed. 'How could you tell?'

'Oh, nothing obvious, just the fact that you crushed my vital organs the whole way here.'

She laughed loudly at this comment.

'I am so sorry. I wasn't scared or anything. I was just being affectionate.'

'Yes, that's what I thought,' he said, smiling coyly.

'Oh, I almost forgot,' she told him, reaching into her handbag. 'I have a little thing for your birthday.'

She handed him a small suede pouch gathered at the top by a drawstring.

Aslan appeared surprised, shocked even, staring for a moment before he took it.

'Thank you so, so much.'

'You haven't opened it yet. You may hate it.'

'No, I would never hate anything that you gave me. I can't believe that you did this for me.'

Earlier that morning, when she had bought her red dress from the market, she passed a stall selling high-quality silver jewellery. Looking at the wonderful selection of items for sale, she was reminded that George would never even wear a wedding ring. He despised jewellery on men. Unsure of Aslan's taste, she had decided to pick something that she would like to see him wearing. George's hatred of men wearing any kind of decoration was perhaps her inspiration for the purchase.

Pulling open the drawstring top, Aslan tipped the contents into the palm of his hand. It was a chunky silver bracelet. It was obvious from his face that he loved it.

Winding it around his wrist, he reached out his arm towards her.

'Please, may you fasten this on?'

Using her thumb to pull back the silver clip, she hooked it into the silver link.

'It looks good on you,' she told him. 'I knew it would.'

He took her hand in his, bringing it up to his mouth. Slowly he lingered a moist kiss on her palm. The warmth of his breath could be felt on her wrist. As he did this, he looked into her eyes.

'Thank you,' he whispered.

His touch thrilled Lockhart. This simple hand-kissing act was, for her, a highly erotic experience which inspired a burning sensation in several parts of her previously dormant body. It would be honest to say that George had never made her feel like that, even in their early days together. Aslan didn't simply light her fire; he ignited a raging inferno that was already spreading out of control.

Several miles along the coastal road, Aslan indicated before turning left onto a tree-lined, single-track road.

Where is he taking me? What if he is a serial killer that kidnaps young women... and old women? No one knows I'm here. Who will ever find my body? I can't believe how gullible I've been, coming away with a stranger in a foreign country and allowing him to take me down an isolated...'

Her thoughts were interrupted as the bike came to a halt. In front of them stood a large stone house. Lockhart was looking up at the windows for signs of life when the front door was opened by a stout, ruddy-faced gentleman. Some Turkish greetings were exchanged before a ritual of man hugs and back patting took place. The man looked behind Aslan to see Lockhart standing there awkwardly. Great laughter roared from him as he waved his finger at Aslan.

Lockhart's face reddened with embarrassment. Feeling deeply hurt by the stranger's reaction to her, she wondered why he found her so amusing.

'Lockhart, this is my uncle, Demir.' He laid his hand on Lockhart's back, edging her forward. 'Demir, this is my friend, Lockhart.'

The two shook hands. Again, Demir laughed. Lockhart eyes began to sting. She felt old and unattractive.

Demir spoke to Aslan in Turkish, then turned to Lockhart, saying, 'It is good to meet with you. This is my... eh, Aslan how you say in English?' he asked, gesturing with two hands at the property behind him and grapes growing around him.

Aslan turned to Lockhart, 'This is my uncle's vineyard.'

'Yes,' Demir took over. 'This is my vineyard. Come, I show you around.'

Demir gave them a tour of the endless rows of vines heavily laden with grapes.

'Always, I am asking Aslan to come work for me, but he say no every time.'

Lockhart smiled, 'Do you not fancy working in the wine business?' she asked Aslan.

'Oh no, I have big plans for myself in the future. I would eventually like to study Physiotherapy, perhaps even open my own business.'

Demir threw his hands up in dismissal, 'Sachmalik!'

'It is not nonsense.' Aslan walked on ahead to avoid any disrespectful confrontation.

After the tour of the vines, Demir led them to the cellar, where he uncorked several bottles for them to sample. With the help of Aslan's excellent English language skills, he gave Lockhart a full explanation of the body and flavours of each wine.

It was not long before Lockhart realised that Demir was, in fact, a warm, humorous person. Despite the earlier introduction, she conceded that she really liked him

Feeling slightly unsteady on her feet from the overindulgent wine-tasting session, Lockhart followed the men to the main house, tripping twice on the uneven flagstones adorning the floors in the hallway. Demir pulled a chair out from a solid wooden table, instructing Lockhart to sit.

They stayed for a few hours, and although much of the conversation between the men was in Turkish, she could tell that their relationship was good. Hearing Aslan talk in his mother tongue was pleasing to her ears. She also enjoyed watching him tell a story using his beautiful, brown, strong hands. His laugh thrilled her, and she found herself joining in the hilarity of the jokes without understanding a word. When Aslan rose from the table, she followed the cue, standing up and straightening the skirt of her dress.

Demir walked them outside to where the motorbike was parked. Again, he kissed Lockhart on both cheeks.

'You are nice lady, Lockhart,' he said, before turning to Aslan to give him a short but stern speech in their own language.

Aslan replied, but not in English. He glanced over furtively at Lockhart.

The power of the bike engine roared up through Lockhart's body. Aslan threw his arm in the air, waving goodbye behind him to his dear old Uncle Demir before heading off along the road which was flanked by vines growing on either side.

On the open road, Aslan accelerated the bike to full throttle. The speed was terrifying for Lockhart. 'Aslan, slow down. Please slow down!' she shouted, but the wind carried her voice in the opposite direction.

Her grip tightened around his waist; her fingers locked together for extra security.

I'm going to die. What will George think when he hears that I died on the back of a young man's motorbike in Turkey? Would he be jealous? Would he cry? Probably not.

To her great relief, Aslan slowed to a stop outside an open market.

Outstretching his hand, he helped her off the bike, saying, 'Come, this place sells the best fruit in Turkey.'

He led her to the many stalls which displayed a colourful array of cherries, figs, peaches, tangerines and melons. The young girl serving smiled sweetly at Aslan as they approached her stand. He pointed at the freshest fruits whilst she filled the brown paper bags.

Aslan stored the fruit in the pannier on the back of the bike before climbing back on and starting up the still-warm engine. With her enthusiasm dwindling, Lockhart painfully swung her leg over the seat to take up her position.

'One more place I'd like to take you,' he told her, before donning his black helmet.

The day's final stop was at a deserted beach, where they sat together on the sand as the sun slowly took its place below the horizon. The colours spreading across the sky were like nothing Lockhart had ever seen before. Pale blue, purple, pink and, of course, the usual spectrum of yellows and reds blended as a backdrop to the rays arcing crown-like above the disappearing fiery ball. Completely awestruck, she sat staring up at the unpolluted sky, then to her delight, Aslan slid his arm around her, pulling her in close to him. In this incredibly romantic setting, they sat in silence, eating the fruit from the market.

If I could choose one moment in time to freeze frame, it would be this.

Sitting on the sand, they leaned on one another until night had completely fallen all around them. Lockhart felt like they were the only humans left alive on the planet. It was wonderful. She would have happily stayed there all night before turning in the opposite direction to see the sunrise in the morning.

Aslan was first to rise to his feet, brushing the sand from his jeans. He offered Lockhart a helping hand, and although she would never have told him so, she badly needed it. Feeling sore all over, she wasn't exactly ecstatic at the thought of getting back onto the motorbike.

Aslan turned to her. 'We have travelled quite far from the hotel, but don't worry, I'll drive at top speed to get you back as quickly as possible.'

Oh God no, please no.
Dread filled her.

'I'm in no rush to get back, so you can just take your time.'

Thinking that she was being polite, he did not heed her suggestion but instead drove at full pelt around hairpin bends and past sheer cliff edges. Lockhart closed her eyes tightly, waiting for it all to be over, whichever way it would end.

When the bike finally came to a stop, she thanked God for sparing her life.

When, at last, she stepped onto the solid ground of the hotel car park, a sigh of relief escaped her.

'Thank you for a lovely day, Aslan.'

'No, thank you for agreeing to spend my special birthday with me. I'll walk you to your room just to make sure you get there safely. You can't be too careful these days.'

Lockhart laughed nervously, knowing there would be a decision to make when they got there. It wasn't a case of being a bit out of practice with these matters, she had never been *in* practice. She was possibly overthinking the situation, but the territory she was now in was unexplored.

Does he want to come into my room, or is he simply seeing me home safely?

She pondered this thought as they entered the lift to the third floor, where her room with the large, sumptuous bed would be waiting.

They walked in silence along the hallway, stopping at her door. Aslan made no move to return to the lift once he had delivered her safely. Fumbling for the key card in her handbag, she began to feel clumsy and embarrassed.

'Would you like to come in?' she whispered, knowing exactly what that question meant.

He nodded his reply, taking the card from her hand. Swiping it with a purpose, he pushed her ahead of him into the room. His arms wrapped around her in a tight embrace for a few moments before swiftly turning her around to face the bed. Under her dress, he gently ran his fingers up and down her inner thigh, barely touching her flesh at all. He could feel her tremble as his touch flitted gently between her legs. This teasing lasted some time, until he was certain that she was ready for him. On her exposed neck, he kissed, licked, and bit at her skin while he reached around the front to open her dress. The small buttons were difficult to open, frustration caused him to become somewhat rougher, ripping her clothes to get at her breasts. When he found her hard, erect nipples, he knew it was time to push her forward and lift her dress.

Lockhart's breathing had become erratic as she shook with pleasure. Then, using an experienced hand, he pushed her lacy knickers down, allowing them to fall to her ankles. Bending her over further, he slid easily inside her. She moaned in pleasure as he held on tightly to her hair. Lockhart never knew that the act of sexual intercourse could last this long. Climaxing during sex was another revelation. Tonight had been a night of many firsts and she simply could not get enough of it. They lay together on the bed, arms entwined. Just when Lockhart thought it was over, sex in one form or another would begin again, with an equal measure of passion. It was comfortable, easy, and devoid of inhibition.

Chapter 5

Lockhart opened her eyes in the morning to see the sun filtering through the muslin drapes. Aslan was no longer beside her. He was either working or had gone home for a well-earned rest. The events of the previous night filtered into her thoughts. Hiding her face in the pillow, she yelped with sheer joy and a little embarrassment.

What a night! I didn't know I had it in me. So that's what I've been missing all these years.

A primal scream appeared in her throat; she released it into the silence of her room.

I was a tigress to Aslan the lion.

Laughing hysterically, she thumped her heels off the mattress on the bed. Two things she now knew for sure, he did not see her as a mother figure, and she now knew exactly what a shagathon was.

The walk from the bed to the bathroom was not easy as her bow-legged gait had returned, only this time she had earned it for more pleasurable reasons. Singing at the top of her voice, she stepped under the hot jets of the shower. Today, she felt different. Something had switched on within her, illuminating her. Every fibre in her being was awakened, like an active volcano ready to blow. It was a feeling that she had never experienced before; it was glorious. Worryingly, her desire to stay in this euphoric state was way stronger than her fear of being hurt again.

Using the palm of her hand, she wiped the steam from the mirror. She critically analysed her slightly pointed, ordinary features.

What can he possibly see in me?

The phone on the bedside cabinet rang, startling her. The woman on the other end of the line spoke the moment the phone was lifted.

'Hello, this is reception. I have a message for Lockhart.'

'This is Lockhart speaking.'

'You have been booked for a complimentary massage today at 11am.'

'Oh, how wonderful!' Lockhart giggled, with a tingling sensation moving through her. 'Thank you.'

The phone call from reception banished all her feelings of self-doubt. For whatever reason, this young man appeared to desire her. After everything they had done last night, he was still coming back for more.

Unbelievable.

Putting the final touches to her make-up, she wore a pale blue top and cotton skirt. Her outfit was a little dated, but her choices were limited, linen trousers with a drawstring waist were out of the question.

Her damp hair was hanging loose when she casually wandered into the restaurant for breakfast. Most of the tables were taken by what looked to be honeymooners or retired couples. Within minutes of entering, it became obvious that several people were looking at her as she passed them. A scenario such as this would have embarrassed her in her previous life, but not today.

Today she was confident, sexy, and desired by a young man. The attention from the other guests may have been her imagination, but in that moment, she loved it.

Coffee and a slice of toast were all she could stomach from the buffet. The churning excitement in her stomach had completely suppressed her appetite. In fact, even the smell of the sausages frying made her want to throw up. Food was certainly not the focus of this Turkish holiday.

Leaving her toast half-eaten, she drained the last of her coffee and left the other guests replenishing their plates for the umpteenth time. Something far more fulfilling was going on in her life, and she planned to partake in it until she was replete.

When the elevator door opened, Lockhart was again engulfed in the wonderful aromas of the spa as she headed over to the reception. She gave her name and room number to the girl at the desk, who then escorted her to the massage room. Aslan was standing there wearing his work tunic, his face expressionless. He pretended not to know her as he addressed her with professional politeness. Following his lead, she played along with the scene he had set. When the receptionist had left, he locked the door behind her. Silently, he stripped her naked, then instructed her to lie on her back on the massage table. She complied with all of his requests. Lying back, he spread her legs apart. He then darted his tongue gently around her most sensitive, feminine area. Teasing her, he softly licked, then plunged with his tongue deeper into her. He brought her to an intense climax when he felt the moment was right.

Guiding her off the table, he bent her forward to enable him to feel the same relief.

Lockhart's legs were unsteady as she climbed down from the massage table to reach for her clothes.

'Thank you for that,' she told him, continuing with the role play.

'You are most welcome. I think you would benefit from regular sessions with me. I would be able to release much of your built-up tension.'

'I will bear that in mind and possibly take you up on your expert advice.'

Over the days that followed, Lockhart's appetite for Aslan was insatiable. They met for short periods in the day, in fairly public places, taking risks for thrills. Lockhart didn't care who saw them. The thought of being caught only intensified the desire. Sex between them was adventurous, with no awkwardness. Aslan knew what she wanted and how she liked it. How long this relationship was going to last, she had no idea and no expectation. This was the time of her life, and it was all thanks to Judy Bailey!

*

One evening, in the second week of her trip, Lockhart ate dinner alone in the restaurant before taking wine with two glasses out to the terrace to wait for Aslan to finish his shift. Through the glass doors of the dining room, she saw him walking swiftly to meet her. His physique was strong, his posture straight. The sheen on his wavy black hair was one of the things she liked best about him. Well, that and his brown hands, the twinkle in his eye, his lips, the length of his legs and a few other adorable characteristics.

A wide smile spread across his face as he approached her on the terrace, kissing her on both cheeks. The herbal smell from his hair caused a rush of adrenaline through her body. Calming her feelings of desire, she poured him a glass of prosecco, which he drank down immediately. They discussed the events of their day, both interested in what the other had been doing.

There had been a pause in their conversation, after which Aslan asked unexpectedly, 'What went wrong in your marriage?'

She was taken by surprise.

Would it spoil things between them if she told him? Will he see me differently, maybe lose respect for me?

'You don't have to tell me,' he said, sensing her reluctance to share her experience. 'I was just curious as to why a man wouldn't hang on tight to a woman like you?'

This comment gave her the confidence to open up to him.

'I have never actually told anyone about the events of that day. I think I have locked them away so tightly that I have never even revisited them fully myself.'

For a few moments, she sat silently, recalling that time.

Eventually, she continued. 'I was preparing the evening meal as I always did. I even remember it was a ginger beef dish I had never made before. I generally sought out new recipes to try. I then poured a drink for George, my husband. His tipple was whisky, Famous Grouse, in fact. He liked it with three ice cubes to water it down a little.'

She realised that she was beginning to babble, perhaps stalling for time before facing the painful part of the memory. 'Anyway,' she continued, her hands clasped tightly on her lap. 'He came in from work at the usual time but headed straight upstairs and didn't come down for his drink or dinner. I thought this was odd because he always went straight to his old, leather chair, put on the television and reached for his whisky. I remember stressing that if he didn't come down soon, the ice in his drink would be melted. It all sounds so ridiculous now.'

Aslan leaned forward, listening, remaining silent to let her talk.

'Eventually, I went up to see what he was doing. I stood in the doorway and watched him remove all of his suits from the wardrobe. He emptied his set of drawers and packed everything into two suitcases. I knew he wasn't going on a business trip because I always packed for him. He was aware that I was standing there, but he didn't offer any explanation.'

She stopped momentarily, took a sip of her drink, then took a deep breath.

'I asked him where he was going. He turned around, staring angrily at me as if I were stupid for not understanding it.'

'Did you understand at this point what was happening?' Aslan asked.

'No, I really and truly didn't. Looking back, I must have been pretty dense, but I really did not know. He told me to sit down, and he started saying things like, *we are not in love, we are not happy, we are not good for each other, we both need to start a new life*. The thing was that I thought I was happy and in love. I thought we *were* good for each other, and I didn't want any other life but the one I had. I told him I loved him and that if he wanted things to be different, we could work on it together. I explained to him that we had too many years under our belts to just throw it all away without trying.'

The wounds of that day began to feel exposed again, making her feel hurt and embarrassed.

Aslan reached over, laying his hand on hers for support.

She continued, 'George explained that he didn't know how to say it gently, but he was bored. He said I had nothing to say for myself, and he needed more from a relationship. Then he told me he had met someone special through work and that she was so much fun, and that they had everything in common. Then he had to make it more painful by saying that he had felt young and alive again since he'd met her. For the final blow, he told me she was his soulmate.'

Aslan shook his head in disbelief.

'These were roughly the words he used to describe her. I may have paraphrased or repeated them in a different order, but the sentiment was the same.'

At this point, Lockhart expected to break down and cry because she had never aired that conversation to anyone, not even to herself. She did not cry. Yes, it was painful, but she felt nothing but anger towards him, herself, and Little Miss Perfect Soulmate, whoever she was.

'What happened then?' Aslan asked.

'I can't even bring myself to admit it. Let's just say, I fell to the floor crying like a pathetic baby while he stepped over me with his cases. The last thing I heard was the front door closing. I haven't seen him since.'

They both sat quietly for a moment, digesting the story. Aslan broke the silence.

'What a fool!'

'Maybe he was right,' she said. 'In hindsight, I hadn't focused on the things that really mattered in a marriage. I thought that if I kept the house nice and prepared lovely meals, then that made me a good wife. I lost the point somewhere down the line. Then habit and routine set in, and I stopped seeing what was in front of me.'

Aslan shook his head. 'No, marriage is for life. You choose a wife, then you love and cherish her always, regardless.'

It was a simplistic view that Aslan held, but Lockhart liked it.

Chapter 6

It felt to Lockhart that the fast-forward button had been pressed on her holiday. The final day arrived before she knew it. This starkly contrasted with her time at home, which dragged slowly with the monotony of repetition. Here in Turkey, she had fallen nicely in step with the relaxed way of life and the routine she and Aslan had created. Their nights were spent together, making love at least twice before the morning. They sat on the terrace, talking and laughing in the evenings. Although she knew very little about Aslan, she had told him everything about herself, no subject taboo. Never in her entire life had she been so open with anyone. It had felt good to have someone to confide in, someone she could trust with her intimate thoughts. Perhaps she had been a bit too wrapped up in herself, but he had released a stop valve within her which had helped her to let go of all the pain of the past. It had been a necessary time of cleansing that seemed to ease her body through the healing process. Back home, she didn't have any close friends, no one to let her guard down to. This holiday showed her many things about herself, good and bad. Whilst reflecting on the old her, she realised that she had manufactured a perfect picture of her life for the outside world. The saddest part was that she too had completely bought into this illusion. It was also painfully obvious that she had allowed herself to become old before her time. Since her early twenties, she had been living a middle-aged lifestyle, simply handing back her youth as though she had no need for it. Now it would seem that the discarded youth had come looking for her, and she was embracing it like a long-lost child.

In the privacy of the hotel room, Lockhart stood naked in front of the mirror, critically analysing her body.

How can Aslan find me attractive? He could have any younger woman he wanted.

Squeezing the flesh around her stomach, she conceded that it was a little softer than it used to be, but at least she had stayed slim. She had George to thank for that. The painful rejection she had suffered over the past weeks had stifled her appetite. Never having any children had also lent a helping hand in keeping things in the right place. George had no interest whatsoever in fathering children. He had made that clear from the start. After they married, she knew there was no point in broaching the subject, his mind was made up. Choosing to spend her life with George meant she would be forever childless.

She remained standing there, looking, scrutinising herself. Cupping her breasts in her hands, she decided they were acceptably firm. In fact, her bust was proportionately large for the size of her frame. The reflection looking back at her was not youthful but neither did it look fifty. Until now, she had no idea that she was attractive. George hadn't properly noticed her in over ten years. She tried to recall a compliment from him, but nothing came to mind. It was obvious to her now that the harder she had tried to please him, the more displeased he had become.

Why did I not create a life for myself? I was a grade-A student at school. I should have reached my own goals. What made me think that my role in life was to support George? How different things may have been if I had gone to university and moved into a high-powered job like his. Would he have respected me more? Loved me more? Stayed for the long haul? Who knows, what does it matter? He was gone now, and Little Miss Perfect Soulmate is the one that makes him truly happy.

All thoughts of George and his newfound happiness were pushed out of her head. He had spoiled enough in her life. She would not allow him to ruin the precious thing she had found right here in Turkey.

Dressed in a sleeveless embroidered top that she had picked up at the market on her first day, she left the room to head downstairs. The hotel was quiet, which freed up a choice of loungers in the sun or in the shade. After weighing up the options, she settled for one that sat under a bay laurel tree. A waiter approached her, taking her order of diet coke with ice and lemon.

On his return with her drink shortly after, he stopped to chat for a moment. She welcomed the company to pass the time.

'You are a good friend of Aslan's?' he asked.

'Well, yes, I suppose I am. We have spent a lot of time together. I enjoy his company.'

'Did you spend his *special birthday* with him?'

'Yes, I did. We had a lovely day.'

She wondered why he had asked that with a nodding smile. Did she detect a smug 'thought so' look on his face. She couldn't be sure.

'Why do you ask?'

'Just enquiring.'

Her reaction to this exchange was to pick up her book, indicating to him that she wanted solitude. The waiter collected his tray and left. He hadn't said anything wrong, but his attitude had given her a feeling of discomfort. This was the final day of her holiday; she didn't want anything to spoil it. Neither George nor the smarmy waiter would get a chance to douse her fire today.

She lay back on the lounger, basking in the warm stillness of the shade, listening to the sound of buzzing insects. Shamefully thrilling memories of the previous night's passion were being welcomed into her mind.

Aslan had brought ice to her room for their routine nightcap on the balcony.

'I can't stand the heat,' she had told him as she stood looking out across the dark ocean. 'It doesn't even cool down in the evenings.' Her complaints had not gone unnoticed.

Aslan had been sitting on a wicker chair beside her. Rising to his feet, he said nothing as he removed her fine nightdress. With a cube of ice from his drink, he gently ran the ice over her nipples until they tingled. The remainder of the cube he used to run up and down the inside of her legs before inserting the cold, melted fluid on his fingers inside her. He had watched her as she writhed with the sheer ecstasy. They remained outdoors on the balcony, pleasuring one another. He whispered softly to her, 'Do you hope that someone is watching us?' She had nodded shamefully to this question.

With a certain degree of urgency, she bolted from the sun lounger, tossing her book to the grass. She entered the hotel, making her way to the reception.

'Can I book a massage please, as soon as possible?'

Chapter 7

Leaving the Blue Lagoon meant saying goodbye to blissful happiness, only to return to misery. Most of her time there had been with Aslan. The remaining hours had been spent thinking about him. Her first-time experiences had been many and the woman she had blossomed into was so far removed from the Lockhart who had arrived two weeks previously. It had been the most wonderful time in her life.

What am I returning home to? I have nothing and no one. I will probably never see Aslan again. No, Lockhart, stop it! You can't let yourself believe that. He shared all the same fantastic experiences. He will get in touch. What we have is special. He could never have found that with a younger woman. It was a once-in-a-lifetime thing. He felt it too… I think.

The taxi dropped her off at the airport where she entered by the automatic doors. Sitting on the marble floor, near the door, were her original travelling companions. On seeing them, a smile spread across her lips. She realised that she had so much to thank them for. They were not conversing with one another, but instead, they supported their aching heads in their hands. It occurred to her that they were closer in age to Aslan than she was, and yet she could not imagine her beautiful Aslan ever wanting to be with any of them. Images of the cheap, drunken sex that they would have indulged in over the past two weeks were a complete contrast to the passionate, caring lovemaking that she had experienced.

Lockhart bought them coffee and a pastry, guessing they had spent all their money.

'Thanks,' Val said, taking the hot drink from the cardboard container. 'Oh, did you enjoy your holiday?'

'It was the time of my life.'

The girls removed their heads from their hands to stare up at Lockhart, who stood above them.

'How? What did you do?' Connie spat, with a tone of resentment.

'Just some stuff that I had never tried before.'

'That's nice,' Val told her.

It was obvious that the girls didn't care enough to ask anything else, and she had no intention of sharing the details.

The flight home was a painful time for Lockhart, with every mile taking her further and further from her new love. Misery tightened its grip on her when she thought of that lonely, soulless place that was her home. If she could have stayed at The Blue Lagoon for the remainder of her natural life, she would have done so without question. Life with Aslan had been perfect in every way. This couldn't simply have been a holiday romance, a memory to drag out on cold winter nights. It had to be more. The intimacy they had shared had not been superficial. It had been like the joining of two souls. An onlooker could be forgiven for thinking that she was an older, inexperienced lady clinging desperately to a dream. But what they shared was real. Her feelings were stronger than anything she had ever felt before. The words *I love you* had not been exchanged between them, but they didn't need to be in Lockhart's mind. They were said in so many other ways.

Mobile numbers had been exchanged before they left, with a solemn promise to keep in touch and to be together again as soon as possible. They were lovers, but she had no idea whether this meant they were in a relationship.

I mustn't build up my hopes. I've been hurt enough. If it happens, it happens. If it doesn't, then it doesn't... oh please, God, let it happen.

Don't forget about me, Aslan.

Chapter 8

It was almost midnight when the taxi turned into Lockhart's treelined avenue. Returning home brought her absolutely no joy, only dread. The rain fell lightly on her as she stood on the pavement, waiting for the driver to retrieve her suitcase from the boot of the cab.
'You're not abroad anymore,' the driver laughed, seeing Lockhart shivering in her lightweight holiday clothing.
'No, sadly, I'm not.'
The temperamental front door lock needed careful working before Lockhart could open it. In truth, she was in no hurry to enter, so, for once, this annoying quirk did not irritate her. She had always loved her home, now she despised it and everything it reflected about her life. Finally, the lock became unstuck, and the door opened into the porch. When she lifted the mail strewn across the doormat, she saw that every letter had only one name on the front, George. She tossed them back onto the floor where they belonged. Nothing of any importance ever came through the letterbox for her.
An unlived-in chill greeted her in the hallway, blended with a stench of rubbish from the bins. Lonely silence screamed in her face causing a churning sensation in her stomach.
I despise this house and all the years it stole from me. What an idiot I've been. I'm more than halfway through my existence on

the planet, and I'm only experiencing life for the first time now.

Leaving her suitcase full of dirty washing in the hall, she entered the kitchen in search of coffee. The click of the light switch illuminated the shocking vision of the state in which she had left it. The hum of bluebottles broke the silence as the creatures flew into the windowpane repeatedly in the hope of escaping. Every foody morsel left on the worktops had long since been absorbed up their proboscises. The dirty dishes were stacked haphazardly in the sink with patches of dried rough texture on the ceramic. Glancing over at the pedal bin in the corner of the room, she saw houseflies flying in a square formation over the vile-smelling contents hidden beneath the lid. Outside the window, an urban fox prowled through the garden activating the security light. The shift from dark to light distracted Lockhart from the disgraceful mess of the kitchen. She glanced out of the window only to be disgusted with herself further. The once beautiful garden was now corrupted by weeds among the knee-high grass.

How could I have been so neglectful of my house? Was I depressed? I must have been, but I didn't realise how bad things had become.

The rejuvenated Lockhart knew that changes had to be made.

I will never be dragged down this low by a man ever again. I am in control of my own happiness, or sadness, for that matter. There is life after divorce, and I have proved that with Aslan. Tomorrow, I will make some considerable changes.

The night had reached the small hours of the following day. Lockhart felt exhausted, but she was filled with a positivity that had been missing in her life. She climbed beneath the unwashed sheets, falling instantly asleep.

Chapter 9

By ten the following morning, the sheets had been stripped from the bed and were now experiencing the washing machine's spin cycle.
Every window was pushed wide open, allowing a fresh breeze to pass through the remotest corners of the house. Wearing her old grey tracksuit, Lockhart scrubbed the kitchen floor on all fours while music from the radio filled the air. The contents of her suitcase had been separated into two piles, one for the washing machine, the other a gift for the charity shop. The linen trousers and flowery blouses were no longer required for her new lifestyle. It was now time for some other woman of a similar age to enjoy their mediocrity.
Lockhart looked around at the transformation of her kitchen.
I never thought I'd think this, but cleaning is good for the soul.
There was a certain joy to be gained from seeing the beams from the overhead spotlights bounce off the granite worktop. It suddenly occurred to her that Aslan could have sent her a message or even phoned her while

she'd been busy; she'd never have heard a thing. She dashed to the hall table where her handbag lay.

Please let there be a text or a missed call. Please, please, please.

There were no text messages and no missed calls. Lockhart slid the phone into the pocket of her tracksuit trousers, keeping it close, just in case.

Dinner time was crawling nearer, and with very little food in the fridge, Lockhart could not decide what to cook. She suddenly had a revelation.

What am I thinking? I don't need to cook if I don't want to. I don't even like preparing meals. It is a totally thankless task. I don't answer to anyone anymore, only myself.

With the twilight dwindling rapidly outside, she grabbed her coat and keys and left the house in the direction of the Main Street. A pizza from the usual carryout shop was exactly what she fancied, and now she only had herself to please. As she walked the short journey to the centre of town, she closed her hand around the phone in her pocket. Oh, how she willed it to ring or vibrate.

The phone remained dormant.

The town was ablaze with weekend socialisers, filling the restaurants and bars. Lockhart could only envy the couples and groups of friends seeking a distraction from their working lives.

I've never had friends to laugh with or confide in. Those girls I went to Turkey with were the closest thing I ever had to friends. I have got to make changes in my life.

On an impulse, she entered the off licence that spread around the corner of the street. The snowy-haired owner of the shop greeted her from the counter.

That little man has worked in this shop for as long as I have lived in this town.

'Hi,' she said, returning his greeting. 'By any chance, do you have any Turkish wine?'

'I will see what I can do for you. Were you looking for white or red?'

'I was looking for red. I have just returned from a wonderful holiday in Turkey, and I got really attached to the red wine in the hotel where I was staying. I even visited a vineyard with a friend while I was there. It was actually his uncle's vineyard.'

'How lovely,' the old man replied. 'I have never been to Turkey. I have never really been anywhere... Oh, except Wales. I went to Wales once. Does that count?'

'Yes, it counts,' Lockhart told him.

'Good. Now, let me see what I have for you.'

A bottle of wine stood alone on a high shelf. The old gentleman pulled over the stool which sat at the checkout. Shakily, he stood on it, reaching up for the wine.

'One left,' he told her, raising the bottle in the air.

Lockhart feared for his safety.

'Great!' she shouted, slightly dubious of the idea that they had all sold out due to popular demand.

The old man flipped the pair of glasses from his head down onto his eyes to enable him to read the label.

Lockhart was not particularly bothered about the description of the wine. It was merely a symbolic gesture to toast the holiday of a lifetime.

He brushed the dust from the shoulders of the bottle and read the label aloud to her.

'It says here that it is a mellow dessert wine with a pleasant bouquet and rich taste.' He peered at Lockhart over the top of his glasses. 'Do you like the sound of that?'

She didn't, but she nodded approval.

'Hold on, hold on, it goes on to say that the wine is pasteurised and is Kosher for Passover. Do you still want it?'

'Yes, I'll still take it. I bet that it's just the ticket.'

He pulled the bottle closer to his failing eyesight. 'You could be right. The alcohol percentage is 15% volume.'

'That sounds like just what I need tonight.'

The man wrapped the bottle in brown paper before placing it in a white plastic bag with the shop's logo in bold letters on the side. Handing it over, he said, 'There you are, now see and enjoy that. You are a nice lady.'

Strangely, the words touched Lockhart, giving her a lump in her throat. 'Thank you, I appreciate that.'

As she was leaving the shop, a small poster on the glass door caught her eye. There was a cartoon drawing of a woman wearing a leotard, sweatbands, and leg warmers. The heading read, *Get Fit With Mags*. It was promoting a local keep fit and Zumba class, two nights a week, in a community hall at the end of the street. Along the foot of the poster ran a mobile number with the name Mags beside it. Lockhart took out her phone and entered the number into her contacts.

'You young ones all care so much about your figures these days,' her new friend commented when he saw her reading the poster.

Lockhart laughed.

Young ones! I like it.

When she left the rather antiquated off licence, she was pleased that she had supported a local business. The supermarkets had pushed so many others out of commission.

The next stop on the main street was the takeaway place where she always bought the pizzas after her Saturday shift at the supermarket.

George loved those pizzas. In fact, I think it was the highlight of his week.

While thinking about George's culinary preferences, she glanced across the road at the Turkish Kebab Carry Out establishment.

Tonight, I think I will go all Turkish as a tribute to my beautiful Aslan.

Looking both ways on the busy street, she ran across as soon as she saw a break in the traffic. It was too early in the evening for the kebab place to be busy. Most of their trade took place after the bars were closed. A donner kebab was the only option she knew the name of, so she ordered one.

Would it be very foolish of me to ask this man if he knows Aslan?

'I just got back from Turkey yesterday,' she announced.

'Aw, that's nice,' he answered, his Scottish accent broader than hers.

'Do you get to visit there often?' she asked, building up to what she knew was a ludicrous question.

'No, I was born here. I don't know anyone in Turkey.'

There didn't seem much point in furthering the conversation. Her Turkish holiday was the only thing she had a desire to discuss.

She paid for her food, thanked him, then left.

Pasteurised dessert wine in one hand and her Turkish kebab in the other, she made her way home to pay homage to the country that had brought joy back into her life.

The fresh, clean smell that met her in the hallway pleased her. From the units in the kitchen, she took a plate and a wine glass through to the lounge. Placing the wine and kebab on George's leather-topped table, she then hurled herself disrespectfully into his beloved chair.

Tomorrow, the chair goes. That bloody table can go with it.

The remote control lay on the arm of the chair where George had left it. Through an act of sheer ownership, she switched on the television even though there was nothing in particular she wanted to watch.

After checking her mobile phone for missed calls or texts, she placed it on the leather-topped occasional table next to her glass of Turkish wine. Using her fingers, she ate the kebab from the polystyrene container. It was a greasy meal, but she simply wiped her hands on the leather arms of the chair. The first glass of the rich dessert wine had gone to her head, and as a result of this, she spilled a fair percentage of the second glass she poured. It made her laugh to see the sticky liquid spread across George's precious little table.

He would hate to see that. Good, she thought.

More than half of the bottle had been drunk, and the lettuce from the kebab adorned her sweatshirt; Lockhart felt replete. The wine was vile, and she despised the kebab, but it didn't matter, she was doing it for Aslan.

Oh, Aslan, why aren't you contacting me?

'Ring, you little bastard!' she shouted at the phone. The phone did not respond.

Lockhart rose unsteadily to her feet, stood for a moment to get her balance, then stumbled towards her bedroom.

It's been a good night. I hope Aslan appreciates what I've done for him.

She was aware that even her thoughts were slurred.

Chapter 10

The following morning, she arose surprisingly energised. A change was coming, she could feel it. Checking her phone once again for messages, she saw that there were none, just as she had expected. Urging it telepathically to ring, she rubbed her temples, chanting, 'Ring, ring, ring. Please ring.'

For a moment, she sat with the phone in her hand. Right, she decided, it's time to phone Mags; I need to get fit. It was surprising how nervous she felt about making the call. Twice she reached out to ring the number, but stopped herself from doing it.

When she finally took the step, there was no reply, but she left a message giving her name and contact details.

Using google search, she looked up hairdressers in the town and booked an appointment with a salon called Nu Yu. The name was exactly what she wanted, out with the old and in with the new. The old Lockhart no longer existed. Her hermit lifestyle had gone on for far too long. It was time to get out and about in the real world, meeting new people. But what the hell was she going to do with her future? She had no skills, no further education.

Am I too old to go out and learn something new? Does anyone ever start a career at the age of fifty?

Fortunately, George had left her financially stable, with no outstanding mortgage on the house, so money was not an issue. However, that did not mean she could sit back and do nothing. There had to be viable options that did not include Saturday supermarket work. Those days were over. She drummed her fingers on the granite worktop, racking her brain for career ideas.

What are my interests? Hmm, I don't have any. What was the last thing that caught my attention and stirred my desire or intrigue? Not including Aslan.

For several minutes she thought about the question she had asked herself. At first, she drew a blank. Nothing came to mind.

Hold on a minute.

She was getting excited.

Before George left, I enjoyed looking in the bridal shop window on the main street. I love dresses. In fact, I love the whole idea of wedding events. Okay, that's a starting point. Something to think about.

Tucking the bridal idea to the back of her mind, she lifted her unresponsive phone from the breakfast bar. A quick search gave the number to dial for the council.

'Hello, is this the council? Do you do uplifts? Great. Could I schedule a day with you to pick up an old leather chair, an occasional table… oh, and a bed too?'

The changes she was implementing in her life awakened an excitement in her. Never before had she taken control of anything in her life. She realised that by allowing George to make all the decisions, she was becoming more and more helplessly reliant on him. Being in charge felt liberating.

A call or text message from Aslan would be the ultimate thrill, but hiring a gardener would have to do for now. While she searched for the contact details of someone in the local area, a text reverberated through her phone, causing it to move slightly on the worktop. Her hand instinctively grabbed it. An initial feeling of disappointment befell her when she saw that it wasn't Aslan. It was Mags inviting her to her seven o'clock class that evening *to get fit*.

The remainder of Lockhart's day was spent rearranging the furniture into two groups; keep and throw away. All the items George had held so dear would now spend the night in the front garden waiting for the uplift the following morning. Manoeuvring the weighty leather chair through the front door proved challenging for her, but when you want something badly enough, it happens. The leather topped table was the next item to be evicted from the premises. This she hurled out onto the armchair. Now with many of the traces of her marriage eliminated, her new Georgeless life could begin.

The next issue to be dealt with was finding suitable attire for an exercise class. From her chest of drawers, she trailed out item after item in the hope that something would look right. Finally, she settled on black leggings and an old T-shirt with the logo Levi's emblazoned across the chest. Just for tonight, she would overlook the fact that it belonged to George. Her intention was to dispose of it as soon as she could replace it with something better.

Wearing the only pair of trainers she possessed, she made her way to the community hall, where she was about to find out how fit or unfit she was. New experiences made her nervous, possibly because she had spent most of her life in the house, specifically in the kitchen. It was difficult for her to comprehend that she had been stupid enough to dedicate her entire existence to looking after a man, but she had.

I wonder if there are any other women out there who have done the same thing as me? I gave him everything, and he left me anyway.

Waiting in the doorway of the hall was a woman Lockhart presumed would be Mags. Her frame was petite, but her upper body looked muscular in her lime green vest top. Lockhart reckoned she was in her late forties, but her healthy lifestyle had allowed her to hold on to a thirty-something glow.

'You must be Lockhart.'

Mags beamed, welcoming her into the room.

'Yes, I am.'

'I'm delighted that you have come along to join us tonight, Lockhart. I aim to get everyone in good shape, but we usually have fun along the way.'

'Can I just explain that I've never been to anything like this before and am really unfit.'

Mags laughed. 'I think you might surprise yourself.'

She took Lockhart's arm, leading her over to a group of older ladies who were standing in their self-designated spots on the floor, waiting for the class to commence.

A woman, advancing in years, and wearing a high cut leotard, pulled the heavy door shut after receiving a nod from Mags. With the bang of the door, the volume of the music was raised a few notches. Mags jumped up and down on the spot, shaking her hands by her sides to limber up. She then shouted instructions through a microphone headset. All the keep fitters sprang into action, some more coordinated than others. Lockhart couldn't help but notice that everyone was smiling. It was a happy place to be.

'Keep doing the leg raises, girls. This will give you super flat tums. That's what we all want, isn't it?' Mags shouted.

'Yes,' came a reply from the ladies, who were now lying on their backs on the floor.

'I can't hear you,' she hollered, putting her hand up to her ear. 'We all want flat tums, don't we?'

'Yes!' came the cry.

'Now keep going, girls, but before I forget, we have a new member with us tonight. So, let's hear a big hello for Lockhart.'

'Hello,' they shouted breathlessly.

'Give them a wave, Lockhart.'

Lockhart gave an awkward wave. Being the centre of attention was not something to which she was accustomed.

On the walk home that evening, she was reminded of that moment when Mags singled her out. Although her cheeks had flushed with embarrassment, she had enjoyed it. Why had she enjoyed it? Because for once, she felt noticed.

What a great night. I can't wait to go back.

Aslan returned to her thoughts as she turned into her street. She reached into her coat pocket, taking out her mobile phone to check for messages or calls. The screen showed no text messages and no missed calls. It had been a fantastic night, but she fought desperately to keep the disappointment from pulling down her mood.

Chapter 11

The following evening, Lockhart was happy to stay home. There was, after all, another fitness night with Mags before the weekend came around. The radio played loudly in the kitchen while she prepared a tuna fish salad.

If I could just get a text message, no matter how short, from Aslan, then I would be truly happy. Could he have forgotten about me so quickly? Has he moved on to some young, pretty girl already?

She began to visualise a beautiful girl lying on a sunbed at the pool, Aslan unable to take his eyes off her. He walks over and takes her in his arms…

I've got to stop torturing myself.

Lockhart had a sick feeling in the pit of her stomach.

He loves me. I know he does. What we had was real.

As she continued to chop the baby tomatoes for her salad, she made a conscious effort to push Aslan from her thoughts. Instead, she focused on her keep fit class.

Tomorrow, I'll go out and get an outfit to wear. Then I can bin the Levi's t-shirt that belongs to George. Once that has gone, there will be nothing left of him. Gone without a trace… was that the doorbell?

Lowering the volume of the radio, she listened in silence.

Ding Dong.

Yes, it is the bell. Who can be coming to my door? I don't know anyone.

Feeling slightly apprehensive, she walked through the unlit hallway to the front door. The safety chain was already on, so she left it that way. Opening the door, she looked out into the darkness of the garden and saw a figure standing there.

'Yes, can I help you?' she said nervously.

The figure moved into the light of the porch.

'It's me, George. Can I come in?'

'Oh my goodness, George, you gave me a fright. You look absolutely terrible. What the hell has happened to you? Have you been sleeping rough?'

Releasing the chain, she opened the door, allowing him to enter what was now her home.

He stumbled over the threshold with an apologetic gait.

She had no idea why he had come or what he wanted; a divorce had already been agreed. With the greatest caution, she observed him for signs of something. He had been a source of pain to her, so her instincts told her to avoid engaging with him. He was the last thing she needed in her life.

'George, I am actually in the middle of something right now, so can we make this brief?'

She led him through to the lounge.

He looked around the room in disbelief. 'Where's all my stuff? My chair? My table?'

'I decided to decorate and replace a few things I never liked.'

He looked wounded at this statement, shocked by her lack of sentimentality.

'We have had those things for so long...'

'Yes, that is precisely why it was time for them to go. Did you come to visit the furniture, or did you want something?' she asked, pushing him to get to the point.

'I just came to see how you were. What is going on? You look so different, and our house has totally changed. In fact, you've changed.'

Would he have been happy if I'd remained broken-hearted Lockhart and kept the house as a shrine to our marriage?

'I could say the same about you, George. You look completely different. What's going on? Why are you really here?'

Now she simply wanted answers.

'Have you got anything to drink?' he asked. An edge of desperation could be detected in his voice.

With a sigh, she left the room, heading to the kitchen, where she knew that there was the remainder of a bottle of his whisky. Pouring a generous measure, she then plinked two ice cubes into the amber liquid.

'What is this about, George?' she asked, handing him the drink.

'I'm starting to believe I may have made a terrible mistake.'

Lockhart sat forward, staring at him.

'Oh, don't tell me Little Miss Perfect Soulmate is actually Little Miss Imperfect and not your soulmate.'

Gloating was not her style, so she fought the temptation.

'Go on,' she said.

'Aitchy...'

'Please don't call me that again,' she interrupted.

She was painfully reminded that when they had first met, he called her Honeybunch. It was a bit corny, but she liked it. He then shortened it to Honey, which soon became Hon and then simply H or Aitchy. He hadn't called her that for years. Sadly, as soon as his feelings towards her had dried up, so did the pet names. There had been a time when she longed for him to call her Aitchy again. But he never had, until now.

'Sorry. The thing is that I miss my home. I miss you and everything we had together. Things aren't the same, and it has made me really appreciate you and our happy life. I have been a complete fool. I love you, and I want a fresh start.'

He put his head in his hands and began to cry.

Lockhart looked at the incredulous scene before her. It dawned on her that she had never witnessed him crying before. All she could do was stare. He made a kind of ugly, piggy face. Suddenly, from nowhere, a bubble appeared out of one of his nostrils. It looked incredibly unattractive.

It was an awkward situation where she didn't really know how to react. She left the room to fetch him a ravel of toilet roll for his nose. What else could she do. A hug was out of the question.

'Thank you,' he said, taking the toilet tissue. 'I've got my stuff in the car,' he added.

There was no pleasure to be gleaned from seeing him so distraught. Had it been a few weeks ago, she would have been elated that he had come to the door with his begging bowl. But things had changed; she had changed. Things had moved on and her feelings for him had evaporated.

'Will I bring in my stuff?' he told her, rising to his feet.

In utter disbelief, she stared open-mouthed at him. At that very moment, a truly magical thing happened. A text vibrated from the phone in her cardigan pocket. With complete disregard for her whimpering visitor, she snatched the phone out to see the message.

Aslan: Hotel season is almost over. I can come and see you if you like. Is next Wednesday any good for you?

Adrenaline sent shockwaves surging through her system. She couldn't hide her smile. There was a temptation to let out a woohoo! But that really would have been highly insensitive.

'George, you've got to go.'

Grabbing him by the elbow, she jollied him up to his feet. Then, pushing him towards the front door, she opened it wide before forcing him out.

'George dear, I hope it all works out for you. Nice to see you, goodbye.'

The door was banged shut before he knew what had just happened.

He lifted the letterbox to shout through.

'I don't want to leave. I want to stay. Please, Aitchy! Help me. My life is a mess. She's having a baby! You know how I feel about that. Only you understand me... Please!'

So that's what it's about.

She walked away from the begging voice pleading through the rectangle on the main door. The volume on the radio in the kitchen was turned up, loud. Picking up the kitchen knife, she chopped frenziedly at the cucumber, her mind in a whirl.

He's coming over to Scotland. He's coming to see me. He loves me. He loves me. I knew it.

The music in the kitchen was blaring as she danced small steps from one foot to the other. Any onlooker would suspect that she needed to pay a visit to the ladies' room , but it was purely the excitement of the text and the news it held. She stopped for a moment, wondering if the whinging had subsided. The volume of the music was lowered in order for her to listen. At last, the front door had now fallen silent.

Phew, he's gone.

All the food she had prepared for her salad was scooped into a Tupperware tub, sealed and placed in the fridge. Eating was the last thing on her mind as her insides were tightly knotted. And now, sitting on a bar stool, she stared at her mobile phone on the granite worktop in front of her, pondering how she would reply to the news that she had waited for weeks to hear.

Lockhart: Great news, Aslan. Wednesday works for me. Just give me all the flight details, and I will pick you up from the airport. I am really looking forward to seeing you.

Another text buzzed through her phone. She grabbed it. Disappointingly, it was George.

George: I will never give up. I will keep fighting until I win you back. We stood up in church and said our vows. Don't give up on us.

There were no words for this ridiculous statement. Shaking her head in irritation, she pressed the delete button, making George's words vanish.

Chapter 12

With only one more day left to wait for her lover, Lockhart decided it was time to fill the fridge with delights to please him. Much as she had grown to loathe cooking, it would be different when Aslan was sitting on one of the stools in the kitchen, chatting to her as she prepared praiseworthy meals for him. Her mind drifted to his visit as she envisaged him sidling behind her while she cooked. She imagined him lifting her dress, then slipping down her new lacy knickers before...Oh, it was more than she could stand.
Pull yourself together woman, she told herself.
Halfway through making a list of the items she would need from the shops for Aslan's arrival, she stopped abruptly. *What am I doing? I am not making any more lists. My life with George was all about making stupid lists.* Tearing the piece of paper into several pieces, she tossed it in the bin. *I won't plan anything. I will act on impulse and buy whatever takes my fancy.*

It was already beginning to get dark by early evening, although the clocks were not due to be reversed for another few weeks. Lockhart walked along past all of the small independent shops on the main street. The assistants appeared to be tidying, getting ready for closing time. A young girl arranged the various occasion cards on a stand in the window of the stationery shop. Two women in the shoe shop stood discussing their window display, which now exhibited a winter boot collection. The bridal shop was next in the row, and as Lockhart passed, she felt compelled to stop. The window had been expertly dressed with an ivory, bejewelled wedding gown dominating the space. Pink bouquets lay around the beaded hem, randomly scattered rose petals covered the floor. *Absolutely beautiful*, she thought, walking on. A few feet along the pavement, she stopped, turned, and headed back to the shop. On the glass door above the sign with information on opening times, she saw the words Princess Bride engraved into the pane of glass. It was barely noticeable, but it struck her as a symbol of permanency. Whoever started this business had planned on being there for the long haul.

The bell above the door rang to alert the assistant that a customer had entered. The inside of the shop was surprisingly spacious. White and ivory dresses hung on rails along every wall, leaving the floor space in the centre of the room clear. A circular Persian rug dressed the polished wooden floorboards. A changing room, indicated by a large sign, was situated at the back of the shop. A faded velvet sofa faced the changing area, presumably for adoring relatives to admire the bride as she emerged from behind the curtain.

In the few moments following her arrival, Lockhart had surmised that although the tired surroundings had seen better days, the shop had managed to hold on to an air of well-established elegance.

'Can I help you?' asked an elderly woman.

'I am hoping that you can. I pass your shop every day and I can't help stopping to admire your dresses. Your window is always a spectacle, whoever dresses it has the most wonderful flair. I would love to be a part of your business, so if you ever have any openings for a sales assistant, I would be delighted if you would bear me in mind.'

As Lockhart spoke directly to the woman, she found herself staring at the pearly-white wisps of hair that framed her face. Her complexion was pale but from her aging face shone sapphire blue eyes filled with vibrancy.

'Can I leave you my contact details?'

'Yes, of course, you can,' she told her, pushing forward a pen and paper from the counter.

Lockhart wrote down her name and mobile number.

The woman outstretched her veined hand to lift the paper near to her face. Her eyesight clearly wasn't what it used to be.

'Lockhart? That is a very unusual name. Nice though. My name is Elsie. I am the owner, sales assistant and window dresser. Delighted to meet you.'

'You have a wonderful shop here, Elsie. I would love to work for you and hopefully bring some ideas with me. It was so nice meeting you.'

'You too.'

Whether Lockhart had made a significant impression on Elsie would remain to be seen. Deep down, she had a positive feeling about it all.

The traffic was building to a crescendo at the teatime rush hour. Lockhart strolled further along the main street, replaying the conversation that had just taken place between herself and the owner of Princess Bride. The way in which she had breezed into the shop, selling herself to a complete stranger had surprised her. Where had this newfound confidence come from? She had left the shop with a distinct feeling that this woman needed help. It didn't take an analyst to work out that Elsie's business was not on an upward trajectory. The fact that she was the only member of staff, told Lockhart all she needed to know. There had to be something that she could bring to the job which would help to boost sales, but she had no idea what.

'Lockhart!' came a shout from across the street.

Lockhart looked over. A complete stranger was waving earnestly with her hand high in the air, her feet balancing on tiptoe to heighten her stance.

The woman began to weave her way through the congested traffic to get to Lockhart, who had now placed her shopping bag on the ground at her feet.

'Phew! That was a bit scary,' the stranger joked, referring to her crossing. 'You probably don't remember me, but I go to Get Fit with Mags. I've seen you there a few times and heard Mags say your name. You've got one of those names that just sticks. I'm Becky, but most people call me Bee.'

'Oh yes, I remember you now. Thanks for taking your life in your hands just to introduce yourself to me. It's good to meet you. I don't really know anyone at the class. It's just a sea of bodies jumping around.'

'Are you going along tonight?' Bee asked.

'Well, I wasn't planning to because I have a visitor coming from abroad tomorrow, but I may pop in if I get organised in time.'

'Great. I will possibly see you there. Good to meet you.'

'You too, Bee.'

Lockhart smiled to herself as she continued with her shopping.

I set out to buy some things for Aslan's arrival, and I now know two new people, Elsie and Bee. This really has been an eventful trip. I think I will go to the class tonight.

In the kitchen, Lockhart placed perishables in the fridge, fruit in the crystal bowl and bottles of wine into the built-in wine rack at the side of the tall unit. Music was playing from the radio, and the kettle was brought to a boil before switching itself off. Above all the noise, she could hear the faint sound of the doorbell.

When she opened the door, she was faced with the most enormous array of flowers. The bearer of the bouquet was not visible as the flowers framed the full extent of the doorway.

'Lockhart Hayes?' the voice from behind the foliage asked.

'Yes,' she replied. The bulging bouquet was immediately thrust upon her.

Holding the flowers in both hands, she managed to shut the door with her foot. Unfortunately, the sender's name wasn't visible from behind the cellophane. As soon as she had placed the bouquet on the counter, she ripped into the wrapping to retrieve the message.

> *My Darling, Aitchy.*
> *My everlasting love,*
> *My true companion.*
> *Forever yours,*
> *George.*

For a few seconds, she stood staring at the card, astonished by his poetic words. Shaking her head, she tossed the card into the stainless-steel pedal bin.

I'll keep the flowers, but as for that nonsense, I have no place for it in my life. Why did the stupid bastard never buy me flowers when we were together? His girlfriend is pregnant, so he is suddenly wooing me with romantic gestures. It is so transparent.

After filling four vases full of flowers, she placed them around the house.

It was nice of George to help me make the house look nice for Aslan's arrival, she smirked to herself.

Chapter 13

Bee ran straight over to Lockhart when she walked through the door of the community hall. The music played softly in the background allowing the ladies to socialise before the class started. The chattering of women could be heard around the room as they removed their coats or retrieved their water bottles from the bags in preparation for the strenuous workout.

'Are you happy to find a space up at the back?' Bee asked.

'Yes, that's perfect. I'll be able to make a fool of myself without anyone seeing me.'

Vibrations rumbled through the floor as the volume of the music rose to signify that the class was about to begin.

Mags shouted through her microphone headset. 'Come on, ladies, let's see you breaking a sweat tonight.'

The class members copied the squatting moves of their leader.

'You can get down further than that, surely! Right, let's pick up a bit of speed. You're not here to enjoy yourself,' she joked. 'Don't make me name and shame the lazy ones.'

'Hey, Lockhart,' Bee shouted above the noise. 'Do you fancy going for a drink after the class?'

'Yes, that would be great.'

I haven't been out for a drink with a friend since… Actually, I haven't been out for a drink with a friend, ever.

Lockhart kicked her height with her left leg, then her right, all to the rhythm of the music.

When Lockhart finally saw Mags removing her headset, a sense of relief enveloped her. It had been a punishing session. Sweat formed drips down her back, soaking her t-shirt through. She was in no state to be going for a drink, but her hooded sweatshirt hid everything when she pulled it on. Bee led the way to the door.

'Hey Mags!' Bee shouted up to the stage area where Mags was packing up. 'You definitely got your pound of flesh from us tonight. That was verging on torture,'

'That's why you love me. Lockhart, are you settling in okay? You seem to be managing fine with the routines.'

Lockhart smiled, 'Yes, thanks, Mags. I really enjoy coming along. In fact, I'm hooked.'

Bee led the inexperienced Lockhart along the main street to a quaint establishment called Decanters Wine Bar. It was acceptably busy for a midweek evening. The music took its place nicely in the background, barely audible over the hum of conversation from the customers.

'You grab us a seat in the booth over there,' Bee suggested, pointing towards the back of the bar. 'I'll get the drinks. Prosecco okay for you?'

'Yeah, yeah, Prosecco's great,' Lockhart said, reaching into her bag for money.

'No,' Bee said, pushing her hand away from her purse. 'I'll get this one. You can get the next. Just go and grab the seats before we lose them.'

Lockhart walked towards the back, repeating *'excuse me'* to small groups of standing drinkers. She slid into the red leather seat of the booth, removing her jacket and scarf. The fact that this experience was new to her meant that she felt awkward sitting alone. On the table in front of her, she spotted a cocktail menu. Snatching it up, she pretending to read its contents.

'Clear a space,' Bee said, when she returned from the bar with a bottle of prosecco in an ice bucket and two glasses.

'Bee, this is great. I would normally be tucked up in bed at this time.'

Bee stared at her in astonishment before looking at her watch.

'But it's only just after nine o'clock. What have you been doing with your life, woman?'

'You wouldn't believe me if I told you.'

'Try me,' Bee pushed.

Lockhart said nothing.

'I'm only joking with you,' Bee told her, sensing she had touched a raw nerve. 'You don't need to tell me anything.'

'No, it's okay. I will explain it in a nutshell then we can move on to more interesting things.'

'Sounds good to me.'

'I dedicated my life to my husband, always trying to be the best wife I could. Then, he came in one day and said he had found someone younger, more interesting and exciting. To be honest, it wouldn't be hard, over the years I had become the dullest person in the world. After he left, I was broken for a while, depressed even, but I signed up for a young person's holiday in Turkey with some girls from my work. It was in a resort full of nightclubs and bars.'

'Oh dear, how did that work out?' Bee asked, screwing up her face.

'Brilliant!'

'Really?' Bee asked.

'No, it could have been an horrendous experience, but I booked into a five-star hotel in a neighbouring town. That is one of the best things about being older, you have a bit more cash than the youngsters.'

'Did you offend the girls you went with?'

Lockhart laughed. 'Are you kidding? If they had noticed that I had gone, they would have been delighted.'

'And how was the five-star hotel?'

'It was just what the doctor ordered. I met someone special and had the time of my life. I rode on the back of a motorbike, had sex in public places and snatched back my lost youth.'

'Sounds utterly fantastic.'

'It really was, and it's not over because the man that I met when I was there is coming for a short holiday tomorrow.'

At this point, she decided not to reveal her lover's age or background. The finer details were private.

'Good for you, Lockhart. If your ex-husband knew that you had met someone else, I bet he would want you back,' Bee commented, pouring them both another glass of wine.

'Well, funny you should say that. There lies a story for another time.'

The conversation continued in a lighter and more general tone. They discussed the keep fit class and the many regulars attending each week. Lockhart laughed as Bee filled her in on all the scandalous backstories of the women who exercised with Mags every week.

The evening ended with Bee turning the empty wine bottle upside down into the ice bucket. They left the bar to head off in the direction of their homes. For Lockhart, it had been not just a night out but a step through the doorway of normality.

Chapter 14

The ring tone from Lockhart's phone played through her dream. It awoke her from her sleep. The first thought to enter her head was Aslan.

Please don't let him be cancelling his trip.

'Hello?'

'Hello, is this Lockhart?'

'Yes.'

'It's Elsie, from Princess Bride, in the main street. I wondered if you had time to come in and have a chat with me today?'

Excitement welled up within Lockhart. *She must have liked me.*

'Elsie, it's lovely to hear from you. Yes, I'd love to come in for a chat. I could be with you in about an hour?'

'That works for me. See you then.'

Within minutes, Lockhart was showered and dressed. Unsure if it was an official job interview, she dressed as though it were, wearing a checked pinafore and white blouse. She intended to change into something more youthful before picking up Aslan at the airport later in the evening. A strong coffee accompanied by a cereal biscuit was consumed hurriedly while she put on her coat, ready to go.

Strolling along the main street, on a wonderful autumn day, she felt truly happy. It had been a long time since she had experienced anything close to this emotion. A few short weeks ago she had nothing to look forward to and now she had a friend, a lover, and a job prospect. If George hadn't walked out on her that day, she would still be coasting along in the rut she had created for herself.

The bell above the door of Princess Bride announced her arrival as she entered the charming little shop.

'Ah, Lockhart! You said you'd be here in an hour. You're early. It's only been forty-seven minutes since I called you,' Elsie joked.

'I wanted to show you how keen I was.'

'Come over and have a seat,' she said, leading her towards the worn velvet couch.

Elsie sat down with her arm along the dimpled back of the sofa. Lockhart sat side-on to face her.

'I am just going to speak quite frankly with you, Lockhart. I opened this shop over 52 years ago and have enjoyed some very prosperous times in those years. It has been a privilege fitting girls for wedding dresses and fitting their daughters and even granddaughters. I have tried to keep up with the latest styles and trends. My range of dresses has stretched from traditional tastes to quirky way-out brides and almost everything in between. I recently fitted an elderly lady for her fourth time as a bride. I have enjoyed every minute of my work; it has been my life. Sadly, I never got to wear any of the dresses. You could say that I was married to my bridal shop.'

She chuckled at this comment, recognising the irony of it for the first time.

'In the early days, I had to hire four assistants to help me because we were rushed off our feet. It was originally appointments only. We are now in changed days, and for whatever reason, I am lucky to make one decent sale per week. The competition is fierce, and I am getting old and tired.'

A silence fell between them. Lockhart did not fill it. Elsie seemed to reflect on how things had become and seemed unsure of what she could offer this woman sitting beside her.

'I would love to hire you, Lockhart, but sadly I can't as I don't have enough money to pay you each month. I could come up with some kind of arrangement for you, but I totally understand if you wouldn't want to take it.'

Lockhart was genuinely moved by Elsie's struggle to keep her small business afloat. However, she understood that Elsie's problem was increasingly common for small businesses. The old man in the off licence was another example of the giants crushing the little guy. For him, the problem lay with the supermarkets being a one-stop shop where parking was never an issue.

'I'm listening,' Lockhart said.

'I was on the verge of giving up when you walked into the shop, and perhaps I see it as a sign. I need help to kick-start my business again. A fresh pair of eyes if you like. I can't pay you now, but I can share the profits if you can help me get the shop back on track. Your hours can be flexible, and I am willing to try any ideas you have, although my funds are limited.'

Lockhart didn't need time to think over the sketched-out proposal, but she paused momentarily before answering.

'Elsie, I don't know how much help I can be, but I'm willing to take your offer and do what I can. I have already thought of some changes you might make.'

'I can't tell you how happy that makes me. This shop is my world. When would you be able to start?'

'Well, I'm itching to get started now, but I have a visitor coming from abroad for a few days, which will take up

all my time. Why don't we say first thing next Monday morning? How does that sound?'
'It sounds like music to my old, failing ears.'

Chapter 15

It was fast approaching time to head off to the airport. Aslan was flying over to be with her. She couldn't quite get her head around it; a gorgeous young man was coming from Turkey just to see her for a few days. How was this possible?
Lockhart finished getting ready. The house looked great, making her realise for the first time that she had good taste. Nothing in the house previously had been her choice. The flowers from George had filled three vases which she placed in various downstairs rooms. Feeling a little fidgety, she decided to make her way to the airport, which was situated on the other side of town.
The engine of her car took a moment or two to start up. It dawned on her that it had been many weeks since she had driven anywhere as everything in her life was within walking distance from her home.
On the drive to the airport, Lockhart thought over something Bee had told her about one of the girls at the keep fit class. The girl was strikingly beautiful, dark wavy hair, pinched features, but in a pretty elfin way,

her figure slim and curvy. Bee had explained that her name was Marnie, and she was engaged to the professional football player, Ashton Brook. Lockhart had heard the name somewhere but knew nothing about him. According to Bee's sources, the young couple were getting married after Christmas. The whole set-up had given Lockhart the foundations of an idea which she was snowballing around in her mind. It would be thrilling if she were able to do something with it, but it would have to wait for the meantime, as all she could really think about was seeing Aslan.

The ground floor of the airport car park was sparsely filled, which meant there was no need to venture up to the next level. Being alone in a deserted multi-storey car park at night would normally have left Lockhart feeling nervous, but not tonight. Her excitement for Aslan's arrival trumped every other emotion.

Once in the main terminal of the airport building, Lockhart headed straight over to the information board situated at the rear of the concourse. The board showed that the flight from Turkey had not yet landed but was due to arrive in the next fifteen minutes. Many of the shops in the airport were shut as it was after six o'clock, but fortunately for her, Starbucks was still open.

With her latte in hand, she found a seat facing the arrivals door. Images of erotic sex filtered into her imagination as she waited for her young lover to arrive. Oh, how she yearned to feel his touch and have his flesh next to hers. The memory of his handsome, youthful face and his brown, strong hands lit a roaring fire in every erogenous zone in her body.

He is coming to Scotland just to see me. He wouldn't come all that way just for sex. He could have any beautiful woman that he wanted. Instead, he wants to be with me, the boring, middle-aged Lockhart Hayes. Why me? Why has he fallen for me?

She sipped on her latte, imagining what would happen when they got undressed at bedtime.

Will it be awkward…?

There had never been any shyness between them, but it had been several weeks since they had been together.

What if he doesn't feel attracted to me when he sees me? Maybe we won't have anything to talk about now that the holiday is over.

Tangled knots strangled her insides.

Oh no, I think I need to go to the toilet.

Panic began to take hold; she looked around for the sign for the washrooms. Bad news, it was in the far corner of the terminal. Sitting her latte down on the table attached to the row of seats, she made a run for it.

The cold coffee awaited her when she finally returned to her seat. A quick glance at her phone told her that the flight must now have landed. Nervous tremors started in her hands, swiftly followed by shaking in her legs. It was a form of pleasurable torture. When the arrivals door opened, she leapt to her feet, running over to the barrier. An elderly couple appeared first, followed by a young family.

Lockhart let out an involuntary yelp when she saw Aslan walk through the electronic doors with a small leather holdall. He wore uncharacteristic clothing, which changed the overall appearance of him. His jeans were ripped on one knee, his black puffer jacket was zipped to the neck. Her first impressions were that he looked gorgeous.

Young, but gorgeous.

He smiled over to her, raising his hand in a slightly awkward waving gesture.

Impulsively, she ran towards him, throwing her arms around his neck. She could feel his muscular strength as he held her tight, lifting her off the ground. Both of them were equally delighted to see one another. For Lockhart, it was an emotional moment which brought tears to her eyes.

I love him. I really, really love him. He is the love of my life.

The grip she had around him tightened. She was in no hurry to let go.

The reunion embrace lasted for a few more moments, after which Lockhart led Aslan by the hand towards the front door and out to where her car was parked.

The conversation was very limited on the short journey to Lockhart's house. However, the air was charged with an almost tangible sexual energy. Idle chat was not flowing freely as there was only one thing that they were both focused on.

The fan heater in the car was turned up to its hottest setting.

'I bet you are freezing?' she asked him.

He slowly turned his head to stare at her for a moment. 'No, actually, I'm red hot.'

Lockhart blushed.

She drove the car into the driveway before fumbling nervously for her house key. Aslan pressed hard against her from behind as she tried to open the front door. It became difficult to focus on the simple task whilst feeling his warm breath on her ear. His erection was now pushing on her hip. Lockhart's hands became useless as she fumbled with the lock. He slipped his hand around, grabbing her tightly underneath her coat between her legs, rubbing and squeezing in a slow rhythm. It was unbearable. The door finally opened causing them to stumble into the hall. In a frenzy, they stripped one another's clothes off and without wasting another second, he plunged deeply into her. This had been the moment that had dominated her thoughts every night and most of the day. By 3 a.m., feeling totally spent, they slept peacefully in each other's arms.

Lockhart was awakened by the doorbell shortly before ten o'clock. With a jolt, she sat up, feeling confused as to who could possibly be waiting at her front door. Reaching for her dressing gown, she slipped it on as she ran down to answer it. Standing in front of her on the doorstep was a young woman with a tear-stained face. Her eyes were red and swollen.

'Hi, can I help you?' Lockhart asked the woman, concerned that she may be in trouble.

'Is he here?' she pleaded in desperation.

'Is who here?' Lockhart asked, remaining very calm.

'Did he spend the night?'

'Did *who* spend the night?'

The situation was becoming confusing.

The young woman broke down in sobs. She began wailing that he had ruined her life and left her broken.

Words such as narcissist and user were also thrown into the rant.

'If you had any sense, you'd throw him out and have nothing to do with him,' she screamed in Lockhart's face. There was no reasoning with her. She was beside herself with grief.

Lockhart heard footsteps approaching from the stairs behind her. Aslan stood there with only a towel wrapped around his waist. She felt his arm go around her shoulder as he stood beside her.

'Who the hell are you?' the young woman screamed. 'If he's not here, then where is he?'

A feeling of compassion came over Lockhart. The grief this girl was displaying was not dissimilar to her own experience. 'Who are you looking for?' she asked calmly, taking a few steps towards her.

'George!' she shouted, wiping her face with her sleeve.

Oh, so this is Little Miss Perfect.

'I'm Lockhart,' she said, reaching out her hand to shake.

'Gemma,' she replied. 'Have you seen him?'

'No, Gemma, I haven't,' she lied.

'I'm pregnant.'

'Congratulations!' Lockhart said, pretending not to know. 'Maybe George has gone somewhere to get his head straight. This is a big step for him, especially at his age. He possibly just needs to get used to the idea. Give him time and space, he will come back when he is ready.'

'Do you really think so?' she sniffled.

'Yes, I really do.'

Gemma bowed her head slightly.

Lockhart wasn't sure whether it was in shame or defeat.

'Thank you,' Gemma said as she turned to leave. 'And I'm sorry.'

Whether it was a sorry for disturbing her or sorry for taking her husband, Lockhart couldn't say.

The experience had been slightly surreal and would have been terribly distressing under different circumstances. What a relief it had been to discover it was George's new woman at her door and not a previous girlfriend of Aslan's. Seeing Gemma standing there, pregnant and distressed, had softened any negative feelings that she harboured towards her. In all honesty, she could now say that wished them well as a couple, especially with a baby coming into the world.

Lockhart led the half-dressed Aslan into the kitchen, where she put on fresh coffee and cooked a breakfast consisting of sausage, eggs, bacon, and a fried pancake. They ate, showered, had sex once more and then headed off for a day of sightseeing.

Chapter 16

'Tell me where we're going?' Aslan asked, getting into the passenger seat of the car.

'Wait and see. I'm in charge now.'

'I kind of hoped that we would be going around Scotland on a motorbike,' he laughed.

'Well, I don't. In fact, I can admit this to you now that I'm back home, I was bloody terrified on that bike of yours.

The speed, hairpin bends, and the sheer drops below still give me shaky legs just thinking about it all.'
'I don't think it was the motorbike that gave you shaky legs. Am I right?'
'I'm saying nothing,' she blushed.
They flirtatiously reminisced the whole way to their destination. Aslan would occasionally reach over to caress Lockhart between her legs as she drove. The pleasure Lockhart felt from this rendered her unable to speak.

This man is driving me crazy. I just can't resist him. He has turned me into a sex fanatic.

Aslan removed his hand when he saw that Lockhart was turning into an area signposted, Park and Ride. He followed her from the car to a machine, where she bought tickets for them to ride on the tram into Edinburgh city centre.

They had boarded the tram and found seats near the back. Lockhart whispered a few sexual ideas into Aslan's ear. Her words were chosen carefully to stir his desire. When she saw him becoming highly excited, she slid her hand under his jacket to caress the swelling in his jeans. She felt his hand down beside hers, undoing his zip. Within seconds his manhood was in her hands. It took very little coaxing to end his frustration.

'Tickets, please,' the guard shouted as he approached.
Lockhart had no idea whether or not he had seen them.
'Oh, here you are,' she said as she handed over the tram tickets. 'Any idea what the weather forecast is for this area?'
'Cold but sunny, as far as I'm aware.'

He punched the tickets with his special clicker before handing them back.

When the guard had walked away, Lockhart looked at Aslan, whose cheeks were obviously flushed. Childishly, they both burst out laughing.

Walking along Princes Street in Edinburgh city centre, Lockhart held tightly on to Aslan's hand. She wanted to show the world that he was hers and they were in love. The age difference between them meant nothing to her now. After all, age was just a number, or so everyone said.

'Look at the castle,' she told him, stopping on the pavement. 'It's built on an extinct volcano.'

'Wow, it is really something.'

'I still marvel at it every time I come into the city. It is over nine hundred years old.'

She glanced at his face staring up, examining every detail of the imposing fortress. Knowing that she had his full attention, she carried on supplying him with information. 'Here's a bit of trivia for you. During the second world war, Hitler continued to bomb the cities, but he told his pilots that they could not bomb Edinburgh Castle under any circumstances.'

Aslan turned in curiosity to look at her. 'Why not?'

'Because he had chosen it as his intended residence when he won the war.'

Aslan laughed. 'I wish I had his confidence.'

Lockhart made a face. 'Are you honestly going to tell me that you are lacking in confidence? Just think about how we first met.'

'Okay, fair enough,' he conceded. 'But there are parts of my life I lack confidence in, things I worry about.'
'Such as?'
He thought for a moment. 'I worry that I won't be able to support myself and a wife. I worry that I will be nothing more than a masseur all my life. I worry about ending up alone.'
On impulse, Lockhart wrapped her arms around his neck in the bustling street. This vulnerable revelation endeared him even closer to her heart. She wanted to tell him that she would look after him financially, reassure him that he would never be alone and that she would be by his side until the day she died. Instead of telling him her heart, she simply said, 'Life has a funny way of sorting itself out. Don't look too far ahead. Enjoy what you have now.'
They walked further along Princes Street until they arrived at the Sir Walter Scott Monument. They stood at the base of the towering structure, looking straight up at the full height of the cone-like stone masterpiece. Lockhart explained to Aslan that Walter Scott had been a very famous Scottish writer and poet.
'Here's another nugget of trivia for you. There are two statues of Scottish men in Central Park, in New York; one is Robert Burns, the other is Sir Walter Scott.'
Aslan listened intently to facts that Lockhart recalled from her school days.
'You might find this interesting,' she continued. 'When Walter Scott suffered from a disease called polio as a child, he was sent to convalesce at an aunt's house in the country. While recuperating in bed, he read about

Scotland's history and folklore. Years later, when he had become an established writer and a poet, he told the King that he had an idea about where Scotland's lost Crown Jewels might be. He asked for permission to search the castle. The king allowed him to do this only because he was a fan of his work. After an extensive search, following clues that he had read about, sure enough, deep in the castle, in a locked box, there was the crown, sceptre and sword of state. They are still on display there today. I'll take you to the castle later this afternoon to see them.'

'That's quite a story. I think before we go to the castle to see the crown jewels, we should climb to the top of this place. We could pay our respects to Mr Walter Scott.' He gave Lockhart a mischievous smile.

'It's *Sir* Walter Scott actually, and no, I'm not very good with heights. There are tiny, winding stairs with people passing you, going down, as you go up. Trust me, you would hate it.'

'We are doing it. I've come a long way to see Scotland, I am not passing up the chance to climb the monument of the man who discovered the Scottish Crown Jewels.'

He grabbed her hand, dragging her over to the ticket desk.

The climb to the top of the monument had been every bit as frightening as Lockhart had remembered it to be, but the view across the city of Edinburgh was well worth the effort. They stood silently together, feasting on every detail of the streets in the city below them.

'Saved your life!' Aslan said suddenly, snatching up Lockhart from behind, pretending to throw her over.

'Hey! That was an incredibly childish thing to do,' she told him with a slap to the chest.
'Don't forget I'm not an old grown-up like you,' he laughed.
Ouch, she thought. *Too near the bone.*

Lockhart continued to tell her visitor yet more tales of the history of Scotland as they walked around Edinburgh Castle in the afternoon. By keeping a close eye on his body language when she talked, she could assess whether she was overloading him with too much detail. He asked many, many questions about almost everything. Although she found this an adorable quality about him, she did find herself adopting a teacher role to her pupil. This was not the way she wanted the relationship to develop.
'Where to now?' he asked her, allowing her to lead him by the hand.
'The shops,' she announced. 'I want to buy you some Scottish things to take home. I want you to remember this day in the big capital city.'
'I don't need you to buy me things to help me remember. I've had one of the best days of my life. I love it here. I love being with you.'
Lockhart became emotional. For the second time that day, she wound her arms around his neck, placing a kiss on his cheek. She had no idea whether people were looking or not, nor did she care. When she was around this young man, her inhibitions fled.
'This is my favourite shop,' she told him, entering the doors of Harvey Nichols. 'Men's department is upstairs.'

'Lockhart, you don't need to do this.'

'I know I don't need to, but I really want to.'

They headed to the escalator, which took them up to the exclusive menswear. A well-groomed sales assistant greeted them almost as soon as they arrived.

'Hello, can I help you with anything today?'

Lockhart thought for a few seconds. 'Yes, yes, I think you can. Firstly, I would like to look at Harris Tweed jackets for my friend here, then we would like to see all the leather brogues you have in his size.'

The assistant turned to Aslan. 'Please tell me your measurements and shoe size, Sir.'

'I'm sorry, I have no idea what the U.K. sizes would be. I am from Turkey.'

'No problem, Sir. Let's get you measured up, and we'll take it from there.'

They left the shop laden with bags, containing a Harris Tweed jacket, Church's leather brogues, two shirts and a red silk tie. Lockhart had spent a small fortune, but he was worth every penny; she would have purchased the moon and stars for him had they been for sale.

'Let's go for dinner before we head home,' Lockhart suggested. 'I know a little place not too far from here.'

'Don't you think you've spent enough money today?'

'Probably, but what is money for if it's not for spending.'

Lockhart decided to hail a black cab as it drove past them. They had walked for miles throughout the day, and her feet, as well as her lower back, hurt terribly. The restaurant she wanted to take him to was in Bruntsfield, which was quite far from the city centre. It was a place that she and George had gone on occasion. There was no sentimental attachment to it, it simply served great food.

The cab driver stopped outside the front door of a little restaurant called The Three Birds. It was intimately small, with a candle on every table. Candlelight pleased Lockhart as she favoured its kind glow, giving the illusion of them being the same age. They chatted and laughed about the day, holding hands across the table. Before their food arrived, Lockhart pulled her hands free from his grip, explaining that she needed to visit the ladies' room. On her return, she saw him writing down something from his phone. As she walked over to the table, he furtively snatched the phone and paper he had written on, hiding them under the table.

'What are you up to?' she asked him as casually as she could muster.

He looked embarrassed. 'Oh, nothing interesting. I was just writing down the details of my flight number for my return home. I like to be organised.'

Her instincts wanted to call him out on his lie. Of course, she would never embarrass him like that, nor would she want to appear jealous and needy. They had spent a wonderful day together; she wasn't about to let anything spoil it. Perhaps George's infidelity had turned her into a suspicious person.

Curse that ex-husband of mine. Am I going to go through life not trusting anyone anymore?

The couple sat together quietly on the tram ride back, each absorbed in their own thoughts. Lockhart rested her head on Aslan's shoulder, shutting her eyes. It had been a tiring day. The lack of sleep from the previous night was now catching up on her.

'Wake up, Lockhart, we're here,' Aslan shook her gently.

'Lockhart discreetly wiped the sleep dribble from the corner of her mouth, hoping it hadn't found its way onto Aslan's jacket.

Chapter 17

'I have chosen my top five films for us to watch while you're here,' she told him when they arrived back at her house. 'You shower first while I get everything set up for our evening of viewing. I even bought popcorn for you coming.'

'Sounds great. Do I get a say in what we watch?'

'No. I've told you before, I'm in charge.'

Whilst Aslan was away, she took the heavy fleece blanket from the cupboard in the hall. She laid it on her recently purchased sofa, which she had turned to face the television. On the new occasional table she had bought to replace George's, she sat two cold beers from the fridge and a bottle opener. The contents of the popcorn bag were tipped into her blue glass fruit bowl, which she brought to the lounge, along with a Pringle tube. On Netflix, she searched for the first movie on her list, Scent of a Woman with Al Pacino. Having no idea what films Aslan had seen or liked, she had made her choices carefully to cover all tastes.

It was after ten before Lockhart was finally ready to press the play button on the film. With the lights out, they relaxed in each other's arms to enjoy the night together. Although they were focused on the story, they were slightly distracted by the erotic fondling which was taking place under the blanket that covered them.

On Aslan's last day, Lockhart introduced him to Robert Burns. They visited the thatched-roofed cottage in Alloway where he was born, and the surrounding area in which his poems were set. As a boy, Aslan had attended English-speaking school, which gave him fluency of the language; however, the old Scots' language of Burns was way beyond his grasp. They visited a local art gallery which displayed paintings depicting scenes from the poem Tam O'Shanter. Lockhart explained the story to Aslan, interpreting the meaning behind the unfamiliar words that told the story.

'You know, Aslan, I would say that Robert Burns is the greatest Scottish figure of all time. Some people may dispute that, but I think he was amazing. He came from a humble farming background, but his father insisted on him having an education. When the popularity of his poetry began to spread, he moved to Edinburgh, where he would attend all the high society parties, reciting his poems to the rich. He became famous at this time, much the same as a rock star or movie actor by today's standards.'

'Really?' Aslan asked, surprised. 'Was poetry really that big back then?'

'Yes, but it didn't end well for him. He died penniless in his mid-thirties. In saying that, over ten thousand people turned out at his funeral.'

Aslan whistled his astonishment. 'Was that fairly recently?'

'No Aslan, it was back in 1796. No phones, no television, no way of effectively communicating, and yet all these people arrived on time to pay their respects to the great man.'

'Unbelievable. Was he as good as Mr, er...Sir Walter Scott?'

'Oh, I think he was far better, but that is just my opinion.'

'Lockhart?' Aslan said, acting somewhat coy.

'Yes,'

'Believe it or not, I write poetry.'

Lockhart stared in disbelief. 'Oh my goodness, you have never told me this before.'

'I have never told anyone this until now. It is probably rubbish.'

'Of course it won't be rubbish. If it expresses your emotions and ideas in a rhythm and comes from the heart, how could it possibly be rubbish.'

'I suppose you're right. I will let you read something I've written before I leave.'

Lockhart smiled. 'I would love that. Please don't forget, though.'

'I promise, and I always keep my promises.'

Chapter 18

The words of Robert Burns flitted through Lockhart's thoughts as she drove Aslan to the airport. *No man can tether time or tide*, she reflected. If only she could tether a time in her life, then it would be the past few days that she had spent with this perfect man. It had been a magical week, filled with so many good things. Before he left, Lockhart searched through the wardrobe for a leather holdall that had previously belonged to George. Aslan was laden with so many gifts from her, it had been impossible to fit them into his own bag.

Carrying a holdall each, they made their way through the glass doors of the airport. His strong, brown hand, gripping the handle of the bag, caught her eye for a moment.

I love those beautiful hands. I'm so glad George's property has come in useful for something.

She accompanied him as far as the security check-in, reluctant to let go. The idea of going home to her empty house without him filled her with utter despair. It had only been a short stay, but they had been inseparable for every moment of it.

Oh no, please no, Please don't leave me. I can't wait for days, weeks or months to be with you again.

She suddenly became aware of him prising his hand from hers. A fleeting memory returned to her, when the stewardess on the flight to Turkey prised her fingers from her bag. That now seemed so long ago.

'I have to go now,' he told her. 'I'm sorry,' he added, seeing that her eyes had welled up.
'Will I see you again?' she asked, hating herself for it.
'Of course,' he said, smiling. He kissed her. 'Thank you for everything.'
They parted in opposite directions. Walking away, she turned to glimpse him once more. He walked straight ahead without a backward look.
For no apparent reason, a sinking feeling developed in the pit of her stomach. Perhaps it was just the end-of-holiday blues. The comfortable bubble they had created over the past week had burst, now she was alone again. Back to staring desperately at the phone, willing a text to come through.

Every detail of Aslan's visit replayed over in her head. He had been attentive, affectionate and loving. She had been made to feel like the most special woman on earth. They had performed wild, exciting sex, indulging in fantasies she would never even have dreamt of. Their conversation had flowed, with never an awkward moment. Movie nights had been intimate as well as fun; in fact, they were perfect. Everything about Aslan's trip was more than she could have hoped for. It had been the time of her life, so why had a nagging doubt crept into her mind and embedded itself there?

Chapter 19

Lockhart drove home from the airport with a deadweight in her chest. A quote from Romeo and Juliet sprung to her mind.

William Shakespeare was so full of shit when he said, 'parting is such sweet sorrow'. There is nothing sweet about this parting. It just hurts.

Going home to a house that was left only with the fragrance of Aslan was not something she could face. A car horn tooted from behind as she veered into a parking place without indicating. Somehow, she had gravitated to the door of Princess Bride. From the busy street, she could see Elsie inside, returning an armful of dresses back to the rails. That was a good sign. There must have been customers trying on gowns. On entering the shop, she was greeted with a beaming smile from Elsie.

'I am so pleased to see you,' she said, unable to hide her joy. 'What a lovely surprise. I didn't think you were coming until Monday. Come in, come in. I'll put the kettle on.'

Lockhart was instantly glad that she had stopped by. It was a pleasant distraction from her sadness.

They sat down together like old friends, both in need of something from the other.

'I have been thinking a lot about the shop,' Lockhart began. 'I believe it's necessary to bring this shop more up to date without losing its small and exclusive charm. One of the biggest assets that we have is you, Elsie. You have over fifty years of bridal experience and have dressed generations of brides. That is one of the areas we need to really focus on.'

Lockhart wanted to start with the positives before discussing the changes.

Elsie's body slumped slightly. 'I know that we have to move with the times, Lockhart. I suppose I have sat back thinking that my expertise was enough.'

'Listen Elsie, most professionals have to evolve and improve their craft over the years. It is an ever-changing world and sadly, if you don't move with it, you get left behind.' Lockhart took Elsie's hand. 'Don't forget that the mother often accompanies her daughter to pick and buy the dress. There are plenty of mothers who still favour tradition. A safe pair of hands, so to speak. However, I think the shop needs a facelift. I think we need to advertise to let the world know we are here. I will deal with that side of things. And lastly, we need a wider range of dresses. I would like to see the shop stocking high-end, hand-finished dresses down to pretty but affordable gowns. We need to cater for every taste, from traditional to contemporary, and everything in between.'

'It sounds great, Lockhart, and you are right about everything, but I don't have the funds to carry out these changes.'

'Well, we'll make an appointment at the bank and draw up a plan for a business loan. I have never done anything like that before, but I will start digging around. I'll get some good advice on the best rates available. We can take the loan out in joint names and get a contract drawn up from a local lawyer.' As Lockhart sat explaining her ideas, she was surprised by her own confidence.

Elsie appeared nervous. 'I've never borrowed money before. My parents funded this place for me all those years ago. I think I am a little afraid to get into any debt, but on the other hand, financially, I am only scraping a living. I can pay my bills but am left with little to live off. I don't know, Lockhart. Maybe it's not worth it. Perhaps it is time to call it a day.'

'Okay, I don't want to push you into anything. It has got to be your choice and commitment. If this little shop is going to succeed, then we need to make some serious adjustments. If you don't want to do that or feel uncomfortable about it, we can shelve the idea, just forget all about it. Think it over and call me when you decide. Either way is fine by me. Please don't feel under pressure.'

'Thank you, Lockhart. I will give it some very serious thought.'

Lockhart glanced at Elsie's furrowed brow as she stood to leave. This was a big decision for someone of her age to make, but it was an all-or-nothing situation. All she could do now was wait for her call. Either way, she would see it as fate. Doors open, doors close, and it is all part of life's big tapestry. The problem was that Lockhart had already started to visualise pearl-embellished bridal gowns embroidered on her own life's tapestry.

Chapter 20

A deep sense of loss befell Lockhart as she entered the front door of her empty home. It had been wonderful waking up next to someone, especially one as handsome as Aslan. He looked so fresh in the mornings, hardly a hair out of place. Showering with him, listening to his breathing beside her in the night, stoking his muscular flesh.

I can't allow myself to dwell on these matters.

A thought entered her head as she walked into the kitchen.

Out of all the things that I love about being with Aslan, it's the companionship that I will miss the most now that he has gone.

There had been no companionship with George latterly. They did nothing together. They didn't even eat dinner as a couple.

I think that I had become invisible to him, apart from the times when he was irritated with me. I also think we were just playing the roles we had created for ourselves. None of it was real, not genuine heartfelt love that you can actually feel when you look at someone. We were just two strangers going about our routine in the same house.

The kettle clicked off the boil. Lockhart stirred the hot water into her sachet of latte powder in the mug. She knew she could make it extra frothy by whisking vigorously with the teaspoon. Her head was full of new bridal shop ideas as she sat swinging her legs on the bar stool. Tomorrow night was keep fit night, so she would make a conscious effort to seek out Marnie, who had recently become engaged to the footballer.

Maybe if Bee suggests going for a drink to Decanters, then I could possibly invite Marnie to come along. It would be hopeless trying to explain things to her in the noisy…

She stopped mid-thought. On the far end of the breakfast bar was a folded piece of paper with the letter L written on the front. Snatching it up, she unfolded it and saw the rhythm of a poem on the page before her.

Lockhart,
Look not thou on beauty's charming;
Sit thou still when kings are arming;
Taste not when the wine-cup glistens;
Speak not when the people listens;
Stop thine ear against the singer;
From the red gold keep thy finger;
Vacant heart and hand and eye,
Easy live and quiet die.
Yours,
Aslan xx

Oh, my goodness! Lockhart stared in disbelief. *Thou? Thy? What the heck!*

When he told her that he wrote poetry, she never dreamt that it was a highbrow piece of work. It was amazing! She read it over several times to feel the sentiment behind it. It was something that needed to be analysed carefully to find the meaning behind each line. The last line was so haunting; easy live and quiet die. How could her Aslan have written such beautiful words?

'Yours, Aslan,' she read aloud.

Was she his? Did his family and friends know that she was his?

She stared at the words, written in beautiful handwriting. Oh, the layers that were hidden within this man. Layers that she was slowly beginning to peel away. It was thrilling. When she lifted the paper up to her nose to extract the scent of Aslan, she noticed, in the smallest of lettering, a message which read:

Please turn over

She turned to the other side, where she saw that he had written more.

'Sir Walter Scott's not a bad poet, is he? I would have quoted Mr Burns, but I couldn't understand a word of it.'

A smile came to her lips.

He must have been copying that poem from his phone when I returned from the ladies in The Three Birds. Yes, he really got me there, she thought. *Like a fool, I believe everything he tells me.*

In truth, the only line of the poem she delighted in, was the only part he truly wrote, Yours, Aslan.

Chapter 21

Lockhart retrieved her phone from her handbag to plug it into the charger beside her bed.

'Three messages!' she screeched aloud.

I've never had three messages in my life.

They could not be from Aslan, as he would still be travelling.

Bee: Are you going to GFWM tomorrow night? Has your visitor from abroad left?

Decoding the lettering, she managed to work out that it was Get Fit with Mags. Replacing letters for words was not something she particularly liked, but there again, she was old school. Yes, she would be at the class tomorrow, and yes, her visitor was gone, was her response, all written out in full.

George: We need to talk!

Oh no we don't. All those years that I was there, desperate to talk, but you didn't talk. Now you need to talk. Well, I don't want to talk anymore. I think I'll ignore you. I'm done with talking.

Message deleted.

The Gardener: I won't manage to do your garden this week. I am taking my wife to an appointment.

Having a friendship with Bee changed everything for her. She no longer felt awkward about walking into the community hall each week on her own. Going for a drink after the class had also added a new dimension to her life. They were all simple additions, but Lockhart was experiencing them for the first time. At long last, she felt like she had entered the human race.

Bee was standing waiting at the door for Lockhart. They exchanged some idle chat as they entered the hall, taking their places at the back of the room. The class was busy, more so than usual. Lockhart scanned the room for Marnie, but she was not there. This was disappointing because she was keen to move forward with her idea for the bridal shop.

The elderly lady in the animal print leotard, pulled the heavy front door closed. Up went the volume of the music. Those first few moments before Mags took over always gave Lockhart a nervous thrill. Each week, at this point, a few of the ladies would shout sayings such as, 'here we go!' or 'let's do this thing!' but Lockhart was too reserved for this. Mags adjusted her headset, counting in the introduction to the high-energy song.

'Who's here to get fit?' Mags shouted.

'Me.'

'We are.'

'Yes, yes.'

Lockhart lacked the confidence to shout anything. Glancing along the row, she saw Bee joining in with all the audience participation banter.

Mags had everyone doing squats for the duration of the song, blasting out of the speakers. Some ladies sat on the floor in defeat before the music had ended. Lockhart kept going, pushing herself through the pain barrier. Her legs ached, but she persisted to the very end, even when more than half the class were beaten. Through the muscular agony, she saw the front door opening. Marnie was sneaking in, her head lowered.

'Better late than never, Marnie,' came the shout from Mags.

'Sorry,' Marnie mouthed.

'You've missed all the hard work. Just pick up from here.'

Marnie began squatting.

With legs the consistency of jelly, Lockhart rejoiced when the class finally ended.

Bee walked over towards her, wiping sweat from her brow. 'Boy, that was tough tonight.'

'The toughest yet,' Lockhart managed to reply.

She stood for a moment, bent over with her hands on her knees.

'Prosecco at Decanters?' Bee suggested.

'Definitely. Would you mind if I invited Marnie? I'll explain more later.'

'Course not. The more, the merrier. She's nice.'

Lockhart introduced herself to Marnie, asking if she would like to join them in the wine bar along the street. Lockhart sensed her pausing for a few moments before she answered. Lockhart tried to read Marnie's expression.

'If you have other plans, then it is absolutely fine. We can do it another night.'

'No, no, it's not that… It's just that, oh, nothing. Yes, I would love to come.'

'Great, we're heading along now. I'll just grab my stuff.'

Lockhart walked back to where Bee was standing. From the floor, she retrieved her water bottle and jacket.

Bee looked on, awaiting the news. 'Well, is she coming or not?'

'Yes, she's coming. She was hesitant initially, but I think she seems keen to join us.'

As they made their way to the front door, they passed Mags, who was packing up her equipment.

Bee shouted over, 'You're killing us, Mags, killing us.'

'You know what they say, Bee, no pain, no gain. See you next week.'

The three women walked together along the almost deserted main street to Decanters. It was surprisingly quiet inside, with only a few couples sitting in the booths. One lone regular sat on a stool at the bar, staring into his beer as though looking for answers. Bee laid her jacket down at a table near the window. Marnie and Lockhart joined her.

Lockhart pulled at Bee's sleeve as she made to walk over to the bar.

'No, it's my turn, you got it last week. You sit with Marnie.'

Bee reluctantly sat back down.

Lockhart returned soon after, carrying the bucket with a bottle of Prosecco in ice. She took peanuts and cashews from her pocket, tossing them down on the table to share.

The barmaid followed closely behind, carrying three glass flutes. Bee took over, pouring them all an up-to-the-brim share of the wine.

Lockhart focused on Marnie's features as she sat across from her at the table.

She is probably the prettiest girl I have ever seen. And that hair…

Marnie's black hair sat in large, soft curls on her shoulders. The dim lights in the bar created an aura around her, which Lockhart thought gave the impression of a Rembrandt portrait.

'So, Marnie, where do you work?' Lockhart asked.

'I just work for the council. Basically, I answer the phone all day. I hate it, really, but I don't know what else I can do.'

Bee stepped in at this comment, saying, 'Oh, Marnie, there must be so many things you could do. I bet you have skills that you haven't even discovered yet. Have you ever thought of going to college?'

'Yes, I thought about it once, but Ashton wasn't very keen on the idea.'

Lockhart's ears pricked up at this comment from Marnie. Changing the subject, she asked, 'Have you set a date for your wedding yet?'

'We haven't got an actual date, but Ashton said that after the football season would be best, around June or July.'

'Do you have your dress yet?' Lockhart asked, leading into her business idea.

'Oh, no, I haven't thought that far ahead. I always look in bridal shop windows but never see anything that would look nice on me.'

Bee laughed at this comment. 'Marnie, you could wear a potato sack tied around the middle with string, and you'd still look great.'

'I agree,' Lockhart nodded.

Marnie dropped her eyes, her cheeks looked flushed. 'I don't know about that.'

'Marnie?' Lockhart said, seizing the opportunity to talk dresses. 'I have a friend who owns the bridal shop at the far end of the main street. It has some wonderful gowns, but like many other businesses, it needs a bit of energising.' She moved forward, resting her elbows on the table. 'I had a bit of an idea that may help both of you. The exact details need a bit of ironing out, but I will try to explain the gist of it.'

Marnie sat quietly without making eye contact with Lockhart.

'Oh, this sounds exciting. I'm all ears.' Bee said, moving in close to the group.

'Well, I thought that if we could ask the local paper to get involved in a sort of competition which involves you as the bride-to-be. Here's how it would work; we choose several different bridal gowns for you to wear at a photo shoot with a professional photographer. The local paper could display the pictures, introducing you as Ashton's fiancé. We would say that you were in a quandary about which dress suits the best. We could then set up a website…'

'Oh,' Bee interrupted, raising her hand, 'I can do that. I'm in the IT business.'

'Brilliant, you're hired!' Lockhart laughed, before continuing with her plan. 'The readers would be able to look at you in various dresses and styles, then they can go on the website to vote for the dress that looks the best on you. By doing this, they would be entered into a prize draw to win a massage in a nearby spa or dinner for two in a local restaurant, you know, that kind of idea.' She paused for a few seconds to gather her thoughts and gauge her friends' reactions. 'As I said, I haven't quite ironed out the finer details.'

Bee clapped her hands gently. 'It's brilliant! I love that it will unite the community like something from decades ago. And Marnie, you will not only get a wedding dress that the people of your local area have chosen for you, but who knows what publicity or career could come from this?'

Marnie sat quietly, clutching her glass of wine.

'Also,' Lockhart added, spurred on by Bee's enthusiasm. 'My friend who owns the bridal shop will get free advertising and hopefully have everyone talking about her dresses. And don't forget that a certain prestige will come with the fact that the fiancé of Ashton Brook, the famous footballer, bought her dress in Princess Bride.'

Lockhart turned to Marnie. 'What do you think?'

'Well, I have to admit that I find the idea quite exciting, but I am quite shy. I don't like being in the spotlight very much,' she explained apologetically. 'I am not sure whether Ashton would approve of all the attention.'

Lockhart patted Marnie's hand, the hand that was adorned with the ring containing an oversized diamond. 'I would never want you to do anything you weren't comfortable with. The last thing I want to do is cause trouble between you and your fiancé. Can I just explain that you wouldn't be in the spotlight. Only your photographs would be on display.'

'Oh, go on, Marnie, it will be fun,' Bee pushed. We can all be involved in one way or another.'

'Okay, I'll do it,' she said, half smiling.

'Well, I had better order another bottle of fizz then to celebrate,' Lockhart said, thrilled by the completion of this phase of her plan.

'My next hurdle is getting the local newspaper to agree to do it,' Lockhart continued, feeling quite unable to drop the subject.

Bee snorted, 'Are you kidding? Have you read any of the headlines in that local rag lately, bearing in mind that the most exciting story is usually put on the front page. 'Residents complain about dogs fouling the pavement' or 'Council challenged over potholes in the road.' They are going to chew your hand off for this feature about Marnie and the wedding dresses.'

'Maybe you're right. I will reach out to them in the next couple of days.'

The three women felt quite tipsy by the time they finished the second bottle of wine. During the course of this eventful evening, Lockhart realised that Aslan had been absent from her thoughts for at least two hours.

Chapter 22

Walking home from Decanters, Lockhart reflected on the events of the past few weeks. The dreaded holiday to Turkey had been the best thing that had ever happened to her. Every good thing that she now had in her life had all started with the chance encounter with Aslan. She stopped as she approached her front garden. This house had been home for most of her life. During this time, she had loved it, then grown to despise it, but now there was nowhere she would rather be. If only Aslan was by her side, it would be the most perfect place on earth. She wriggled her temperamental front door key into the lock to open the door. Taking a deep breath in the hallway, she inhaled the last traces of Aslan's smell. She missed him.

If I could just get a text from him tonight, it would round off the perfect evening.

She took her phone from her coat pocket. No messages.

That was asking too much. I can't go back to checking my phone every five minutes. It is so unreasonable of me to despise the little device for not delivering a text that hadn't even been sent. I need to change my focus. I love him but I can no longer allow my life to revolve around him contacting me.

Lockhart lifted the small saucepan of hot milk, pouring it into the mug of powdered chocolate. After giving it a vigorous stir, she reached into the drawer, taking out a notepad and pen. It had been a long day and she hadn't had much sleep lately so carried her things upstairs to bed. Business ideas had been flitting in and out of her head since that first day when she walked into the bridal shop. These precious ideas needed to be captured and written down before she forgot them. Her new business venture turned out to be the perfect diversion.

The phone ringing at half past seven the following morning wakened her.

'Hello,' she said sleepily.

'Lockhart, it's Elsie here. I've thought it over, and I'm in. Let's get to the bank.'

'Elsie, that's great news. Deep down, I knew you would say that. I have lots to tell you. I have an exciting plan which is cooking along nicely.'

'Oh, how thrilling! Come down to the shop, and we'll talk.'

That afternoon the ladies were in the bank waiting to see one of the advisors about a loan. That was one of the benefits of living in a small town with three local banks. More often than not, you could arrange an appointment for the same day.

The business loan was approved, with the funds going into a joint account within 24 hours. Lockhart was astonished by the simplicity of borrowing several thousand pounds.

A phone call to the editor of the local paper was all it took to secure a meeting with him later that day. Over the phone, Lockhart gave very few details about her proposition, but it was obviously enough to keep him intrigued.

When Elsie and Lockhart left the bank, they talked over one another with excitement. It became apparent that all fears that Elsie held about borrowing money had completely left her. Lockhart took her arm as they walked back to the shop. Initially, Lockhart had decided to attend the meeting with the editor alone, now seeing her colleague and friend glowing with the promise of success, she dismissed the idea completely. They were in this thing together, facing all hurdles side-by-side.

'Okay, okay, I'm lovin' reader participation. I think there might be something in this, ladies,' he told them excitedly. His ideas began flowing faster than his mouth could relate them. 'We could run this feature for several weeks, you know, drag it out, keep them waiting for the next selection of dresses. We could even take it to a grand live final event in a hotel. I'll get in touch with local businesspeople in the area to encourage them to donate prizes. In return, I'll promote their shop, restaurant, or whatever they have to sell. Everyone stands to be a winner in this. I like it. There is a very good chance that it will increase the circulation of my paper. Yeah, yeah, well done, ladies. Let's move on this as soon as possible.'

Elsie and Lockhart walked silently out of the newspaper office. It was not until they were out in the street that they looked at one another, laughing.

Chapter 23

Lockhart made a salmon salad for dinner. She sat in the kitchen, writing as she ate. Her phone was placed beside her. Still nothing from Aslan, but things were different now. Her time was taken up with arranging the revamp of the shop and organising the newspaper competition. Aslan remained in her thoughts, but he no longer dominated them, he was simply a hovering presence.

She sent a text to Bee.

Lockhart: The newspaper loves the idea. Can you get started on a website? Give me the estimated cost of how much it will be. L xx

A text came back almost immediately.

Bee: I will start the basic outline tomorrow. Free of charge. Not surprised that the editor liked the idea. B x

Lockhart: I will not allow you to do it for nothing. You can give me friends and family rate, but I insist on paying for your time. L xx

Bee: I'll think about it and tell you at GFWM. B x

Lockhart then sent a text to Marnie.

Lockhart: Hi Marnie. The editor of the newspaper is really keen to run the bridal feature. We will arrange a fitting for you next week at Princess Bride. L xx

Within in the hour, a text came through from Marnie.

Marnie: Lockhart, I think I'm taking cold feet over this. I am so nervous about it. Maybe we should just forget it. Sorry.

Lockhart analysed the message. I *think* I am taking cold feet. *Maybe* we should forget it.
I don't want to push her if she doesn't want to do this. But if it is a lack of confidence, then I think I can give her a gentle nudge of encouragement in the right direction. She'll be sold

131

on the idea when she sees herself in the dresses. I won't mention it until we go to Decanters.

There was nothing more to be done, it was impossible to move forward without Marnie. Drumming her pencil on the counter, she read over her proposal for the editor. It was thorough and professional. Once again, she felt astounded by her capabilities. For now, all she could do was wait.

Her newfound empowerment prompted her to do something unexpected. Lifting her phone from the breakfast bar, she sent a text message.

Lockhart: I miss you, Aslan

As soon as she had pressed send, she wished she hadn't. No reply came.

Chapter 24

Elsie had the kettle on, ready for Lockhart to arrive that morning. There was no need to put the *closed* sign up for the meeting because customers were so few that it was unlikely that there would be any interruptions. They sat down on the worn sofa with their coffee whilst Elsie listened intently to Lockhart as she ran through her plans for the newspaper feature. It was only fair at this point to warn her of the doubts Marnie was experiencing. A look of disappointment had befallen Elsie's face, but Lockhart assured her that the doubts were temporary.

Elsie waited until Lockhart had finished before she made her own announcement.

'Lockhart, I've made a decision. We are going on a trip. We are going down to London to buy a selection of bridal gowns from a supplier I used to buy from years ago. He has a small business designing very exclusive and unique dresses. In the old days, I would travel down at least twice a year to purchase gowns from him. The problem was that, over time, it became easier to order in bulk from big companies that mass-produce the dresses. It meant I didn't need to travel alone down to London. It was also a damn sight cheaper. I think I just lost sight of what my shop was all about. I took the easy option. Anyway, what do you think about taking a trip?'

'I reckon it's a great idea. We could stay somewhere nice and maybe see a show. Do you know for a fact that this guy is still in business?'

Elsie face turned sheepish. 'Yes, I've already been in touch.'

'Great, we can go later in the week if you like. There is no point in wasting any more time. Neither of us is getting any younger!'

They looked through brochures for new furniture, finally agreeing on two golden-coloured, high-backed armchairs, complemented by a decadent purple velvet sofa with golden rope trim. The next stage was to arrange a meeting with a reputable decorating company to come in and give the place a badly needed makeover. Appointments were fixed in the diary for several local joiners to come in and supply quotes for laying oak flooring throughout the premises. The final touch was to order a magnificent chandelier to hang in the main area of the shop. This would be visible from the street.

Sorting through the rails of stock, Lockhart laughed at several dresses as they began clearing out the discoloured or dated gowns.

'I loved these Lady Di collars back in the eighties,' she mocked, holding the dress up against her frame. 'It was such an outrageous era for fashion. Big hair, shoulder pads, oversized earrings. I had it all. Looking back at it now, it was all in such bad taste.'

'Don't knock the eighties,' Elsie told her. 'The Princess Bride was a movie in the eighties. Believe it or not, it brought a lot of business my way.'

'Eighties movies were the best,' Lockhart said. 'Pretty in Pink, The Breakfast Club, Some Kind of Wonderful, Uncle Buck, there were so many.'

Elsie stared at her blankly, 'I was all grown up by that stage, fashion and movies weren't really part of my world.'

Several of the dresses were put together in a pile for dry cleaning. The dated gowns were heading for the local Cancer Care charity shop. The remainder were size coded before being displayed on the rail towards the back of the shop. The rails nearest the door were left clear for the new stock yet to be purchased.

Outside, in the street, darkness had fallen. A steady glare from car headlights flashed across the shop window. Lockhart looked out to see passers-by, combating the harsh wind that had whipped up in the past hour or so.

'Elsie, I think I'll call it a night,' she shouted through to the changing room at the back.

'Me too. I'm done.' Elsie moved her aching back from side to side to prove her point. 'It's been great today, Lockhart. I haven't felt this motivated about the shop since I first opened it. I feel like everything is getting a new lease of life. It's all thanks to you.'

'I can say exactly the same thing to you. I think it has been a fortunate twist of fate for both of us.' Over her coat, she wound her knitted scarf around her neck twice. 'I'll be back along tomorrow morning. We can finish things then. Now, do you want me to book flights for London tonight?'

'Oh no, dear, the travel agents will all be closed. Wait until tomorrow.'

'Elsie, I can do it online.' She saw a look of confusion on Elsie's face, 'I mean on my laptop... you know, my computer.'

'Yes, yes, that's right. I forgot that you could do that on a device now.'

'Why don't I book us a hotel? We'll just share a room. I could also get us tickets for a show if there is anything on.'

Elsie laughed, shaking her head, 'Can you really do all that from an armchair in your own home?'

Lockhart furrowed her brow. 'Elsie, we need to get you computer trained. It will change your life. See you tomorrow.'

Lockhart headed off, leaving Elsie to set the security alarm for the shop.

The wind was biting. Lockhart raised the collar of her coat up around her ears. Her cheeks began to sting with the cold. The smell of pizza suddenly enveloped her nostrils. Seeing a gap in the traffic, she dashed across the street to the pizza parlour. Leaving the shop doors wide open was a profitable sales tactic. People like Lockhart were heading home, feeling hungry. The aroma of fresh oven baked pizza had sent out its tendrils into the streets, drawing the customers in like the Pied Piper.

'Hello, stranger,' the assistant said. 'Is it the usual?'

'No. I'll have a cheese and ham pizza with a few pieces of pineapple on the top, please.'

'No problem,' he replied, gathering the tubs of ham and pineapple. 'Is your other half not having anything tonight?'

'Fortunately, I don't have an other half anymore.'

The assistant became embarrassed, unsure of how to answer. Instead of offering condolences or congratulations, he simply spooned extra topping onto her pizza.

Carrying the box flat in front of her, she salivated for the remainder of the walk home.

For once, I have to agree with George. This pizza might well be the mealtime highlight of my week.

Aslan entered her head unexpectedly.

Maybe there will be a message on my phone from him.

It had been several hours since she had checked.

Surely it's just good manners to send a few lines to say that he was home safe or that he had enjoyed his time in Scotland. Why did he not reply when I sent the message saying that I missed him?

It was mystifying to her.

It's not like I'm asking him to sit down to write a five-page love letter, and then take it to the post office. Keeping in touch now couldn't be simpler, so why doesn't he?

'Hello,' came a voice from the bushes.

Almost dropping her pizza, a scream escaped her. The house key fell from her hand into the hydrangea bush at the side of the step.

'It's okay, Aitchy, it's only me,' George announced reassuringly, appearing from behind the hedge.

'Oh no, that's what I was bloody afraid of,' she mumbled, searching in the darkness for her key.

'It's time we sat down together for a long talk to figure this out.'

An exasperated sigh exhaled from her, but she said nothing. Pizza and Aslan were the only priorities on her mind, not necessarily in that order. Calmly, she reached into the plant to retrieve her key. He attempted to follow her as she opened the door, but she blocked his way.

'George, go home. Gemma seems like a nice girl. She deserves better than what you are offering. Face up to your responsibilities. People are depending on you.'

The front door shut, leaving George standing on the doorstep.

The letterbox flap opened whilst Lockhart made her way to the kitchen.

Oh no, he's doing that shouting through the letterbox thing again. I can't stand it.

'George!' she shouted. 'Go home!'

A text vibrated from her phone, lying on the breakfast bar. She snatched it and read it. It was George.

She screamed.

George: You can't ignore me forever.

'Do you want a bet?' she muttered.

Chapter 25

Elsie wandered back into the shop to turn off the light in the changing room. For a moment, she stood looking around at her precious little empire. The words of her long-deceased father echoed in the silent space around her. She could still hear his words all those years ago, advising her that having her own business meant she would always have a pound in her pocket, she would be a free woman and she would answer to no one. It had been good advice. He had been right about everything. There was always a steady flow of cash, and no one told her what to do. Only now did she see the heavy price she had paid for her hard work. No husband to share her world, no children to watch growing up. Now in her seventies, she was alone with nothing left but a shop full of bridal gowns. The question she often asked herself was, had she known how it would turn out, would she still have opened Princess Bride. It was not an easy question to answer. Still, the new energy that Lockhart was bringing to the business meant that she could say truthfully that she was content. If given a chance to travel back in time to the day she opened the doors of the business on that first day, she wouldn't change a thing.

That said, it would have been wonderful if she had been lucky enough to have it all.

Going to London with Lockhart was going to be a memorable trip. Reconnecting with that special person was filling her with excited optimism.

Who knows what might come of it? Stranger things have happened. Perhaps fate allows you to claim your prize whenever the time is right. The thought filled her with hope.

Chapter 26

The hum of a text message from her phone on the bedside table awoke Lockhart with a start.

Aslan?

Snatching the device from its charger, Lockhart rubbed the blur of sleep from her eyes. She focused on the name of the sender. It was Bee. As she clicked on the message, it crossed her mind that she was pleased it was Bee rather than disappointed that it wasn't Aslan.

Bee: Started designing the website. How do you feel about calling it Marnie's in a Quandary?

'Marnie's in a quandary, Marnie's in a quandary,' Lockhart repeated aloud to herself. 'Marnie's in a quandary.'

Lockhart: Bee, you're a genius. I love it! Hold fire, though. Marnie is not on board yet.

Bee: She will be. We'll talk tonight in Decanters.

Lockhart smiled. Bee's enthusiasm was contagious.

The sun beamed through the space where the bedroom curtains should join. Lockhart lay back in bed, watching the dust particles dance in the laser of light.

Oh Aslan, please, please get in touch today. I would be so happy.

Her mind travelled back to the holiday in Turkey and the wonderful time they spent together. A delicious memory came into her head of him gently fingering her under the table as they sat in a pavement café, passers-by oblivious. She also relived the time he followed her into the luxurious ladies' room in the hotel. He told her to stand up on the toilet. He then reached in with his face under her skirt, giving her a powerful orgasm.

He was such an unselfish lover. Everything was about pleasuring me. If we ever get to spend time together, I am going to make it all about him. I will give him everything he likes. In fact, I'll go into the Ann Summers shop and pick out some incredibly sexy outfits. I know he likes stiletto shoes, so I'll get a pair of strappy high heels.

Her heart began to race with thoughts of the role play they could get involved in. Sweat formed on her forehead, and she reached down under the duvet to massage away the built-up tension.

'Phew!'

She breathed heavily. 'That feels a whole lot better.'

The clock on her phone said it was almost 8.30.

That was an unexpected morning call. First job to do, book tickets for London.

Reaching for her dressing gown, she headed straight to the kitchen, where her laptop sat open on the breakfast bar.

Scrolling through the list of available accommodations in her price range, she settled on The Purple Orchid Hotel. It was small but stylish, set in a perfect location in the heart of the city. Everything they wanted to do was within walking distance of the front door. A realisation came to her as she began looking at possible shows to visit whilst they were there.

It was my fiftieth, and I didn't celebrate. Not even George remembered. Had we been together, he would have told me to buy myself something from the joint bank account. That's what he always did.

It was difficult to believe that several weeks had passed without her acknowledging that she was fifty. Her special birthday had come and gone just like any other day.

That's what happens when you start to get a life. You forget about the boring stuff.

Chapter 27

Lockhart walked through the doors of the community hall. Mags could be seen on stage, setting up her equipment for the evening's class. Lockhart booked her space on the floor with her water bottle, before heading to the door to wait for her friends.

'Leaving so soon, Lockhart,' Mags shouted down. 'You must have heard that tonight was going to be tough!'

'I don't scare that easily. I'm just going out to wait for Bee and Marnie.'

'Okay, but don't go making a run for it.'

Lockhart shook her head, putting one hand on her heart with her other mimicking the girl guide's honour.

Bee was crossing the busy road when Lockhart looked out. Her face broke into a smile at the sight of her friend at the door. In her hands, she held a grey flat case. Lockhart saw that it was a laptop when Bee held it up, pointing relevantly at it.

'Have I got something to show you!' Bee announced. 'Wait till you see what I've done with the website so far. I think it's one of the best things I've ever done.'

'Bee, you're a marvel. I can't wait to see it.'

'Is Marnie inside? When she sees this, she'll be saying, where do I sign?'

Lockhart laughed. 'No, she's not here yet, but you know Marnie, she's always late.'

They looked both ways along the main street but there was no sign of their friend.

The elderly lady, who had claimed the job of closing the heavy door, asked them if they were coming inside.

Lockhart headed over to where her water bottle was standing on the floor, Bee stood to her left. The music cranked up, the two ladies got ready for action, keeping one eye on the door.

Mags adjusted her headset.

'Okay, tonight we are working on bums and tums, so watch me and join in when you've got it.'

The music system played an eighties classic, which everyone in the hall sang along to.

Halfway through the bums and tums routine, Marnie walked apologetically into the hall. Lockhart's first thought when she saw her was that something wasn't right.

Marnie weaved her way past the bouncing keep fitters, in order to get to the back of the room. She threw her jacket behind her, then picked up the moves of the routine from the women in front.

'Well done, everyone. I know that the session was tough tonight but if you want flat tums and pert bums, you have to work for results. See you all next week.'

Mags reached for her gym bag to get a towel to mop the sweat from her face.

Bee passed the stage, shouting, 'Is that perspiration I see glistening on your forehead, Mags? I think you need to join a get fit class!'

'Get out my sight, Bee, or I'll put the music back on and make you do it all over again.'

Mags enjoyed the banter from the regulars. She was proud of the fact that the class had been running for almost ten years, with the original members still turning up week after week.

The women were relieved to be outside in the wintry cold air. With very little ventilation in the community hall, it could get blisteringly stuffy after a strenuous work out.

Lockhart was aware that Marnie was quieter than usual. Her furrowed brow didn't go unnoticed either.

I don't think it's the right time to ask her if there is anything wrong.

Instead, she linked arms with Marnie, walking silently beside her in a supportive role. They both listened as Bee chatted away, hardly taking a breath, about her ideas for the website.

'My turn to get the drinks,' Marnie said, walking straight over to the bar. 'Is it just the usual?'

'Yes, one bottle, three glasses.'

Placing her laptop on the table, Bee took a seat before pulling up the screen. In the same vein as a concert pianist, she cracked her fingers before bringing up the website.

'Tah dah!'

Lockhart pulled the wooden chair up next to her. A gasp of astonishment escaped her.

'Bee, it's fantastic! It's so… so professional. I can't believe you created this. You are some girl.'

Bee sat back, lapping up the praise. 'There is some information that I couldn't fill in without you, but apart from that it's almost ready to run.'

'Oh Bee, I love it. You must have put hours and hours of work into it. I need to pay you.'

'I don't want paid. I have actually really enjoyed doing it. In fact, it has crossed my mind that I may go into business for myself doing this full time.'

Lockhart stared at her for a moment. 'I think you definitely should, you are so talented. As for payment, I will think of something nice to do for you if you won't accept cash.'

'Oh, forget it, friends do things for friends.'

That phrase moved Lockhart almost to tears.

Friends. What did I ever do without friends?

An image flashed through her mind of herself, walking alone to the shops to buy food to take home to cook for her ungrateful husband.

I was so incredibly friendless back then. I was a purposeless shell, and I didn't even know it.

'Here she comes,' Bee whispered excitedly.

Marnie sat the ice bucket down on the table, before returning to the bar for the glasses.

'Hurry up, Marnie,' Bee shouted as she approached the table. 'We have some really exciting stuff for you to see.'

Marnie looked over Bee's shoulder at the open laptop. The title, in bold lettering caught her eye, Marnie's in a Quandary. Looking extremely anxious, she sat down on the seat next to Lockhart. Her head fell into her hands.

Lockhart rested a motherly arm around her shoulders.

'Marnie, talk to us. What's going on? We're your friends, we want to help.'

'Just stuff at home. I'm sorry for ruining the night. The website looks amazing, but I don't know if I will be able to do it.'

Lockhart was so saddened by Marnie's demeanour. She could not understand how someone so beautiful could be so cowed.

'Marnie, this is not worth getting upset over,' Lockhart said softly. 'You don't need to commit to anything yet. I want you to take your time to think it over.'

'Yes, Lockhart's right, don't stress yourself. You obviously have a lot going on.'

Lockhart decided to lighten the mood a little. 'Bee, pour the wine. Marnie, I am going on a trip to London with Elsie, the owner of the bridal shop. We are going to buy exclusive gowns from a designer she knows.' Taking a small notepad and pen from her handbag, she said, 'Give me some ideas of the type of dresses you like. You are in the know about fashion. Tell me what you would choose.'

Perking up considerably, Marnie became quite animated as she described her favoured wedding dress styles. It became apparent that Marnie was impressed by the bridal gowns of the rich and famous. She explained in great detail the necklines, trains and veils worn by celebrities she admired.

To Lockhart, it was golden information and every detail of Marnie's dress desires were scribbled down frantically.

They were on to the second bottle of Prosecco, and Marnie's cheeks were glowing. The alcohol was revealing an outgoing side to her nature that was normally suppressed.

'What was your wedding dress like, Lockhart?' she asked.

'Too hideous to talk about,' Lockhart replied, grimacing.

They all laughed.

'How about you, Bee? Tell us about your dress.'

'Okay, this was twelve years ago, remember. I was looking through a magazine in the doctor's surgery when I saw an advertisement for a Harley Davidson motorbike. The big, hairy, rough, tough biker sat on the bike with a girl on the back wearing the most beautiful wedding dress. She had tossed her veil in the air, ready to ride off with her new husband. I absolutely loved the dress she was wearing, so I tore the page out of the magazine when no one was looking. I took the picture to a local dressmaker who was a friend of my mum's, and I asked her if she could copy it. After staring at the dress for ages, she said, I'll give it a damn good go.'

Marnie loved this story of Bee's. 'How did it turn out?'

'Honestly?' Bee asked.

Marnie and Lockhart nodded.

'Much, much nicer than the one the girl on the motorbike was wearing. I framed the picture, which still hangs in my hallway.'

'Bee, that's a great story. A truly original dress, apart from the one the girl on the bike was wearing,' Lockhart commented. 'I bet your husband was bowled over on the day. What's your husband like?'

'I am married to the best man on earth. He is a big six-foot cuddly teddy bear, and he is the kindest man I have ever known. He is my best friend and my hero.'

A smile remained on her face as she described him.

Lockhart clutched her heart.

'Oh, Bee, you're going to make me cry. You're so, lucky.'

Bee nodded. 'The best bit is that I know how fortunate I am. I would never take him for granted.'

Chapter 28

When Lockhart turned in to bed later that night, she mulled over the words Bee had used to describe her husband.
My best friend and my hero.
Pulling the charger cord out from her phone, she sat up in bed, device in hand. There was no will I or won't I? she simply wrote out the words in her mind.

Lockhart: Please let me know if we are something or should I move on?

Without hesitation, she hit the send button.
This time she did not regret her decision to contact him. Being in limbo was torture. Things had to be brought to a head.
Lockhart's sleep was deep. Dreams featuring her and Aslan together were the main content. They started out being deliciously sexual, with the two of them writhing naked at the poolside. It began to take a darker turn as women approached him, kissing him, touching him. He became distracted, leaving her alone, naked. She saw him with the other women and felt painful jealousy. A cold chill spread across her flesh, causing her to curl up in a foetal pose. In the dream, he did not seem to care about her feelings. Her phone began to ring in the dream, but as she looked around the pool area, there was no sign of it.

With a jolt, she sat upright, confused, and groggy. Her phone on the bedside table had vibrated with a text.

Aslan: Of course we are something, don't dare move on without me. A xx

Her night dress was soaked in perspiration. A loud thudding came from her chest. Closing her hand around the phone, she clutched it to her breast.

Oh, Aslan. I love you. I knew it had to be real. We will have a wonderful life together. I know there is a big age difference, but we will figure it out as we go along.

Tears rolled from her eyes onto the pillow. This was everything she had longed to hear.

Slipping her feet into her sheepskin slippers, she went to the kitchen. There was no way that sleep was going to visit her now.

Chapter 29

The flight to London was leaving at midday, so they had to be at the airport at around half past ten. Lockhart called a taxi and arranged to swing past Elsie's house to pick her up.

The taxi driver gave a blast of the horn to alert Elsie that they were outside the front door.

Lockhart laughed affectionately when she saw Elsie trundling out the front door with her pull-along suitcase. Her outfit was not dissimilar to something a mother-of-the-bride would wear. The little sausage-shaped sections made by heated rollers, were still visible in her hair. When she walked towards the taxi, Lockhart saw that her face was painted with blue eyeshadow and pink lipstick.

The driver exited the cab to meet Elsie, relieving her of her case.

'I'll get your luggage, darlin'. You get in.'

'Thank you. It's a bit heavy. I think I've packed way too much stuff,' Elsie babbled in case the driver cared.

Scrambling into the back seat of the cab, she exhaled.

'Oh, Lockhart! I've been up all night. I couldn't sleep a wink. I'm so excited.'

Her breathing became laboured, which concerned Lockhart. Reaching over, she took her hand in hers, patting it gently.

'Elsie, take deep breaths. Sit back and relax. Now breathe in through your nose, out through your mouth. We are going to have a wonderful time.'

Shutting her eyes, Elsie sat back as the driver set off towards the airport.

*

The shuttle flight to London was almost full. Lockhart found the correct seats before turning to Elsie.

'Window or aisle?'

'Aisle seat, please, Lockhart. I'll be up and down to the toilet the whole flight.'

Once in the air, Elsie beckoned the stewardess over.

'Hello, Dear, would it be possible for me to order two glasses of champagne? You see, my friend and I are celebrating.' She turned to Lockhart, giving her a smile accompanied by a wink.

'I will go and see what I can do for you.'

*

Elsie was, once again, hyperventilating with excitement at the thought of going to London again after all these years. There was such a thrill to be had in picking out exclusive dresses which were all hand finished.

Seeing Bartlett again will be so wonderful. Will there still be the same magic between us?

The stewardess returned with two glasses of champagne in plastic glasses.

'Here you are, ladies. Congratulations on whatever it is you are celebrating. Enjoy the rest of the flight.'

'Thank you, my dear,' Elsie said, raising her glass to the young woman.

When the attendant left them, Elsie turned to face Lockhart, 'Let's do cheers.'

'Yeah, good idea. What would you like to drink to?'

'Let's drink to the success of the shop. Oh, and let's drink to the day you walked through the doors of Princess Bride.'

They tapped the plastic receptacles together, making a clinking sound with their voices before saying, 'Cheers.'

'I'll add another one then. Here's to you believing in me and giving my life a new focus,' Lockhart added.

'Clink. Cheers.'

For the remainder of the flight, Lockhart brought Elsie up to speed on all the details of the Marnie's in a Quandary feature.

'So, I have tentatively booked a photographer for next Monday. Marnie is not totally on board with the whole idea, but I feel she will change her mind when she sees the dresses. She has reluctantly agreed to come along to the photo shoot. Of course, we will have to rearrange if the dresses cannot be delivered before Monday.'

Elsie listened to Lockhart's plans, feeling quite in awe of her.

'Lockhart, you have come up with such wonderful ideas. I would never have thought of anything like that. What I needed was some young blood in the business.'

'Elsie, did you just say young blood by any chance? I turned fifty a few weeks ago.'

'Well, you're young blood to me. How will we celebrate your birthday?'

Lockhart gave her a sly smile. 'I've got it all planned out. I booked an early dinner at the hotel, then we are going just two streets away from the hotel to the London Palladium to see The King and I. How does that sound?'

Elsie clasped her hands together. 'This is the best time I have had in many years,' she confessed.

'How do you know? We're still on the flight there!' Lockhart told her, laughing.

An airport taxi delivered Lockhart and Elsie to the hotel in the city's centre. The hotel and its location were perfect. Lockhart suggested they get settled into the room before dinner, then possibly indulge in an early night. They had a meeting with Bartlett Northcote, the bridal gown designer, at his shop early in the morning.

'If we get a reasonably early night, Elsie, we will be refreshed for our buying excursion. We have plenty of money in the business account, so I don't think we should scrimp on dress choices. If we both see it and love it, we'll get it. Do you agree?' Lockhart suggested.

'Definitely, I don't want to scrimp on anything. I want to stock the most exclusive dresses in Scotland. Lockhart, I once had a mother and daughter in the shop to look at bridal gowns. The bride-to-be tried on several dresses and then decided on a most beautiful ivory brocade design. The mother studied the label, entering all the details into her phone. I asked if they wanted to purchase the dress, she replied she could get it online at a fraction of the price. They left the shop.'

'Oh, Elsie, that must have felt awful. This is the problem nowadays, people complain that their town centres are looking rundown, but it's because the small businesses are not supported. When the exclusive shops in a town have to close, charity shops or pound shop businesses take over. People don't understand that you can't have it both ways.'

Lockhart didn't realise until that moment just how passionate she felt about the independent traders being the heart of a community.

'Well, when we get a shop full of Bartlett's original gowns, no one will be able to buy them cheaper online, eh Lockhart?'

Lockhart laughed, 'Yep, we'll soon put a stop to that nonsense.'

The ladies freshened up in their superior room, with a view overlooking the city. Elsie laid the white towelling bathrobe, supplied by the hotel, across the foot of her bed. Using her teeth, she ripped the plastic wrapping from the matching slippers. They were going to come in very handy when she visited the toilet in the night. A further two special occasion outfits appeared from her pull-along case to be hung up in the wardrobe. Next up were the matching shoes, with Elsie sitting them together under each co-ordinated outfit. Toiletries, face creams and foam rollers were carried in her two hands to the bathroom, where she lined them up on her side of the sink.

A smile spread across Lockhart's lips when she thought of the girls that she had nearly shared a room with in Turkey. Every outfit they tried on was discarded on the floor, with a free-for-all rule.

I would choose Elsie as my travelling companion any day.

From the bathroom, she could hear Elsie singing, Shall We Dance, from The King and I musical.

The waiter showed the ladies to a table at the window in the dining room. Lockhart felt a twinge of embarrassment as they walked past the other guests, not because Elsie was somewhat overdressed but because she clung to her arm. To Lockhart's mind, it gave the impression of them being a couple of old spinsters.

Maybe something in between the girls in Turkey and Elsie in her seventies, would be the ideal companion.

A wonderful dinner was enjoyed by both ladies, with conversation plentiful. The bridal shop was surprisingly not the main topic of the evening. Stories of past experiences were exchanged, sharing sadness and laughter in almost equal measure.

Elsie was talking in depth of a significate memory from her past, when mid-sentence, she shouted, 'Waiter!'

'Yes, madam?' he asked, approaching the table.

'I know this is not on the menu, but could you please make me a great, big, knickerbocker glory? You see, my friend and I are on this trip to celebrate, and I haven't had a knickerbocker glory in years. I'd be so grateful.'

'I'm not sure,' the waiter answered. 'I'll find out from the chef.'

Elsie continued with the story of her youth.

Night had fallen, but the city lights illuminated the streets outside. Lockhart was beginning to lose the threads of Elsie's long-winded childhood tale. Suddenly, something caught her eye as she raised her hand to stifle a yawn. It was a young man walking hand-in-hand with an older woman. The couple were side on from where Lockhart sat, but the young man's jacket made her take notice. It was identical to the tweed jacket that she had bought for Aslan when they were in Edinburgh. She may have been mistaken, but she could have sworn that she also saw him wearing a red tie. Rising to her feet, she walked over to the window to get a closer look. He was Aslan's height and build, his hair was identically black and shiny, exactly like his. The couple crossed the road, Lockhart looked on for confirmation that it was definitely him. Yes, he walked with the same confident air.

'Lockhart, Lockhart! What's going on?' Elsie's voice said from behind.

A violent trembling took over Lockhart's body. She could not control it. Hysteria was rising in her throat whilst her shoulders rose and fell with every breath she drew.

A comforting arm guided her into her seat, whispering in her ear.

'Breathe in through your nose, out through your mouth, come on, love, deep breaths.'

Lockhart could not answer Elsie, nor could she see the other guests staring curiously.

Sobbing heavily, she covered her face with her hands. The emotions she was experiencing were out of her control.

Elsie fidgeted nervously, staring at her friend's reaction.

'Lockhart, please talk to me. What has upset you so terribly?'

A calmness was beginning to pass over Lockhart, although on the inside, she felt devastated. Removing her tear-stained hands from her face, she lifted her napkin to dry her eyes. She inhaled deeply before deciding to disclose the source of her pain to her new-found friend and business partner.

'Oh, Elsie…'

At that moment, the waiter arrived with a ridiculously oversized knickerbocker glory adorned with a lit sparkler pushed into the cream. With an exaggerated gesture, he removed two long-handled spoons from his apron. There was a pause as he waited for the ladies to laugh and lavish their praise upon him.

Talk about bad timing.

Elsie thanked him.

'Go on,' Elsie coaxed, as soon as the waiter had left.

After a few more deep breaths, Lockhart shared the details of her trip to Turkey. They both managed to laugh at the escapades of the young girls, and how ridiculous it was that Lockhart had been with them in the first place. She described the luxury of the five-star Blue Lagoon Hotel on the hill, with its elevated sea views. This led her to discuss the spa treatments and how she first met Aslan. Missing out on the intimate details, she told Elsie of their connection, which blossomed into love. Her heart began to beat wildly as she moved on to the reason for her distress. She described the jacket of the young man that strolled past the window, his walk, his hair, and his profile, all resembling Aslan.

Elsie listened intently to Lockhart's tale of love. 'Did you see his face?' she asked her.

'No, not his actual full-on face.'

'What was the most convincing feature of this young man that made you think it was Aslan?'

'The jacket, the tweed jacket that I bought him. I also bought him a red silk tie, and I could swear I also caught a glimpse of that.'

'Where does Aslan live?' Elsie knew the answer to this question, but she wanted to secure it in Lockhart's mind.

'He never took me to his home, but he lives in Turkey. I'm not sure if he lives with his parents or if he lives alone. He

tended to avoid speaking about himself. He would ask all the questions.'

Elsie paused momentarily before summing up her thoughts on the matter.

'Well, based on what you have told me, I don't think it was Aslan.'

Lockhart rolled her eyes in a gesture that inferred that Elsie was just saying that to make her feel better. In truth, it was exactly what she wanted to hear. It did make her feel better.

Elsie continued. 'There must be thousands of Harris tweed jackets identical or similar to the one you bought for Aslan in Edinburgh. I doubt you saw a red tie on the boy who passed by. I think you expected to see it because you associate the jacket with the tie. I'm going to tell you about when my father died. I was devastated. He was on my mind constantly. Everywhere I looked, I imagined that I had seen him. I would see men in the street with similarities to him. The way he laughed, the way his hair receded, the way he walked with his head tilted slightly to the left. In the early days, amid my grief, I actually followed a man I truly believed was my father.'

'That must have been tough, Elsie.'

'Yes, it was, but I'm not looking for sympathy. I am making an important point. You see, when you obsess over someone, which I suspect you possibly do over Aslan, it is very easy to superimpose that person's traits, or even their face, onto a stranger of a similar height and build. Think about it logically, Lockhart. What would be the chances of you being in London at the same time as Aslan, who resides in Turkey.'

'That does all make sense, Elsie. Thank you for your wise words.'

'From what you tell me about Aslan, I think he truly cares for you. Don't let a destructive emotion like jealousy ruin what you have.'

The ladies retired to their room for the night. Lockhart's heart ached; a churning sensation had started in her stomach. Elsie's words had been comforting but she knew what she had seen, and she was almost sure that it was Aslan. For her, the trip had been tarnished. The image of Aslan with another woman was going to be difficult to erase from her mind. She would keep her feelings well hidden from Elsie as she deserved a wonderful time. No one would suspect how flat she was feeling.

'It's a big day tomorrow, Elsie,' Lockhart commented as she scrambled under the white linen sheets.

'It certainly is. I can't tell you how excited I am about seeing Bartlett again. It's been so long. We have always had something special between us, you know.'

She switched off the bedside light.

'Interesting. You're a dark horse, Elsie. Tomorrow, I want all the details. Goodnight.'

'We'll see. Goodnight, my dear.'

Lockhart lay awake in the dark, tormented by the visions of Aslan with the older woman, laughing together.

I must put these thoughts out of my head. I must convince myself that it wasn't him. Elsie was right, how could it be? He's in Turkey.

She hoped that by morning, she would actually believe it.

The silence in the hotel room was shattered by the sound of loud, cartoon-like snores coming from the bed beside her.

The next time we come to London, we're booking two rooms.

Chapter 30

The outfit Elsie donned the following morning was even more extravagant than the one she had travelled in. Lockhart wasn't quite sure whether Elsie was dressing to impress or if she had simply been around wedding parties for too long. Presumably, it was a bit of both.

In the dining room, Lockhart made her way straight over to the seat she had sat in the previous evening. Her eyes became fixed on the people outside that she could see from the window.

Elsie joined her, after she had collected a bowl of porridge laced with prunes.

The waitress brought coffee and toast to the table. Lockhart wanted no more than that.

'I like a nice bowl of Scott's porridge in the morning, Lockhart. It keeps me regular, and I think that's very important when you get to my age. Don't you agree?'

'What, sorry, what did you say?'

'Lockhart! Are you staring out of that window for any particular reason? I hope not.'

Lockhart rose to her feet, moving to the adjacent seat, which meant she had her back to the window.

'Is this better?'

'Much better,' Elsie said smiling.

Lockhart then asked Elsie to tell her about Bartlett Northcote. A bit of background was always useful when you were about to meet for business.

'Bartlett and I have known each other since the late sixties. Oh, the fun we've had over the years! Parties, theatre shows, concerts, you name it.'

'Were you two ever an item together?'

Elsie turned coy. 'Not as such, but let's just say there has always been a strong connection between us. The funny thing is, neither of us ever married. So maybe we were waiting for each other.'

'That is very romantic, Elsie. I'm sure that I will just adore him.'

'You will. As a designer of wedding gowns, I think he is the best in the business. Just wait until you see his dresses. They are to die for.'

Lockhart glanced at her watch. 'I would say it was time to head off to see him now. We don't want to be late.'

Off the main thoroughfare was the narrow side street where Bartlett Northcote's business was located. Lockhart had already passed the humble frontage of the shop when she realised that Elsie had walked through a door. The small, understated sign above the window read:

Northcote Exclusive Bridalwear

This was not what Lockhart expected from such a reputable business, based in the centre of London.

Once inside, she heard the whirr of sewing machines from the rear of the premises. The seamstresses, however many there were, could not be seen. The main shop space displayed the many handmade dresses in a haphazard way. A cashier's desk was situated to the front of the room. No sales assistant stood there. Only an antiquated till and gold bell for seeking attention were visible. Lockhart absorbed every detail of the surroundings, deciding that the Dickensian style of the business only added to its exclusivity. The lighting was the only modern feature to be seen. The bright spotlights shone strategically down on the sequins and pearls of the dresses below.

A feeling of awe fell over Lockhart, as though she had walked into something incredibly special.

With the palm of her hand, Elsie banged on the bell on the desk. This brought a young woman, presumably a seamstress, from the back shop.

'Hello,' she said. 'Mr Northcote is expecting you. Follow me.'

The ladies were led through a glass-fronted door leading to an office where an elderly gentleman sat behind a table.

'Elsie, my dear, dear friend. Come in, pull up a chair beside me.'

He rose to his feet to greet her with a kiss on both cheeks. 'Don't you look absolutely beautiful, as always. That colour suits you so well. You are one of the last remaining women who really know how to dress.'

Elsie replied with a bashful laugh. 'Oh, Barty, you are such a flatterer. This is my friend and work colleague, Lockhart.'

'Ah, Lockhart, that is a very unusual name. I love it!'

'Thank you.' Lockhart felt strangely shy in the presence of Mr Northcote. His overwhelming charisma charged the room.

Bartlett pulled over a chair beside his own for Elsie, whilst Lockhart sat across the table. He clung firmly onto Elsie's hand, as though he feared that she would run away.

'How about this, ladies? Coffee first, inspect the dresses after, then catch up and talk about old times. In other words, let's get the business out of the way, then we can enjoy ourselves.'

He lifted Elsie's hand to his lips, kissing it earnestly.

The woman who had led them through to the office returned shortly after to take note of tea and coffee preferences.

'I'll have coffee with a level teaspoon of granules, a splash of milk and three sugars. Could you make sure you give it a vigorous stir? There is nothing worse than finding a thick, sugary glob at the bottom of the cup,' Elsie said, laughing.

Lockhart sensed that the woman was irritated, she could see it on her face. Making the coffee was possibly not her job, she was merely doing it as a favour to Bartlett.

Bartlett exaggeratedly sighed, 'Norma, ignore her. She's always been a fussy pain in the ass.'

Norma forced a smile before leaving to make the drinks.

'Here's something you may be interested in, ladies,' Bartlett said as an afterthought.

From a three-tier chest behind him, he reached into the top drawer.

The ladies simultaneously leaned forward in curiosity.

He slapped a copy of *Hello* magazine onto the top of the desk, then began flicking through the pages.

'There we are,' he announced, turning the double page spread around to enable the women to get a better look.

The glossy pages featured the BAFTA-nominated actress Emily Jane Mott. Both women gasped, recognising her immediately. The feature covered her lavish wedding in Sicily. The backdrop showed a Sicilian village with cobbled streets, in the foreground. Emily Jane was laughing as she threw her bouquet in the air.

'Isn't she beautiful?' Elsie asked.

'Unbelievable. What a dress. These are the best wedding photos I have ever seen,' Lockhart agreed.

Bartlett adopted a smug expression. 'Emily Jane is a customer of mine. That dress is one of my own designs. She is actually a wonderful girl, so unaffected by stardom.'

'Barty, the dress is out of this world. You are such a clever boy,' Elsie giggled, kissing the top of his head.

An idea began formulating in Lockhart's head.

Marnie had been so impressed with the wedding gowns of the rich and famous. What if we had one of these photos enlarged and framed for the shop with a caption saying that many of the gowns were by the same designer as Emily Jane Mott's wedding dress.

'Bartlett, how well do you know the actress, Emily Jane?'

'Pretty well. We got to know each other during the many dress fittings. She has also asked me to design her ball gown for next year's Oscar ceremony. My speciality is wedding dresses, but I have agreed to do it, just this once.'

'Do you think she'd mind if we get this photo from the magazine, and have it blown up very large? I'm thinking that it would look great on the wall of Princess Bride.'

Lockhart threw a glance at Elsie as she asked this.

Elsie smiled, 'Yes, yes, that is a great idea.'

Bartlett nodded. 'I actually have her mobile number. Leave it with me, I'll send her a message.'

The ladies whooped with joy.

'You know what that means now?' Bartlett said in a more serious tone. 'You will definitely have to buy several of my gowns.'

The quality of Bartlett Northcote's dresses was exceptional. They had all begun life as a pencil sketch, then moved through several stages until they were hand finished. Every pearl, glass bead, sequin and stitch of embroidery had been sewn by hand onto the fabric. Each dress was inspected closely before it found its place on a rail on the shop floor. Bartlett had never advertised his business; word of mouth had brought more than enough customers to his door.

It was several hours before Elsie and Lockhart settled on their final selection of gowns. They chose a wide variety of styles with various price tags. Bartlett gave them a generous discount on the final sale.

'Would you be able to deliver these dresses to us as soon as possible?' Lockhart asked.

'I can have them packaged and posted by tomorrow or the day after. I always work with the same courier, he's a nice lad, but he seems to be getting busier and busier these days.'

'Just do what you can, Barty. We are so grateful to you,' Elsie said.

'Right, business is done and dusted. Let's go through to my office for a little glass of bubbly to celebrate.'

From a small fridge under the desk in Bartlett's office, he took out a bottle of Moet Champagne.

'Norma!' he shouted through the open door.

Norma appeared soon after.

'Be a love and rinse out these coffee cups, please.'

The stony-faced Norma snatched up the cups. Lockhart couldn't help thinking that it was a blessing that she was tucked away with the sewing machines at the rear of the shop, rather than dealing with the public.

'Weyhey!' Bartlett shouted as he popped the cork of the champagne. The foam swelled from the top of the bottle.

'Hurry up, Norma!' he yelled. 'We're trying to have a celebration here.'

Elsie began to laugh. 'Hey Bartlett, do you remember when we went to that fancy dress party in Kensington Park Gardens?'

Bartlett took over, 'Yes, I do. That was the one to which we weren't actually invited. Hilarious!'

Elsie took the reins of the story back into her possession.

'Lockhart, it was the funniest thing. Barty heard two of his customers talking about this party in a posh part of town. He invited me to go with him but only if I wore a mask. The masks were to disguise the fact that no one knew us and that we weren't supposed to be there.'

Bartlett laughed loudly at the memory. 'I showed you a good time, though, didn't I?'

'You certainly did.'

When a new shared memory emerged in the room, Lockhart took this as her cue to leave. It was only fair to leave the old friends travelling down their reminiscing path without worrying about her feeling left out. There was no similarity to the invisibility cloak she had worn with the girls in Turkey, this was different, and she was not offended in the least.

It felt good to step out into the bustle of the city. Bartlett's Old Curiosity Shop was great, but she was glad to wander around the sights alone. With no idea which direction to take, she invented a system where she would keep turning left. She took a left turn at the top of the street where Bartlett's business was located. The sound of unfamiliar accents fell on her ears as groups of people passed her by. The pavement cafes were filled with customers, wrapped up against the remaining chill of winter.

Lockhart strolled until she saw a turning on her left, parallel to Bartlett's shop. This pedestrianised road took her away from the main thoroughfare. Her interest was piqued by the small quirkier shops, so different from the High Streets stores. The fashions in the window of a vintage second-hand clothing shop caught her attention. The steps leading to the front door had been painted into cuboid shaped Union Jack flags. Lockhart found them irresistible. It would be impossible to pass up this opportunity, she had decided as she climbed them.

The shop was a browser's paradise and she was a born browser. After exchanging a greeting with the unconventionally dressed assistant, she headed over to the rail of jackets, displayed in the centre of the shop floor.

'If you fancy trying anything on, the changing room is just over there.'

Lockhart nodded with a smile.

Incense hung heavily in the air while The Mamas and Papas singing California Dreaming came out of a speaker fixed to the wall with a bracket. The hippy-looking assistant arranged silver rings on a tray at the checkout, leaving Lockhart to look at jackets in her size.

After much deliberation, she finally settled on an up-cycled Joey d jacket. She was delighted with her purchase, made from many different fabrics of old jackets sewn together. Being in her fifties, she remembered Joey d from The Clothes Show. She was also aware that he had opened a business on Boughton Street in Edinburgh City centre.

This will enhance my new wardrobe nicely.

The shop owner wrapped the Joey d in tissue paper before slipping it into a bag with the shop's name, YESTERDAY, emblazoned across it.

Leaving the shop, Lockhart took a left turn because that was the rule. From what she could see ahead of her, the foot of the street appeared to take her out to another bustling part of the city. Above the shop roofs in the narrow side street, she could make out the steeple of a church or cathedral.

I think I'll head into the church and light a candle for my mum.

The thought of this made her a little tearful. Her mum had passed away so long ago, but unexpected bouts of sadness could strike her at any time. The idea of paying her respects to her mum made her quicken her step, anxious to carry out her plan.

Adopting a fast walk, not quite a run, she hurried. A slight jog took over, but she slowed it back to a fast walk. At the end of the street, she realised that if she wanted to get to the church, she'd have to break the rule of turning left. The church, which she could now see was a cathedral, was to the right.

Oh well, rules were made to be broken. My mum is more important than a left-turn rule.

As she turned right, she stopped abruptly. Staring ahead, her eyes could not quite compute what she was seeing. It was Aslan with a woman. Not the same Aslan that walked past the hotel window, but the real Aslan, her Aslan.

The Harris Tweed jacket was slightly different from the one the boy wore the previous night, but she was sure that this one was exactly the same as Aslan's. Rooted to the pavement, she stared in utter disbelief. Aslan had his back to her, but she was certain it was him.

No wonder I have heard nothing from him.

The woman he was with was older, much older. They were deep in conversation, looking at something in the window of the jewellers. Lockhart could see that Aslan's elderly companion was laughing at his every word while she clung onto the sleeve of his Harris Tweed jacket.

I've been such a fool.

It struck her that when she and Aslan were in Edinburgh, they must have looked just as ridiculous as the couple she now saw before her.

He needs to know that I've seen him. The game is up. He will never treat me like an old cash cow again.

With her heart hammering within her chest, she strode angrily towards them. The closer she came, the louder their laughter rang in her ears. The woman saw her before Aslan did, giving her an odd stare.

Standing right behind him, she tapped heavily on his back. 'Remember me?' she spat.

The young man turned in shock. The laughter had dwindled away.

It was not Aslan. Close up, it didn't even resemble him.

'I'm sorry. I thought you were someone else.'

'Obviously,' the older woman scoffed. 'How rude,' she added, turning to her look-nothing-alike Aslan.

Lockhart clutched her Joey d jacket in the bag and ran in the opposite direction.

Why did I do that? Elsie's right. I am obsessed. I need to sort myself out.

In the direction of Bartlett's bridal wear shop, she continued to run. Sweat moistened her forehead and armpits, tears clouded her vision. A feeling of self-loathing consumed her as she put as much distance as she could between her and the scene of the mortifying crime.

I'll say nothing to Elsie about this experience. I will never tell anyone. I feel so stupid.

When she reached the side street where Bartlett's shop was located, she stopped running. Instead, she walked casually as though nothing had happened. Once inside, she made her way past the main area of dresses, through the back to the office. She took deep breaths to slow her heartbeat before entering.

'Ah! Lockhart, lovely to see you back. Did you buy anything nice?' Elsie asked, glancing down at the YESTERDAY bag.

Lockhart saw that Elsie had moved even closer to Bartlett, if that were even possible. Both hands of the couple were entwined at the fingers. Elsie's leg was resting on Bartlett's shin, her shoes had been discarded. The empty champagne bottle accounted for their flushed cheeks and overfamiliar manner.

'Yes, I bought a really nice jacket from a designer who now has a business in Edinburgh,' she babbled, feeling embarrassed just by being there.

'Grab a chair,' Bartlett instructed her. 'Let us tell you about the laughs we've been having, remembering the escapades of our youth.'

A resounding guffaw escaped him.

The last thing Lockhart wanted at that moment was to hear more of their wild, gregarious stories.

'Eh, listen, I am not feeling too well, folks. I have a sore head and an upset stomach. I really need to go and lie down. Why don't you two take the dinner reservation and the theatre tickets? I just want to sleep.'

'Oh, Lockhart! We couldn't. It was to celebrate your belated birthday,' Elsie sympathised, but was clearly reluctant to stand up and release her grip on Bartlett.

'No arguments. I'll see you when you get back to the hotel tonight.'

There was no energy left in her to discuss the matter further. She turned, wished them well, and left. When the door was closed behind her, the sounds of uproarious laughter resumed from the elderly couple.

Chapter 31

Lockhart walked into the hotel dining room alone. Going solo no longer bothered her. The Turkish holiday cured her of that insecurity. The table at the window was free, so she headed in that direction, choosing the chair that would give her a view of the restaurant rather than the city.

If I face the window, I'll just start imagining that I see Aslan again. I've embarrassed myself quite enough for one day. I'm not going to turn around at all.

The waitress took Lockhart's order for a starter, and main course and the wine waiter brought her the previously ordered bottle of Argentinian Malbec.

Sipping slowly on the red wine, her mind drifted back to her life with George. There had been a time when he took her to the best restaurants, but more often than not, she dined alone while he talked on his phone. He told her he needed to take the calls as he had a big case.

Why did I not ask if the call could wait until we had eaten? Why did I not insist that he leave his phone in the car? What happened to lawyers in the past when mobile phones weren't around? How did they manage? I can't believe I just sat there without question. I was a nobody worth bothering about back then. A faint shadow.

The waitress arrived with her scallops. She thanked her. Then looking down at her starter, her thoughts again returned to George.

I really hated the way George would steal food from my plate. He would simply reach over and take a scallop or a chip without asking. That made me so damned angry, but I never said anything.

Her thoughts stayed with George as she tried to picture him as a father.

I can't imagine what would happen if a little mini-George were running around, messing up his papers for court or crying and screaming through his television programmes.

A smile crossed her lips when she visualised the child knocking over George's whisky, sending his ice cubes flying across the carpet.

He is going to hate every second of that messy stage.

Was she jealous about George becoming a father? There had always been a deep longing within her to be a mum, but it was never considered. George had set out his child-free cards on the table when they first met; the case had been closed. With regards to George's new fatherhood role in life, she could say truthfully that, no, she wasn't envious in the least. For her, the motherhood ship had sailed.

Coffee with shortbread was the last course to be brought to Lockhart. During this time of reflection, she found herself stirring the coffee over and over. For a moment, she glanced at the window behind her.

There's Aslan!

Lockhart saw a young man pass the window.

Oh, for goodness sake, I'm doing it again. Time for bed.

Grabbing the piece of shortbread, she abandoned the thoroughly stirred coffee and left the dining room.

Lockhart unfurled the little shower cap supplied by the hotel. It was unusual for her to wear anything over her hair when bathing, but it was free, so she decided to use it. After disrobing, she slid down into the hot bubble bath until the water lapped around her ears. A thought occurred to her as she soaked.

My phone! I haven't checked my phone for messages.

Torn between staying in the luxurious bath and getting out to retrieve her phone, she decided on the latter. Her curiosity was preventing her from relaxing, so she reached for the towel, which had been left on the floor.

Three messages were showing on her phone screen.

George: Where the hell are you, Lockhart? I've been standing here outside the house for three hours. I'm freezing my nuts off. Text me immediately.

George: Okay, now I'm getting worried. Where can you be? I'll sit in the car until you come.

He's going to have a very long night.

Aslan: Hi, Lockhart, Sorry I haven't been in touch. When I save enough money, I will come back to Scotland to see you. Love Aslan.

Lockhart let out a scream of joy.

He wants to come and see me! He can't be in London, or he would have mentioned it. I can't wait until he saves up. I need him now. Oh, I'm so happy that he misses me.

Lockhart: Hi, Aslan. Lovely to hear from you. Let me know the dates you want to come, and I will book your ticket from here. My treat. L x'

Aslan: I can't let you do that for me. I will do some work for my uncle at the vineyard to get some extra money.
Lockhart: I insist.

Aslan: Thank you, Lockhart. You are so kind.

I would give my last penny in the world to have that man back in my arms and back in my bed, for that matter. Love is not about money. The rule should be, the one that hath giveth to the one that hath not.
She chuckled aloud at her own wise saying.
Apart from earlier at the shops, when she hunted down a complete stranger, it turned out to have been a perfect day. Beautiful dresses for the shop and news from Aslan.
'Ahh,' she said aloud as she lay back on the feather-filled pillows. 'Now sleep.'

Chapter 32

Lockhart opened her eyes in the sun-filled hotel room.
What a sleep! I didn't even hear Elsie come in.

Glancing over to the single bed beside her, she was shocked to discover that Elsie had not returned.

Elsie, you old rascal.

She pictured Elsie waking up in Bartlett's bed, her underwear strewn around the room.

Elsie turned up at the breakfast table with no mention of the fact that she had not returned the previous evening. Her hair was wild, her elegant two-piece suit looked crushed.

'I'll just go over and get my porridge, then I'll tell you all about the wonderful evening I had.'

She turned to leave the table but stopped.

'Are you feeling better, dear?' she asked.

'Yes, much better. I'm so glad you had a lovely time.'

The ladies finished their breakfast, catching up on all the news before heading to the room to pack for their return home.

The overhead information board in the airport informed the ladies that the shuttle flight to Edinburgh was leaving from Gate 5. Elsie was wearing her final outfit for the trip home. The turquoise and ivory ensemble consisted of a dress and jacket, set off by a pair of matching shoes. Her heels were high, perhaps a little too high for a woman of her age. It took her all her time to keep in step with Lockhart. When she finally saw the vacant, plastic-moulded seats outside Gate 5, she collapsed gratefully into one.

Lockhart took her phone from her handbag to send two text messages.

Marnie, hope you can still make it to the dress fitting on Monday. What till you see the dresses we've ordered from London.

Aslan, I am booking your flight to Scotland later today. I realised that I don't have your surname, date of birth or any other information that you can think of that I may need.

Why did I never ask anything about him? His surname. I don't even know his surname.

On the flight back to Edinburgh, Lockhart was aware that Elsie was unusually quiet. Allowances could be made because she was tired, maybe a bit hungover. That aside, Lockhart could only presume that leaving Bartlett was difficult for her. She knew that feeling only too well. As an onlooker, it seemed like Elsie and Bartlett had spent their time together over the years, wildly partying instead of sitting down to discuss their future together. There was no doubt in Lockhart's mind that Bartlett was incredibly fond of Elsie. It could even be love. From what Elsie had told her, they had let the years slide away from them without either one of them bringing up the subject of their future.

I never want this to happen to Aslan and me. We mustn't let our future together be left unspoken about. I will do everything I can to ensure that we are solidified as a couple with a lifetime ahead.

Then she told herself off.

I'm so stupid. I'm fifty now, will he still be attracted to me when I'm sixty, seventy... Oh, what does it matter? Age is just a number, everyone says so.

'Are you all right, Elsie?' Lockhart asked, resting a hand on her arm.

'Yes, I'm fine. I had such a wonderful trip, and I'm now sitting here reliving every moment of it. I don't know when I'll see Bartlett again. I'm going to miss him terribly.'

'Are you kidding, Elsie? If these dresses sell the way I think they will, then we will be taking a trip to London every month, at least.'

Elsie brightened up.

'Maybe it's time you told him how you feel.'

Elsie turned to stare out of the window, but she did not give a reply.

When the shuttle flight arrived in Edinburgh, Lockhart switched on her phone as she walked through the airport. Two text messages vibrated through. One was from Marnie.

Marnie: Yes, still coming.

Lockhart smiled at Marnie's typically short, to the point, message.

Aslan: Cerci, my surname is Cerci. Aslan Cerci.

Aslan Cerci. Lockhart Cerci, Lockhart Cerci.
Oh, stop it, you foolish woman.

Focusing on the full text, she was struck by Aslan's date of birth.

I'm celebrating my special birthday today...

They had gone out on that wretched motorbike along the clifftop road. Memories filled her mind of them sitting at a pavement café in a picturesque village. Lockhart had handed him the silver bracelet she had bought earlier at the market at the nearby village.

This is the best birthday I have ever had.

They had indulged in highly erotic sex for the first time that night, and the thought of it was stirring within her.

Wait a minute, she thought, *his special birthday happened in August when I was there. The date of birth he gave me is in March. How could that be? Why would he say it was his birthday when it wasn't?*

It didn't matter what month his birthday fell on, but he had lied to her. This niggled at her.

Chapter 33

Lockhart sat on a stool at the breakfast bar in her kitchen. Using all the information that Aslan supplied her with, she managed to book his flights to and from Scotland. When the task was completed, she began thinking about the date-of-birth discrepancy. It swirled around and around in her mind as she tried to think of a logical explanation. A recollection returned to her of a Greek girl called Lina who attended her high school. From what Lockhart could remember, she had two birthdays, a proper birthday, and a name day. They were equally special days, according to Lina.

That could be it. It may have been his name day. That's if the Turkish traditions are the same as the Greeks. I'm sure that's what it is.

She decided not to google name days in Turkey. Some things were better not knowing.

To take her thoughts away from Aslan in the meantime, she searched Emily Jane Mott's wedding on her laptop. The photos from Hello magazine appeared on the screen. They were incredible. Zooming in on the fine detail of the dress, Lockhart was filled with admiration for Bartlett, especially knowing that every dress was finished by hand. It had been enlightening visiting the shop and seeing for herself the difference between a designer and a mass-produced wedding gown. Bartlett Northcote had been nothing like what she had imagined him to be. He was not tall in stature, and his hairline had receded back to an unacceptable place on the crown of his head. His ginger sideburns were the only clue left that he had once been a redhead. The pompous London designer she expected was far removed from the unassuming gentleman she had met.

On impulse, she typed his name into Google search. To her surprise, there were pages of information about his life. In one article, he described his love of dresses from childhood. He explained that he failed most of his school subjects because he sat in class designing gowns at the back of his jotters. His mother encouraged his passion by giving him old curtain fabric and buying him a second-hand sewing machine. Lockhart scrutinised the images of him in his thirties, and although he had never been classically handsome, he did have something.

Thinking about Bartlett reminded Lockhart of a quote she had heard somewhere. It was by Aristotle. *Give me a child until he is seven, and I will show you the man.*

George once told her he had always intended to be a lawyer. He said he had a notebook at school that he used for writing rules and regulations. He explained that he had always believed in fairness. If someone had been wronged in the playground, he would take them to the teacher and speak in their defence. It made Lockhart laugh to think of George as an obnoxious young man, brandishing his notebook in the playground as he touted for victims to defend.

Memories drifted back to a time when she would have been around six or seven. Her dad had built a Wendy house in the garden as a surprise for her. The disappointment she felt when she saw it must have been apparent on her face because her father suddenly said, 'Why don't we turn it into an office?'

When he saw that she liked the idea, he built a sign over the door and supplied her with a rubber stamp and some old cheques. Perhaps playing in houses with baby dolls was never meant to be for her. The idea that she was destined to be a businesswoman suited her nicely.

She clicked back to the photos of Emily Jane Mott's wedding. Another idea was forming in her mind which would be far more effective than a framed photo for the shop's wall. Into Google search, she typed *companies that turn pictures into wallpaper.*

Chapter 34

When Lockhart arrived at Princess Bride early on Monday morning, the courier who had been hired to transport the dresses, was pulling into a parking space outside the door. The driver and his colleague carried the newly purchased wedding gowns together. Lockhart followed behind them. She was met with the smell of oak from the newly laid floors, blended with the aroma of freshly ground coffee from the percolator in the corner.

'Ah, Lockhart, just in time to help me with these mirrors. They arrived yesterday. I've unwrapped one of them to take a peek. It's gorgeous. I want them beside the changing rooms. Oh, and before I forget, Bartlett called late last night to say that Emily-Jane Mott was delighted to be displayed on the wall.'

'That's great news. I hoped she would agree because I've already ordered something special, in anticipation.'

'You little minx! What is it?' Elsie asked, unable to hide her excitement.

'Wait and see.'

Lockhart walked over to get a closer look at the mirror, which stood six feet tall with an ornate gilt frame.

'I love it,' Lockhart said, unravelling the plastic wrapping from the other mirror. 'They were a perfect choice, and if we position them carefully, the brides can see the front and back of their dresses. Okay, grab the other side and lift after the count of three.'

'I'm ready,' Elsie announced.

'One, two, three, lift!'

The mirror did not move a millimetre from the ground.

'Give it all you've got, Elsie. One, two, three, lift!'

It was hopeless. The ladies were no match for the mirrors.

'Boys!' Elsie bellowed to the young men who had delivered the dresses. 'Can you help a couple of damsels in distress, please?' She comically fluttered her eye lashes, making Lockhart laugh out loud.

The men lifted the gilt-framed mirrors like they were made of cardboard.

A resounding ding came from the bell above the front door. Lockhart's initial thought was Marnie. She ran through to the front of the shop and met a long-haired, youngish man with a camera on a strap around his neck and a tripod stand in his hand.

'Hi,' Lockhart welcomed him. 'Thanks for coming. Our model has not arrived yet, but she does have a tendency to be late. Come in and have a cup of coffee.'

The photographer unloaded his equipment, then introduced himself to the two women as Andy Morris. They all shook hands before discussing the expectations of the day.

The cups in the shop were small, so Lockhart replenished everyone's coffee as they waited for Marnie, who was now almost thirty-five minutes late.

Elsie asked the photographer questions about himself and his career. She was genuinely interested. He was happy to share his story with her, although it contained no particular *wow* moments.

Lockhart arranged ten possible dresses on a rail set up in the changing rooms. These were for Marnie to wear for the photographs, if she ever turned up.

Elsie decided to phone the council to uplift the old, faded sofa, as the new furniture would arrive within the next few days. While Lockhart busied herself around the shop, she debated whether to call Marnie. She decided against it knowing that she would be frightened off easily.

While she pondered her next move, the overhead bell at the door rang. It was Marnie. Lockhart put her hands to her mouth, letting out a gasp, not only from relief but from the sheer beauty of the girl. At the keep fit class each week, she wore no make-up and old joggers. Now, for the first time, Lockhart was getting a look at the polished-up Marnie. Her beauty was stare worthy.

'Oh my goodness! What a beautiful young lady you are,' Elsie told her. 'Lockhart told me you were beautiful, but you are actually exquisite.'

Marnie was embarrassed. Lockhart was aware that as Marnie stood bashfully looking down at the new oak floors, the photographer's jaw was almost hitting them.

'I'm so sorry I was late.. 'It was a frantic morning.'

'You're here now. That's all that matters,' Lockhart told her, taking her arm. 'Come through to the changing rooms. I'll help you with all the dresses. Some of them have difficult little pearl buttons.'

The photographer snapped photo after photo of Marnie; he was reluctant to wrap the session up at the end of the day. Finally, Lockhart found herself stepping in to halt the proceedings. They had enough to choose from. Every dress that Marnie wore for the shoot looked like it had been specially made for her.

The public will have a hell of a time choosing which dress looks the best. Every dress looked like 'the one'.

Chapter 35

That same evening, when Lockhart got home, she ran herself a deep bath. Usually, her preference was a shower, but tonight, her feet hurt, and she felt rather distressed. As she lay soaking in the soothing water, she knew what she saw in the changing rooms at the shop could not be ignored.

Whilst helping Marnie on and off with bridal gowns, she had seen some horrific bruising on her body. It was also obvious that she had attempted to hide the marks with foundation make-up.

Has this been the reason for her reluctance to take part?

Lockhart had noticed that Marnie masked unhappiness from within; until now, she couldn't figure it out. Anyone looking at her would think she was the girl with everything. The problem that now faced Lockhart was how to deal with what she'd seen.

The photos were in her inbox of her computer by the time she rose from the bath and donned her pyjamas. They were sensational. Marnie was elegantly beautiful, with an endearing vulnerability in her eyes. It was almost impossible to pick the best photos as they were all outstanding. Lockhart zoomed in on Marnie's beautiful face.

How dare some animal beat on this perfect creature. I despise bullies. I will fix this, I don't know how, but I'll stop it from happening again.

The photographer had added a little post-script at the foot of the email asking if she would mind passing his mobile number to Marnie. He wanted to offer her more modelling work.

Yes, I will pass his number on to her. This could be the confidence boost that she needs.

With her mug of hot chocolate and a slice of buttered toast, Lockhart sat on the stool at the breakfast bar, pondering over the photos. It was not an easy task, but she emailed her favourites off to the editor. Although the hour was late, she decided there was no time like the present for getting things done. The pictures would be waiting patiently for him when he arrived at the office in the morning.

She checked her phone for messages before heading off to bed.

Chapter 36

The following morning, the editor emailed back saying that the main newspaper, of which they were a subsidiary, also wanted to run the feature. This newspaper was based in the city of Glasgow, so it had a much wider circulation. He then listed all the small local businesses that had donated prizes for the entrants in the free draw.

Lockhart replied immediately, saying she was delighted with the progress and fully on board with the Glasgow paper being involved. However, she explained to the editor that she would like to add additional information to the feature. Namely, the designer of the dresses, Bartlett Northcote, who also designed the wedding gown of actress, Emily Jane Mott. Photos could be found in the September edition of Hello magazine.

Packing her laptop into a holdall, Lockhart headed along the main street to the shop to show Elsie the photos of Marnie. She couldn't wait to tell her how the feature had grown arms and legs!

The decorator arrived at Princess Bride to discuss quotes for an overall freshen-up of the premises. This allowed Lockhart to talk to him about her idea for the wall behind the till. He listened with reservation as she explained.

'I have ordered a wedding photo of actress Emily-Jane Mott to be made into black and white wallpaper. There will be enough rolls to create a mural of her on this wall here.' She showed him the area that would be covered. 'Are you able to do this for us?'

'Well, I'm not saying it's going to be easy, and it will cost you extra, but I'll give it a go,' he told her.

'I would really appreciate that. I don't think it will be any more difficult than matching up the pattern on regular wallpaper. Also, I will make sure that I mention the name of your business to anyone who comments on the mural.'

Dates were entered into the diary for a possible start for the painter and decorator. This was, of course, dependent on the wallpaper arriving on time.

It was around lunchtime when Lockhart and Elsie finally got the shop to themselves. Three doors along from Princess Bride was a delicatessen which sold filled rolls. Lockhart went out to fetch them lunch before they sat down to look at the photos from the previous day's photo shoot.

The ladies sat until almost dinner time, discussing a grand reopening of the shop; a launch, as it were. They agreed to hold a champagne reception with a live musical trio playing in the background. This event would be advertised in advance, and anyone wishing to attend would have to phone with their details. Exclusive invitations would be sent to a selection of guests as well as local businesspeople of the town.

When Lockhart had exhausted all of her ideas with Elsie, she wrote down a list of people to be contacted when she returned home. The date of the event would ideally dove-tail nicely with the completion of the redecoration, the arrival of the new furniture and the introduction of Marnie's in a Quandary article in the newspapers. Once a date had been set, Lockhart would alert Bee so that the website could go live.

It was a Get Fit With Mags night, so Lockhart made her apologies to Elsie for dashing away so sharply. They had covered almost everything, and Lockhart promised to email the necessary people and return to the shop early the following morning.

A thought entered her head as she ran most of the way home to get changed.

I can't believe how full and busy my life is now. I hardly get a minute to myself!

Bee was standing with Marnie when Lockhart appeared in the hall for the class with Mags.

'I've brought my laptop to show both of you the photos later,' Lockhart told them, patting her holdall. 'Marnie, you won't believe how gorgeous you look. Andy, the photographer, has asked me to pass on his number if you are interested in more modelling work. I think you are a natural. Obviously, so does he.'

Marnie was clearly embarrassed, saying nothing, as they joined the fast-moving flow of women heading through the door.

When the self-appointed door woman completed her job, Mags cranked up the music. The song was a nineties classic with a fast beat.

'Join in when you've got it, ladies. There is going to be less chat and more action tonight. I've been letting you off lightly for too long now. No more Mr Nice Guy.'

By the end of the hour, the keep fitters were done. It had been a non-stop, energetic session with no let-up. Lockhart, Bee and Marnie left the hall, red-faced and breathless.

In Decanters, the women laid their belongings down at their usual booth before Lockhart headed to the bar to order the Prosecco.

Bee played her usual part of being mum as she shared the wine evenly between them.

Lockhart brought the photographs of Marnie up on the screen, then turned the laptop to face her.

'Wow,' Marnie gasped with her hand over her mouth, 'I can't believe it's me.'

Bee was equally aghast by the breath-taking beauty of the bride on the screen. 'Oh my goodness, Marnie. These pictures are incredible. Wait until Ashton sees them. He'll be so proud.'

Marnie bowed her head. 'No, he won't. He is dead against me being involved.'

'Why?' Bee asked.

'He said that I shouldn't be parading around, flaunting myself. But, you don't know what…'

Marnie's sentence trailed off.

'What's going on? Talk to us, Marnie. We are your friends. You can trust us,' Lockhart said gently.

Marnie started to cry and simply said, 'I can't.'

Lockhart decided this was her moment, 'I think I've got an idea about what is going on, and it is not acceptable.'

Bee was bewildered. 'Can someone explain to me what is going on here?'

'I saw the bruises on your back and arms when I was helping you with your dress,' Lockhart said to Marnie, clarifying the situation to Bee.

Bee gasped, putting her hands up to her face. 'The bastard!' she screeched, feeling enraged at the thought.

Lockhart was the first to speak after a lengthy pause. 'What are we going to do about it?'

'I still want to do the bride feature. I loved dressing up in the bridal gowns and getting photos taken. This will sound silly, but I felt like a different person.'

'It doesn't sound silly at all. You are a beautiful girl who can enjoy a bit of attention.' Bee was still feeling furious from what she had heard about the bruises. 'You know, Marnie, you always seem to look for the darkest corner to hide in. Life shouldn't be like that. You should be standing proud, basking in the light. You are a special girl. I just wish you knew that.'

'Thank you,' Marnie whispered. 'I honestly think things will get better. Ashton said that he is going to get counselling. I know he has said it before, but I think he really means it this time. He is truly sorry.'

'I'm sure he is sorry for a few hours, even days. Marnie, he won't change, and one day he will do you some serious harm. What sets him off?' Bee asked.

'If I knew that, then I'd be able to prevent it from happening. It is often the smallest thing. It can be how I say something or if we go out, he says I am encouraging men to look at me. I can never predict it coming. He has lashed out at me when he seems down in the dumps, but he has also hit me when he appears upbeat and happy. I just don't know. He says that it has never happened to him before. It is only me that brings this out in him.'

'Let's get one thing clear,' Bee said, enraged. 'This is his problem, not yours. You are a victim in this, not the cause of it. Never forget that!'

'Do you want to marry him?' Lockhart asked.

'I don't know. I think I love him sometimes, but I'm frightened of him. I don't want a life of fear. Maybe once we get married and have a family, he will calm down, and it will stop. I know someone like me is lucky to have someone successful and good-looking like him.'

'Who told you that you were lucky to have him, Marnie? Him, I suppose?' Bee snarled.

Marnie gave her answer by not saying anything.

'We are going to fix this situation,' Lockhart pledged. 'Meanwhile, see him as little as possible, avoid any situation that may rile him. Don't worry. Your life is about to change for the better. Here, take this, it's the photographer's phone number. It may be something, or it may be nothing. You decide if it's a step worth taking.'

They drained the last of the prosecco, grabbed their things and left. When they parted to go their separate ways home, Lockhart wondered if Marnie felt slightly more empowered by talking about her situation.

Once you let the cat out of the bag, so to speak, you are never going to get it back in.

Chapter 37

Lockhart was awakened the following morning with an excited fluttering in her stomach. In a matter of days, Aslan would be back in Scotland, back in her town, home, and bed. What was it about this young man that made her lose all her inhibitions? The very thought of his skilled hands moving expertly over her body made her shudder. She was insatiable when she was with him. Her libido had dwindled down to a non-existent level latterly with George, but now, her home fires were burning brightly. He had a way of making her feel like she was driving him wild, which was an incredible turn-on.

Never before had she felt as though she had any power in the bedroom. It was more a case of lying there and doing as you were told.

Aslan had changed everything about the way she saw herself, and for that, she would always be grateful. Yes, there were a few unanswered questions in her head, but she had no right to doubt him. He had not broken any promises or let her down. George's infidelity had possibly made her more distrustful of people.

I need to work on being a more trusting person. The last thing I want is for George's betrayal to have left damaging scars. Aslan is the one who pulled me from the painful mire that I was caught in. I owe him my full trust.

A text vibrated through her phone, causing it to wriggle slightly across the granite worktop. Her eyes rolled upward when she saw that it was from George.

What does he want now? Why won't he leave me alone to get on with my life?

George: Can we meet? It is important. Please.

The thought of meeting him filled her with dread.

Lockhart: I am free right now for half an hour. How does that suit you? You can come round.

I should have said, 'you're more than welcome to come around.' Here's hoping right now is inconvenient.

George: I'll be there in five minutes. Thank you.

Lockhart: Make it ten.

She was sitting in her pyjamas.

George: Ten it is, then.

Her joggers and sweatshirt were lying on the floor from the previous night. She slipped them on, then wound her hair up in a band. The door knocked as she was changing.

That was about six minutes. What a pest! He must have been sitting outside the whole time.

A painfully thin, gaunt George stood on the doorstep. The sight of him took her quite by surprise.

'Thank you for seeing me. You look beautiful,' he said.

She laughed. Beautiful was not a word that suited her look at that moment.

'No problem. Come in. Do you want coffee or something a little stronger?'

Everything about him looked broken. 'No, thank you, I don't want anything.'

Lockhart led the despondent figure through to the lounge.

Through force of habit, he sat on the new sofa seat where his leather chair had once been. With his eyes fixed on the carpet, he ran his fingers through his hair several times. The unwashed hair stayed firmly in place as though his fingers had contained Brylcreem.

Eventually, Lockhart said, 'What's wrong, George? What did you want to talk to me about?'

'I don't know what to do or where to turn, Aitchy.'

'Before we go on, George,' she interrupted. 'Could you please not call me that ever again? The Aitchy days are over. I don't want to hear it.'

'I'm sorry,' he said. 'I won't do it again. I'm on medication for depression. I am not coping with things at all,' he continued.

This was not the George she had known since she was a teenager. It saddened her terribly.

'What, in particular, do you find hard to cope with?'

'Everything. I hate myself for hurting you, not appreciating you. Life is not worth living without you. Oh, Aitch... eh, Lockhart, I can't stand not having you anymore.' At this point, he broke down crying into his oily hands. 'The thought of becoming a father at this age and living with Gemma for the rest of my life fills me with misery. She is too young for me, and we are worlds apart in every way. I've realised that I don't love her. I had everything, and I just threw it all away.'

He lifted his head, revealing his tear-soaked face.

'I am in a living hell, Lockhart, and I can't see a way out. I just want to come home and start over.'

Taking a deep breath, he then looked her directly in the eye.

'I am begging you with all of my heart and soul. Please give us another chance!'

Lockhart could feel his agony. She hated seeing him like this. She didn't want to say anything that would crush him, but she needed to be frank.

'George, I will always have a place in my heart for you because we have had good times together, and I have spent most of my life with you. I want you to forgive yourself for leaving and not being terribly kind to me because something had to change. Our marriage had gone stale. Life is too short to stay in something that is no longer good. It took strength to leave, and I can tell you, hand on heart, that although it hurt at the time, you set me free to become the person I am happy with, the person I was always meant to be. I have created a great life and experienced things I would never have dreamt of. You have to stop texting and coming around. There is no alternative option for you here. Nothing will make me change my mind. While you are hanging on to hope that life will return to the way it was, you are not facing the future you have created. There is a little baby coming that needs you. The child will need your love and support as a dad. There are enough damaged people in the world who have lived with rejection from a parent. Don't let your baby be a statistic of abandonment. You must have been in love with Gemma at some point, so reach down deep, and find what you saw in her initially. She really needs you to be with her at this time. Life is full of shocks and surprises, but they happen for a reason.'

George stood to leave, knowing there was no hope of a lifeline.

'I'm sorry, George. You won't believe this, but one day you will see I am right. You may even thank me.'

'I doubt that,' he said, as he headed to the front door.

When he left, she felt drained. A great sorrow engulfed her. It was the end of an era.

Chapter 38

Speculation around town was rife about why the bridal shop had remained closed for the past couple of weeks. Elsie had even witnessed passers-by pressing their faces against the window to get a closer look inside. For as long as the locals could remember, Elsie opened Princess Bride every day except for Sundays. She barely took a holiday.

Lockhart and Elsie sat drinking coffee in the closed shop, discussing the finer details of the grand re-opening reception.

Elsie suddenly changed the subject, saying, 'Lockhart, I have been wondering what gave you the idea for Marnie's in a Quandary?'

'Well, let me think. I put together a few ideas to come up with it. I saw Marnie at my keep fit class and thought she was beautiful, then when I heard she was getting married to a well-known footballer, I thought we could somehow get in on that action.' Lockhart paused for a moment with a faraway look. 'The actual feature idea was a flashback from my childhood. My grandmother bought The Sunday Post newspaper every week. When I visited her, she asked me to choose *the fashions.* They ran this competition for years, with eight photos of a model wearing different outfits. My grandmother would ask me to put my favourite fashions in order. She would fill out the attached coupon and post it using my answers. If your coupon contained the winning combination, you won a good sum of money. My grandmother pinned her hopes on winning, not for herself, but to help her family. Anyway, I loved it. It was fun.'

'Did she ever win?'

Lockhart laughed. 'No, she never won, even though she must have entered every week for ten years.'

'Do you think people nowadays will be too sophisticated for a competition like ours?'

'I think if the public were asked to fill out a coupon, buy a stamp and then find a post box, we wouldn't get many entrants. The fact that we are asking them to choose by clicking buttons on a computer is definitely in our favour. People will always love competitions, especially when there are prizes involved. There is no way of knowing how successful it will be until we launch it.'

'What will be the actual day that it goes... what was it you called it again?'

Lockhart smiled. 'Live, until it goes live.'

'Oh yes, when will it go live?'

'I meant to talk to you about that. Do you remember I told you about Aslan?'

Elsie nodded.

'He is coming to Scotland on Wednesday for a week. This means that I won't be available until he has left. So, we will aim for the opening and the competition to happen on the Friday following Aslan's trip.'

'Oh, Lockhart, does that mean I won't see you while he is here?'

'I'm sorry, Elsie, but I need you to understand that it is my hope that Aslan will be my future. We hardly see one another, and I must fully commit to this relationship for it to work.'

Elsie was crestfallen. 'I understand. I'm just disappointed. I've been thinking about my future too. I wish I had shown the same commitment towards someone I care about.'

Lockhart smiled, knowing that she was talking about a future with Bartlett.

Chapter 39

Aslan's flight was due to arrive late, but this would not stop Lockhart from setting off early. It was better for her to be pacing up and down at the airport than hanging around the house, letting her nerves get the better of her. As she lifted her car keys from the table, she caught sight of herself in the mirror, which hung near the door.

I look so wrinkly. Not being able to sleep last night hasn't helped matters. Still, the truth is I am not young anymore. I'm way too old for a man of thirty. What if he sees me as an old lady? Maybe he won't be attracted to me anymore. This lined face of mine is only going to get worse.

Reaching into her bag, she searched around for her lipstick. She applied it to her pursed lips, then smacked them together, looking back at her reflection.

That's a bit better, not great, but better.

Parking places at the airport were plentiful as the Turkish flight was the only one arriving that night. Lockhart clicked the button for the central locking on her car before heading into the airport building. Apart from what appeared to be a maintenance man moving boxes on a trolley, there was not another living soul in sight. The gift shop, along with Costa Coffee, was shut. Instead, Lockhart saw a vending machine against the back wall of the building. Not eating all day meant that her stomach was beginning to let out occasional hunger growls.

She bought crisps and a bottle of sparkling water with the coins she had in her purse.

All she could do now was sit and wait for the time to pass. Nerves were multiplying in her stomach at the thought of her Aslan walking through the arrivals' door. The past weeks had been busy with so many things to fill her time, but she had still managed to physically ache for him several times daily. But now, she would have him all to herself with no interruptions.

A distant rumble vibrated through the floor. Only the silence allowed her to hear it and feel it in her feet.

That must be the luggage conveyor belt.

Rising off the chair, she ran to the board near the check-in desk to see if the flight from Turkey had arrived.

Yes! It had. She slipped off her jacket, laying it over her arm. Using her fingers, she gave her hair a ruffle.

He's here.

From where she stood, she saw the arrivals' door opening. She ran to find a place that would give her the best view of the emerging travellers. An elderly couple strode out of the door, hand in hand. They were followed by a woman with what looked like her teenage son. There was a lull where no one came out for a few minutes. She stood, eyes fixed on the door, hoping to see

Aslan's silhouette through the frosted glass. Her armpits began to feel sweaty; nausea was rising in her throat.

Where is he? Come on, Aslan, this is torture.

The doors opened once again to allow two Turkish-looking men through. Closely behind them was a family of four, then a woman alone. Lockhart's legs felt shaky, causing her to move from foot to foot. It was a horrible experience, not exciting at all.

A few more people walked through the door, and then there was silence. The conveyor belt rumbling had stopped, all activity had ceased. Lockhart stood alone in the empty airport building, feeling sick.

Unsure what to do, she tried phoning Aslan's number. The phone had been switched off.

Another maintenance man wearing identical overalls to the man with the trolley appeared out of the arrivals' door.

'Excuse me, excuse me,' she shouted, as he headed in the opposite direction.

He stopped, turned, and waited for the question he knew she was going to ask.

'Is everyone off the plane from Turkey?'

'Yep, that's the lot.'

Tears blurred her vision as she walked to the front door to make her way home alone.

I am done with this.

Painful sobs escaped her.

I will never let a man hurt me again. This was exactly what I was afraid of, getting my heart broken. I'm finished, I'm through, it's well and truly ov—

'Lockhart! Lockhart!' came the familiar Turkish voice. 'Wait, Lockhart!'

Lockhart felt like her feet had lifted off the floor as she ran, full speed into Aslan's arms. Smothering him with kisses all over his face, she said, 'I missed you so much. I didn't think you were coming out. Where were you?'

'I was taken into a room by two border control men so that they could ask me questions about my trip. Do I look like a suspicious character?' he asked her, making a mean face.

'Very.'

'I was so worried that you would return home without me.'

'I would never do that, although I was heading out the front door alone.'

'Look,' he said seriously. 'Take me to your house. We have some business to take care of.'

Lockhart felt a burning thrill between her legs because she knew exactly what he meant.

In the car, they were both silent. The anticipation of what lay ahead filled her thoughts. Lockhart could not wait; she reached her hand over, placing it on the swelling in his trousers. 'Oh, my goodness, you really did miss me.'

When she finally managed to unlock the front door, they ran at full speed to the bedroom. Undoing the buckle of his belt, she released him from his jeans. He stood before her, swollen and wet. Not a word was exchanged as he ripped her dress at the cleavage, exposing her bare breasts. They moaned in unison when his fingers slipped into her lacy knickers. Passion had completely overtaken them, and both knew they could not hold on much longer.

Aslan pushed her back onto the bed, raising her parted legs. He knocked against her making her scream out in indescribable ecstasy.

It was over all too quickly, but Lockhart was left thinking, *I can't believe I have a whole week of this to look forward to.*

They lay in bed until noon. The previous night had left them exhausted. It had been a spectacular night with some pretty remarkable highlights.

Wearing only their night time attire, they sat eating breakfast in the kitchen.

'So, what have you been up to since I last saw you?' she asked him.

'Oh, nothing much, really. A bit of this, a bit of that. I've been thinking about you mostly. What have you been doing?'

The bridal shop was her passion, but she was unsure if he would be interested in it. Testing the waters a little, she told him she was busy planning an event. To her surprise, he asked all the right questions, showing a real interest in her plans to revamp Elsie's shop.

'We even went to London to meet with an exclusive wedding dress designer. His dresses are unbelievable. Oh, and I must tell you this funny thing that happened. I thought I saw you there. I saw a guy just like you. He was wearing a Harris tweed jacket and red tie!'

Aslan became awkward. He shifted around on the bar stool, saying nothing.

Lockhart had expected him to make a joke, possibly saying that it was him, or ha ha, you've caught me out. But he didn't. Instead, he sipped on his coffee.

'I stopped the guy that looked like you. It was so embarrassing. He looked nothing like you close up. I was mortified. His lady friend wasn't pleased at all.'

On hearing this, Aslan appeared to loosen up and began joining in the joke.

'They must have thought you were a mad woman,' he laughed.

'They did. I was beginning to think it myself.'

'Tell me more about the event you're organising.'

'Here, it's better if I show you.'

She opened up her laptop, clicking on the photos of Marnie wearing Bartlett's dresses.

'Wow!' Aslan said, moving closer to the screen. 'She is absolutely stunning.'

To Lockhart's horror, she felt crippled with jealousy. It made matters so much worse that they were of a similar age. 'I know, she really is. The best bit about her is that she is just as beautiful on the inside as she is on the outside.'

'What's her name?'

'Marnie. She is engaged to be married to a footballer who is quite well-known in these parts.'

At this point, she wondered if she had added that last piece of information to let him know that she was taken.

'He's a lucky guy. The dresses are really nice too. It all sounds great. I hope it is a big success.'

'I hope so too. Right, enough about my thing. You must be involved in *something* back home, surely.'

'Actually,' he eventually divulged, 'I've been doing courses on sports' injuries. I thought it was time to further my career because I can't massage old ladies in a seasonal hotel forever. I have to earn money all year round.'

'That sounds great. You are so good with your hands!' she said suggestively. This was only a flippant throwaway line to cover her reaction to his statement about massaging old ladies. Was she one of these old ladies? When she was his age, she thought fifty was ancient. Turning her back to him, she walked over to switch on the coffee machine. That was two wounding comments within half an hour. As she fiddled away with the sachet of ground coffee, she gave herself a serious talking to.

Lockhart, you stupid woman. You are being oversensitive. Stop ruining your time with him. He didn't mean anything bad. Marnie is stunning, and he does massage old ladies. It doesn't mean that I'm one.

'Brrr!' Aslan shivered, 'I'm just going to get my sweater from my case.'

When he left the room, Lockhart felt herself relax. Her shoulders had become tense.

What am I doing? I am allowing myself to get hurt. How can there be a future with this young man? What will I feel like in ten years if I feel needy and jealous now? What should I do, I can't go on like this, but I can't give him up.

Two strong arms came from behind, wrapping around her waist. She felt her dressing gown open, and both hands slowly massaged her breasts. All thoughts of ending the relationship vanished in an instant. One hand stayed on her breasts, and the other slid down to the inside of her leg.

Of course, we'll make things work between us. I was just being silly.

Loud moans escaped her as Aslan pressed hard against her.

Chapter 40

'What have you got planned for me today?' Aslan asked on day two of his holiday.

Lockhart loved his enthusiasm. 'I'm going to take you to the town of Stirling. I'm going to educate you on the Scottish Wars of Independence.'

'Independence from what?'

'England, of course.'

'I thought that Scotland was in England,' he told her.

She shook her head. 'You really need a Scottish history lesson.'

It took just over an hour to reach Stirling by car, during which time Lockhart explained to Aslan that in the 1300s, battles were fought to gain independence from the English. William Wallace and Robert the Bruce made an appearance in her history lesson.

'The Scottish were totally outnumbered with no armour or horses. Many of the Scottish soldiers were just local farmers fighting with pitchforks and broom handles. Anyway, to cut a long story short, Scotland remained in union. The real irony is that our country had a referendum recently to decide if we wanted our independence now. No one lost their lives, and no one had to fight. We simply had to turn up at a local primary school and put a cross in a *yes* or *no* box. How times have changed.'

'So, is your country now independent?'

'No, that was the crazy thing. The people of Scotland chose to remain part of the United Kingdom. We decided not to be free from England.'

'I wonder what William Wallace and Robert the Bruce would think about that, Lockhart?'

'I wonder. They were probably turning in their graves.'

Stirling Castle was the first stop on the itinerary. They saw the banqueting hall, bedrooms, and kitchens. They also walked outside the castle building with its battlements and portcullis. Aslan absorbed every detail. He asked questions, listening carefully to every word.

'I want to ask you something,' he said, once they had seen every corner of the castle.

'Go on,' Lockhart replied.

'Why did Adolf Hitler not want this castle for his home when he won the war? I think I like it better than Edinburgh Castle.'

'I have no idea. Perhaps he didn't get a chance to see this one.'

They returned to the car to drive to the next attraction, the Wallace Monument. There was not much to see, but it was important to say they had been.

Next stop, the Battle of Bannockburn Visitors' Centre.

Lockhart smiled when she saw Aslan behaving quite childlike with the weaponry handling. He did not appear to care who was watching him. She found his earnest interest in everything incredibly endearing.

'Are you hungry?' she asked him as they left the centre.

'Yes, I'm starving.'

'Let's go into the town centre for some lunch.'

It was already almost three o'clock, and the sky was turning wintry grey. Lockhart noticed that Aslan was shivering. His teeth chattered as he spoke. There had been a considerable drop in the temperature. She could feel it on her cheeks.

The town centre was bustling with wrapped up, red-nosed shoppers. Aslan's hand felt cold in hers. She was also aware of his trembling from the icy wind blowing head-on.

She stopped. 'I think before we find somewhere to eat, we'll go into this shop to see if you like any jackets. My treat.'

'No, don't be mad. You don't have to buy me anything. You've done enough for me.'

Pulling him by the hand, she took him into the shop, which sold every kind of outdoor wear.

Lockhart sat on the backless seats provided while Aslan tried on a selection of four jackets that he liked. She enjoyed getting the chance to stare at him without seeming strange. Whenever she got a chance to admire him from afar, she was left asking herself the same question. *Is he really mine?*

Eventually, Aslan chose a stylish winter jacket by a Canadian company.

Lockhart had to agree that it was the nicest jacket of the four, and he really suited it.

While she took the jacket to the checkout, Aslan walked around the store looking at the tracksuits. The sales assistant waved her wand over the ticket before folding the jacket into a large bag. It came as quite a shock when she told Lockhart what she owed. It had been the most expensive jacket by far.

I could never justify spending that on any item of clothing for myself. Oh well, I did tell him to pick any jacket, it's not his fault that I'm out of touch.

When they left the store, Aslan took the jacket from the bag, slipping it on over his own ill-equipped-for-the-weather jerkin.

'Thank you so, so much, Lockhart. You really didn't need to do that. I feel really warm now.'

He wrapped his arms around her, kissing her on her cold lips.

They walked into a quaint coffee shop which served simple items like soup and toasties. While she was reading the chalky specials' board, Aslan reached his hands across the table to hold hers.

Looking directly into her eyes, he said, 'Do you know that I love you?'

This was the first-time love had been mentioned in this way since their relationship had begun. Lockhart became overwhelmed with emotion. Tears gathered in her eyes.

'Aslan, I love you too.'

'I think of you every minute of every day,' he told her.

During this declaration of love, she was finding it difficult to hold it together. 'Me too,' she whispered tearfully.

When the food was ordered, they sat holding hands across the table. Lockhart may have imagined things, but there appeared to be a few stares and whispers from customers sitting at nearby tables. Not only did she not care, but she was shame-facedly proud.

Aslan brought his phone out of his pocket, checked it for messages, presumably, and then laid it on the table beside him.

It had been years since Lockhart had seen such an antiquated-looking phone. She had no idea that this type of phone was still available.

'Aslan, your phone is very old looking. I haven't seen anything like it in years.'

'I know,' he said, looking embarrassed. 'Being here in such a beautiful country is frustrating, and I can't even take photos to show my family.'

Maybe this explains the lack of communication when we are apart. I would love him to show me to his family.

Giving the waitress the signal that they were ready to pay, Lockhart held her bank card at the ready.

'Come on,' she said to Aslan. 'I'm going to get you a new phone.'

'Lockhart, keep your money. I can't let you do it,' he argued.

'I want to. Everyone deserves to have nice things. Maybe I'll get a few more messages from you now,' she hinted.

'I promise that it won't always be like this. In the future, when I am established in a career, I will pay for everything. I will buy you wonderful gifts.'

Lockhart didn't want anything from him. The fact that he said *in the future* was more than enough pay back for her.

Chapter 41

Lockhart ensured that not a moment of her week with Aslan was wasted. They braved the bracing winds, which held freezing temperatures. She took Aslan on forest hikes as well as deserted beach walks. Aslan photographed every scenic view around him with his new phone. It was only on the last day when they trekked across a field to a ruined castle, she suggested that he might like a photo of her standing in the foreground or even a selfie of the two of them together. He agreed, telling her to pose as he snapped the shot of her standing in front of the crumbling castle remains.

They ate out in restaurants in the afternoons, she cooked dinner for him at night. Her cooking was well received, with high praise for every meal. They watched movies in the evening with the lights out in the lounge. This time, she allowed him to choose from the viewing options. Their lovemaking was adventurous and plentiful. Lockhart kept the black lacy outfit she had ordered online until their last night together. He had been taken completely by surprise when she left the room during the film, reappearing in a basque, stockings and stilettos. His reaction to her outfit told her everything she needed to know.

A painful sadness weighed on Lockhart when she watched Aslan pack his holdall in preparation for the flight home. Having a new jacket meant he had to find room for his old one in the tightly packed case. After rolling it up, squashing it down, then sitting on the case to shut it, he finally gave up, telling her that it would be best if he left it behind for his next visit. This comment brought joy to her heart.

'Wait a minute!' he told her, suddenly remembering something. He unzipped the pocket on the side of his bag. 'I meant to give you this last week when you picked me up.'

'Happy belated birthday,' he said, handing her a small package wrapped in tissue paper. 'I remembered that you told me back in the summer that it was coming up your special birthday.'

Lockhart was incredibly touched. Peeling the sticky tape from the wrapping, she opened up the present. Inside was a small, oval-shaped ceramic pot with a lid. In silver, handwritten letters, were the words, *Within You See What Pleases Me*. To her delight, she removed the lid to find a small mirror stuck to the base of the pot. It was such a sentimental, old-fashioned idea, and she loved it.

'Aslan, you are full of surprises. I totally adore it. Thank you so much for thinking of me.'

He shrugged his shoulders, telling her that she was worth it.

Glancing up at the clock in the kitchen, Lockhart saw that it was time to leave, or Aslan would miss his flight.

Now there's an idea. Perhaps I should just keep him talking.

It was a sad farewell at the airport, but Lockhart took comfort from the thought of Aslan having his new phone, making it easier to keep in touch. The more time they spent together, the tighter the bond had formed between them. This time, she felt that their relationship had really moved forward. He was now talking about love and the future together. She knew she would miss him terribly, but her feelings of insecurity were slowly dispersing.

Back home, in the quiet of her house, she could still feel Aslan. The citrus smell of his aftershave and the herbal scent of the bodywash, were a tonic to the nostrils. Then, in the bedroom, she inhaled the pillow at his side of the bed.

I refuse to wash this pillowcase until the smell has faded.

She sat on a stool at the breakfast bar, phone in hand. The first text she sent was to Elsie.

Hi Elsie, I will be in the shop early tomorrow. Hope everything went well over the past week.

Her second text was to Bee.

Hi Bee, I'm back in circulation. See you tomorrow night at GFWM.

The novelty of having friends was ever present in her daily life. How she ever managed to live in a friendless world, was a mystery to her. The time she spent with Aslan had been unforgettable, but she had missed the girls and the excitement of the shop. Marnie's situation had also crept into her mind several times over the past week. Now that her romantic bubble confinement was over, she would find out what was happening with her friends on the outside world.

The delicate trinket box was sitting on the worktop. Lifting it carefully, she cupped it in her hands, admiring it with love. When she turned it over, she saw a stamp on the underside of the pot. She reached for her reading glasses, lying next to her laptop. The writing read, Handmade by Panache Pottery, London.

Don't even think it. He wasn't in London, so don't even go there.

Chapter 42

The event designers were working their magic on dressing the shop. The grand opening started at 7pm but they had pledged to have completed the finishing touches by five. Elsie hired two local girls she knew through a customer to work as waitresses, serving drinks and canapes to the guests. Boxes containing bottles of Prosecco had arrived from the off license on the corner of the street. It was the shop where Lockhart had bought the Turkish dessert wine several months before. She knew that it would have been cheaper to buy from the supermarket, but she chose not to. She was going to champion small businesses at all costs.

The invitations to the local businesspeople had been sent out, to which most people had accepted. Marnie and Bee would be special guests of Lockhart's because she appreciated everything they had done to make the event a success.

Imitation blossoms surrounded the front door outside the shop in the shape of a bridal arch. Two large olive trees stood in pots at either side of the entrance creating an illusion of pillars. A double-sided sign out on the pavement advertised the event. Helium balloons were tied on to attract attention. A banner under the Princess Bride sign with the words Grand Opening would leave the town's people in no doubt that an exciting event was taking place.

The newspapers' editors advertised the Marnie's in a Quandary feature. The list of donated prizes had grown considerably; every business saw an opportunity for free prime-time advertising. To whet the readers' appetite, the prizes and the rules of the competition were listed. Everything was set in place for the new and greatly improved Princess Bride business.

'I'm going to slip away to get changed now, Elsie. I'll be back before six. The first guests should arrive around seven. Are you all right here alone for a couple of hours?'

'Yes, yes, you go. I'll get changed here in the shop. Oh, Lockhart, I can't believe this is really happening.'

'Well, you had better believe it because this is the start of something big!'

The ladies had a celebratory hug before Lockhart headed home to get changed.

On the walk back to her house, Lockhart reached into her handbag to check her phone. There were no messages, which was disappointing.

I bought Aslan a new phone, and I wasn't looking for anything in return, but I thought he would be able to contact me more. I haven't heard a thing since he left.

Lockhart searched desperately for reasons why he wouldn't send her a quick message.

Could he be living a double life? What if he has a wife and children back home waiting for him. Stop being so silly, you foolish woman. He will hardly leave his family for a whole week just to get a free jacket and phone. He loves me, he told me that. I have to have a little faith in him. Put it all out of your mind, there's a big event happening, and I organised it all.

In her wardrobe, hung two formal occasion dresses that had never been worn. They had been purchased years ago on the off chance that George would invite her to something and mean it.

Using a pair of kitchen scissors, she cut the label from the black velvet dress. She knew she had a pair of black velvet shoes somewhere in her wardrobe that would suit perfectly. As she slipped on her dress, she heard the vibration of a text coming through her phone in the kitchen. The granite worktop had amplified the sound. With her dress only halfway up, she ran to see if the message was from Aslan.

Bee: I'm so excited about tonight. I wish you all the best in this venture. You are a dear friend.

Bee's kind words removed the sting of disappointment that it wasn't Aslan.

Chapter 43

Lockhart returned to the shop, wearing a warm coat over her dress. From across the street, she looked on with admiration at the decorative, little premises, ablaze with lights. She saw Elsie looking out from the window, probably wondering where she was. She hurried her pace to put her friend out of her misery.

When she walked through the door, the band were tuning up by practising a few musical numbers. The sparkling wine had been poured into crystal flutes, which were lined up in rows on a silver tray. Lockhart smiled when she saw Elsie. Her outfit was, yet again, in the style of the mother of the bride.

Lockhart marvelled at how the event designers had decorated the main area of the shop. A red carpet ran from the front door to the changing rooms. Twinkling fairy lights hung across the room in rows from the ceiling, changing the whole atmosphere of the venue. Realistic artificial flowers were displayed in tall silver cone-shaped vases against the main walls. The place looked professionally elegant and worthy of its long-established bridal business.

Bee and Marnie were the first to walk through the doors. Marnie wore a red dress that flattered her curves, Bee wore a green velvet trouser suit.

'Elsie, you know Marnie already, but this is my good friend Bee. She designed the website for Marnie's in a Quandary. Bee, this is Elsie who owns this wonderful shop.'

After Elsie had been introduced to Bee, she told them to hold tight for a moment. She ran through to the back of the shop, reaching into a box containing a bottle of vintage champagne.

'I have been keeping this champagne for a special occasion, and tonight is the night. So, let's drink up before the other guests arrive.'

Lockhart popped the cork, catching the overspill in a flute as it frothed over.

Holding her glass in the air, she said, 'Here's to the success of the shop.'

'Cheers,' they all said, clinking together.

Bee held up her glass, saying, 'Here's to a rosy future for us all.'

'Cheers,' they clinked again with their glasses.

'Oh look,' Marnie announced excitedly, seeing two dressed up couples passing the window, 'Here are the first guests arriving.'

Chapter 44

The launch had been a highly sociable affair. Lockhart had the opportunity to meet the town's businesspeople, the majority of whom she liked and a couple of whom she was unsure.

The following day, a steady stream of browsers visited the shop. Elsie left Lockhart in charge while she visited the newsagent along the road. She couldn't wait any longer to see the feature in the local paper.

'I've got it!' she shouted, waving the newspaper in her hand when she returned to the shop.

'Have you already looked?'

'No, I promise I didn't. We'll look together.'

The two ladies stood at the counter, flicking through the pages of the local paper. To their delight, it was right there, in a middle page spread. Marnie looked incredible. The header read: Marnie is getting married to footballer, Ashton Brook, but she is in a quandary over which wedding dress to choose. Help her make her mind up, and you could win one of the following prizes.'

Each prize listed came with a generous advertising plug for the business that supplied it.

The article continued with information on Princess Bride, designer Bartlett Northcote and Emily Jane Mott's wedding dress, as seen in Hello magazine. Finally, there were simple instructions to follow to enter the competition. The photos of Marnie wearing eight exquisite dresses were set out in two columns across the double pages. Beside each picture was a capital A – H letter.

At the foot of the page were details of the website.

'It looks fantastic, Lockhart. I am thrilled with it. Bartlett's dresses are beautiful, and so is Marnie.'

Lockhart stared at the photos on the page.

'Yes, it is all perfect, even better than I dreamt it would be. All we can do now is sit back and wait to see if the readers think it's as great as we do.'

During the day, Elsie sold a straight, ivory dress to a third-time bride-to-be. Lockhart took a phone booking for a dress fitting at the end of the week. Then just before the close of the day, a grandmother came into the shop with her granddaughter to make an appointment for the following Saturday.

'What made you come in today to see us?' Lockhart asked before they left the shop.

'We've passed the shop many times and noticed it was closed. Then last night, we saw the sign and all the flowers for the grand opening. So, we thought, right, let's go in and set a date for a fitting.'

'Well, I'm really glad that you did. Oh, and have you seen the competition we are running in the local paper?'

'No, dear, we haven't.'

Lockhart handed over the newspaper that Elsie had bought earlier.

'Take this, have a read when you get home. It's in the middle pages. It's called Marnie's in a Quandary.'

The granddaughter took the paper from her grandmother and began flicking through the pages before they were out of the front door.

When the shop finally emptied of customers, Elsie turned the sign to closed.

'One sale, two bookings. I would say that that was an incredible day. I haven't had that many people in my shop for twenty years.'

Lockhart smiled. 'Yes, Elsie, I would say that we achieved a one hundred per cent improvement in our sales today, and this is only the beginning.'

Later that evening, Lockhart received a text message.

Marnie: I can't believe it! Two separate strangers have stopped me in the street to ask if I'm Marnie's in a Quandary. I'm almost famous, ha, ha.

Lockhart: Marnie!!! I have just this second read an email from the paper's editor. He says that the response to the feature has been unbelievable. According to him, everyone is talking about it.

Marnie: I'll never sleep tonight. See you at GFWM tomorrow?

Lockhart: Yes, I'll be there. Definitely before you!

Heavy tiredness came over Lockhart as she sat at her computer screen reading over her emails.
It's been a really good day today. Things are really starting to happen. I feel it. I can tell that Marnie is happy. Her text was so upbeat. She deserves it. It was lovely to see Elsie in her element among brides. What a day!
Her phone vibrated in the silence of the kitchen.
Oh, joy of joy, it's my darling Aslan.

Aslan: Within, you see what pleases me.
Underneath was a photo which she had to tap on.
She laughed aloud. It was a photo of her sleeping. Although she was incredibly touched, she couldn't help noticing how wrinkled she looked.

Chapter 45

Elsie was dealing with a customer while Lockhart answered the phone, which had rung four times since they opened that morning. Lockhart had booked two appointments in the diary, one for the following day, the other for the following week. As she stood taking a phone call at the desk, Marnie breezed into the shop.

Lockhart tried to wrap up the call because it was plain that Marnie was excited about something. She looked like she would burst if she didn't relay whatever information she was storing. The caller at the end of the line simply would not stop talking about the colour scheme for an upcoming wedding.

'That sounds just lovely,' Lockhart told the caller. 'You can tell me all about it when you come in.'

Marnie continued to step from one foot to another with a broad smile that Lockhart had never seen on her before.

'Yes, yes, how wonderful,' Lockhart answered before saying, 'Oh, we have just received a delivery of dresses, so I will need to go. I will look forward to your visit on Friday. Goodbye for now.'

'Finally!' Marnie screeched.

'You look like the cat that stole the cream. What do you want to tell me so urgently?'

'Firstly, I contacted the photographer, and he has some work for me, paid work.'

'Marnie, that's great. I am so glad you plucked up the courage to call him.'

'Wait, there's more. The paper's editor has asked me to do more Marnie's in a Quandary features. Hotels have approached him about running a feature on which venue to choose for the wedding. Oh, Lockhart, he is now talking about which wedding car, which florist, which honeymoon. I can't believe it! He told me that the wedding dress feature had been an amazing success. I was stopped by more complete strangers on the way here to see you. One of them said that I looked the nicest in dress E.'

'I am so happy that good things are happening for you. You deserve it.'

The bell above the door announced a customer, and to Lockhart's surprise, it was three generations of family members.

'We don't have an appointment, but would you be able to squeeze us in?' the mother of the bride-to-be asked.

Lockhart knew that they were not at the stage of turning away drop-ins.

'Of course, come in,' she welcomed them.

'Excuse me,' the elderly member of the party asked. 'Are you Marnie from Marnie's in a Quandary?'

'Gran, well spotted,' the bride-to-be laughed.

Marnie smiled.

'We love your feature, and we've all voted. So, what does Ashton think of all this attention about his big day?'

'He loves it,' Marnie lied.

The customers were shown through to the back of the shop while Marnie slipped out, blowing Lockhart a kiss as she left.

Chapter 46

Lockhart was running late for the exercise class. Grabbing her coat from the stand in the hall, she dashed out of the door, slipping her arms into the sleeves as she went. While running, it dawned on her that her fitness levels had significantly increased. She was neither fatigued nor breathless on the jog to the hall.

Bee stood at the door, tapping on her watch as Lockhart approached.

'Sorry, I got caught up with customers at the shop. Elsie was off to an appointment in the afternoon, so I was on my own. Has Marnie told you all her good news?'

'No, Marnie's late as usual. The news will have to wait until we get to Decanters. It sounds like business is booming for you, though.'

'Oh Bee, you wouldn't believe—'

Just then, the self-appointed doorwoman appeared.

'Are you coming in or staying out?' she barked.

'We are coming in,' Bee told her, rolling her eyes at Lockhart.

The music volume raised, Bee and Lockhart ran to their usual places.

'Okay, you lot, I've been too soft for too long. It's time I got you really working,' Mags shouted into her headset.

Marnie did not turn up to class late or otherwise. This was unusual for her, but Lockhart figured she had a busier schedule now with the extra modelling work.

When Mags wrapped up the class with a couple of relaxation exercises on the mats, Bee mouthed to Lockhart.

'What's happened to Marnie?'

Lockhart shrugged her shoulders.

The music stopped, and the class had ended. The women packed up their belongings and headed for the door.

'Great class, Mags. Could you make it a bit tougher next week?' Bee joked.

'I'll remember you said that. You may live to regret those words.'

Decanters was busier than usual. Lockhart recognised a few of the regulars, but a different crowd stood at the end of the bar. When she ordered the wine, she asked the bartender if she had seen the dark-haired girl that was usually with them.

'Is that the girl in the newspaper, Marnie or something?' the barman asked.

'Yes, Marnie, has she been in tonight?'

'No, I'll ask the others, but I haven't seen her.'

Lockhart and Bee sat in a booth at the window. Bee poured the prosecco into two flutes.

'I'm going to call her,' Lockhart said, feeling slightly concerned. There had been no reply to a previous text she had sent in the afternoon asking her if she was going to the class. Marnie's phone had simply rung out.

Bee asked about the response to the wedding dress competition as the sipped their prosecco.

'The editor said that it has been incredible,' Lockhart explained. 'Not only that, but the shop has also been going steady every day with customers. It's been... Oh,

Bee, I can't relax. I am worried about Marnie. Any idea where she lives?'

'Yes, I do, because we shared a taxi home the night of the grand opening for the shop. She lives with her parents in a housing estate near the airport. Do you want us to go to the house?'

'Yes, I think I'll call a taxi.'

Lockhart took her phone from her handbag.

'Don't bother. I'll phone my husband, Billy. He won't mind taking us.'

The car, with Billy at the wheel, pulled up outside Decanters minutes after Bee had called.

Bee introduced Billy to Lockhart, although they both knew plenty about one another.

Lockhart noticed that Billy drove with one hand on the wheel, the other hand gripped tightly to Bee's.

George would never have held my hand while he was driving. What am I saying? George would never have held my hand, full stop.

To the best of her recollections, Bee directed them to the housing estate, street and, with any luck, the house where Marnie lived. The two women decided to go to the door together.

After two robust knocks on the door, a man stood before them. They felt instantly intimidated. The can of lager in his hand and neck tattoos did not help.

'Does Marnie live here?' Lockhart asked.

'Who wants to know?'

'I'm Lockhart, and this is Bee. We are her friends.'

'Are you the bride-dress woman?'

'Yes, I suppose I am. Are you her father?'

'Yes, I suppose I am.'

'Is she here?' Bee enquired, smiling sweetly to keep on the right side of the man.

'No, there's been a… sort of a, well, you could call it an accident. She's been taken to the hospital.'

'Right, I see,' Lockhart said abruptly. 'Thanks for your help.'

I know exactly what's happened, and it's been no accident.

Lockhart made her way to the car.

Billy had heard every word, so as soon as the women were in the car, he screeched off in the direction of the hospital.

Chapter 47

In the hospital's main foyer, the reception desk was located to the left. Unfortunately, only one receptionist was on duty, singlehandedly answering the queries of an ever-growing queue. Lockhart, Bee, and Billy joined the line behind an elderly couple.

'Could you please tell us which ward Marnie Taylor is in?' Billy asked when they finally reached the desk.

The receptionist checked down the list of patients. Next to Marnie's name, there was a series of letters. They obviously made sense to the woman behind the desk.

'Are you family?' she asked.

Lockhart stepped forward to reply on behalf of them all.

'Yes, we are.'

'In that case, she is in ward seven. Go straight along the corridor, up the stairs and ward seven is facing you.'
'Thank you.'
They walked silently along the corridor, each wondering what they would see when they reached ward seven.
'He fucking did this!' Bee said, climbing the stairs two at a time.
'Who did it?' Billy asked, 'I thought her father said she had an accident.'
'We'll explain later. Let's just say that her boyfriend is a heavy-handed thug.'
'But why would—'
'We'll talk later, love. Let's put on a brave face for Marnie,' Bee suggested, wiping her moist eyes.
Lockhart still had not spoken. She feared that she may throw-up if she opened her mouth.
Standing in the corridor, Marnie's three friends looked through the window into ward seven. In the bed nearest the door, they saw Marnie's beautiful raven-coloured hair spread over her pillow. Lockhart realised, as did the other two, that the hair was the only recognisable feature of their friend. Vomit rose into Lockhart's mouth when she looked closely at the facial trauma Marnie had suffered.
'I don't think I can go in,' Lockhart told the others. 'I worry that I won't be able to hold it together.'
Billy took the hands of both women. 'We have to be there for her. It seems like she has no one else. Be strong, we'll walk in together.'
'Marnie, we've come to see you. It's Bee and Lockhart. This is my husband, Billy.'

With her eyes closed shut from the swelling, Marnie could not see her friends, but she attempted to smile through her puffy, burst lips.

'Thanks for coming,' she whispered. 'I must look a state.'

'Don't try to talk, angel.' Lockhart took Marnie's frail hand, her manicured nails broken off. 'Can you just nod or shake your head to a question I want to ask you?'

Using mainly her chin, Marnie nodded as best she could.

Lockhart looked down at the lacerations and swelling on Marnie's face. She could hear her struggling to breathe from her damaged nose bone. Visions of her smiling in the photos where she wore Bartlett's dresses flashed through Lockhart's mind. *What kind of monster does this to another human being?*

'Marnie, did Ashton do this to you?'

Marnie nodded.

Chapter 48

During Lockhart's regular visits with Marnie, it became clear that she had no intention of pressing charges against Ashton Brook. Her parents had called the hospital only once since the attack. Their visit had been to warn her to keep her mouth shut to the police. Ashton had been incredibly generous to them with money and football season tickets.

Both Lockhart and Bee had sent a clear message to Marnie that if she didn't report him, then he would continue to hurt women.

When Lockhart entered the ward one evening, Marnie sat up, hair combed, looking more like herself.

'Oh, Marnie, it's good to see you looking so much better.'

'I've made a decision. I'm going to give a statement to the police. I know my family won't speak to me again, but I've decided to do it anyway.'

'I am so proud of you. You are doing the right thing. But don't forget that we are like a new family now. You'll never be alone. I have a spare room for you at my house, and you can stay as long as you need to.'

'I feel very afraid,' Marnie confessed, somewhat fearful of the potential repercussions.

Chapter 49

The editor soon received word about the vicious attack on Marnie by her fiancé, Ashton Brook. This was tabloid gold, especially in light of the fact that the locals had helped her to pick her wedding dress. Although he could no longer use the Marnie's in a Quandary feature, the editor was rubbing his hands together with glee at this unexpected twist in the story. Marnie's trauma became the front-page story for all the newspapers in the chain. When the nation became outraged, the editor fed their fury. Ashton's abusive behaviour towards his fiancé made the six o'clock news on all the main television channels. The editor had a win-win situation on his hands, and he bled it for everything he could get.

Lockhart, accompanied by Bee, drove to the hospital to collect Marnie. The spare room in Lockhart's home had been prepared with brightly coloured bedding and flowers in a vase by the window. The idea of Marnie living with her pleased Lockhart, except for a nagging worry about any future visits from Aslan. Still, she would cross that bridge when she came to it.

Apart from thanking them for picking her up, Marnie was quiet on the car journey to her new home. A nurse at the hospital had informed her that Ashton had been dropped by his football team. This news worried Marnie as she knew he would somehow blame her for his misfortune. She no longer felt safe knowing she would become the focus of his revenge.

Marnie stayed in her bedroom for several days, sleeping. She had asked Lockhart to leave her meals outside the bedroom door.

Lockhart knocked on Marnie's door every few hours to check if she needed anything. Occasionally, she would invite her through to join her or suggest that they go for a walk. Marnie was not interested in leaving her bedroom.

Lockhart respected her privacy until she felt it had gone on too long.

I'm not being a good friend if I just leave her in there indefinitely. Sometimes tough love is the only way. I'll make this her last day of being a recluse. Tomorrow, I'll shake things up.

The morning that followed, Lockhart made scrambled eggs for Marnie. She stood outside the bedroom, carrying a tray which held her reclusive guest's breakfast.

Knocking gently on the door, she said, 'Marnie, I'm coming in.'

'No! Don't come in. If it's breakfast, then leave it outside the door.'

'I'm coming in, Marnie. You've been away too long.'

'Lockhart! Do not come in. Please, give me some privacy.'

'I'm coming in,' she told her, turning the handle of the bedroom door. 'It's time.'

Marnie hid her head under the duvet.

In utter disbelief, Lockhart looked around the darkened room. Only a narrow line of light shone from between the curtains. The bedroom was unrecognisable from the pretty spare room she had prepared before Marnie's arrival. The air in the room smelt stale with a hint of dampness from the pile of wet towels on the floor. Then, Lockhart noticed Marnie's opened suitcase in the corner of the room. Inside the case, she saw the carefully folded clothes she had brought to the house. From this sighting, Lockhart could surmise that Marnie had lived for the past few weeks in her pyjamas. Setting the tray down on the chest of drawers, she sat on the bed where Marnie lay, head still out of sight.

'Marnie, I want you to get up, showered and dressed. Once you've done that, we will go for a walk. We may even stop in somewhere nice for a coffee and a piece of carrot cake. How does that sound?'

'I'm not ready to come out. I want to stay here in the bedroom for a few more days,' came the muffled reply.

'I can't let you do that, Marnie. I care too much about you. Come on, up you get.' Lockhart pulled back the duvet to see her tousled-looking friend. 'Come on, I'm not leaving until you are up.' Lockhart then walked over to the window, pulling the curtains wide open.

Marnie screeched at the blinding sunlight, throwing her hands up to cover her eyes. She had not been acquainted with daylight for some time.

Lockhart laid a clean towel over the rail in the bathroom before switching on the shower.

'Shower's running, so don't waste hot water. Hurry up and get in.'

With great reluctance, Marnie stumbled out of bed, heading towards the shower.

Lockhart noticed that although her face was healing nicely, there were still signs of yellow bruising and some scarring around her eye.

I wonder if her face will ever heal completely.

Lockhart also noticed a dent on Marnie's head when she tied her hair back.

After stripping the bed and gathering all the wet towels together, Lockhart left Marnie to get ready.

As she busied herself around the kitchen, she wondered if Marnie would simply go back to bed, and then she remembered that she had removed all the sheets and pillowcases.

Would it stop her scrambling under the duvet if no covers were on it? Hmm, probably not. I think I'll go and check on her. Or should I? I don't want her to think I'm hounding her, but I suppose I have been hounding her. It all comes from a good place, though. Oh, what the heck? I'm going to peek in.

Just as she approached the kitchen door, Marnie appeared from the bedroom. Her brushed hair lay wet on her shoulders, her pale face wore a sad expression.

Lockhart's heart was aching for her. 'Come on. You look so much better. I'll make you a fresh cup of tea.'

'Thanks,' Marnie whispered, looking tenderly raw by being out of her safe place.

They sat together in comfortable silence. Lockhart was unsure whether Marnie wanted to talk or listen.

Eventually, she seized the moment and asked, 'Do you want to tell me about what happened?'

Marnie nodded. 'I don't remember everything, but I know how it started,' she explained, swallowing hard. 'He always looked through my bag to check my phone. I forgot to hide the piece of paper with the photographer's number on it. He found it.'

Lockhart felt a piercing pain cripple her chest because she had been the one that had written that number down and given it to Marnie. That small innocent act had changed the course of Marnie's life.

'He then checked my phone and saw I had called the guy.' She winced, remembering what happened next. 'He grabbed my hair and shouted in my face that this whole bride thing had to stop. I saw his fist coming and a blinding light, then I don't remember much more after that.'

She sobbed into her hands.

Lockhart cried with her.

'Let's take things a day at a time, Marnie. I know you don't believe me right now, but you will find happiness again. Things in life always happen for a reason, and you can't see it until you look back.'

The positive words of encouragement came directly from her own experience.

'I know it's not the same, but I was devastated when George left me. I saw the future as a dark, hopeless space. Now, I can say honestly that I wouldn't change a thing. Although it hurt at the time, George leaving that day opened up a new, exciting future that would never have been available to me otherwise. I promise you, Marnie, you won't always feel this way.'

Marnie climbed down from the breakfast bar stool and walked around to where Lockhart sat. She wrapped both arms around her wise friend's neck, crying onto her shoulder.

'Okay, be strong and let's call this day one of your new beginning. Fancy going for coffee and carrot cake now?'

Marnie wiped her face on her sleeve as she nodded.

Chapter 50

Lockhart and Marnie began every morning with a walk along the lane at the back of the house, then down by the embankment. Marnie pulled her knitted hat down to her eyebrows and, depending on the weather, she would often wear large-framed sunglasses. The collar of her coat was always raised, with her long dark hair tucked within. They rarely met anyone at that early hour, but Marnie's disguise gave her confidence, nonetheless.

On their return home, Lockhart left for work at Princess Bride. The success of the shop meant that she had to work every day, which she was happy to do. All the newspaper coverage on the Marnie and Ashton story had kept the shop and its dresses in the public eye. Princess Bride was mentioned in every news story that followed the attack on Marnie. Lockhart had appointments booked in the diary for almost every day for several weeks ahead.

Marnie remained at home cleaning and even cooking for Lockhart coming home in the evening. She wasn't the greatest chef in the world, but the gesture was very much appreciated.

On many occasions, Lockhart attempted to coax Marnie along to Get Fit With Mags, but she was adamant about not being ready to return to the class. Lockhart met Bee at the door to the hall each week, but they did not indulge in Prosecco at Decanters without Marnie. Instead, Bee came back to Lockhart's house for drinks. Sometimes, Billy came along to join them.

Chapter 51

'Marnie, since it is Saturday night, why don't I go and buy us our dinner from the local pizza place. When I was with George, I brought home pizzas every Saturday after my work. It was a kind of ritual. It seems like an eternity ago now.'

Lockhart's thoughts drifted to her life back then. She felt nothing except a craving for a pepperoni pizza.

'That's a great idea,' Marnie said, rising from the sofa. 'I think I'll come with you.'

Lockhart's spirits levitated within her. However, she did not reveal this surge of emotion to Marnie for fear of her changing her mind. Her friend agreeing to walk along the busy street among civilisation was a major leap forward in her recovery.

'Okay, I'll enjoy the company,' Lockhart said, keeping the key low.

The evenings were lighter now, the weather milder. It was a pleasant walk along the main street where the shops started closing and eating establishments began to open. The two women were chatting about nothing in particular when a text message vibrated through Lockhart's phone. Retrieving it from her pocket, she glanced at the sender's name.

Aslan.

I won't read it right now. I'd rather savour it when I'm alone.

A feeling of excitement crept over her as she tried to guess what could be written within the text. Keeping her voice calm, she continued to comment on the windows of the shops they walked past.

'Excuse me, are you Marnie's in a Quandary?' a woman said, stopping as she passed them.

Marnie shrugged her shoulders. This was exactly what she dreaded about venturing out of the house.

'What a bastard that Ashton Brook is. I've heard you are not the first woman he has beaten up. Well, he's finished now. Apparently, he can't even walk down the street without people shouting at him and heckling him. Good! He deserves it.'

Sensing Marnie's discomfort, Lockhart suddenly wondered why they were standing listening to this one-way conversation.

'Come on, we'll be late,' she said, tugging at Marnie's coat.

Marnie appeared dazed, but she followed Lockhart away from the woman.

'Are you all right?' Lockhart asked. 'I don't think she meant any harm. I believe her intention was to be supportive. She won't know how raw everything still is for you.'

'I know,' Marnie agreed. 'Let's just get the pizzas, then go home.'

Linking arms with Marnie, Lockhart said, 'It was going to happen sooner or later, so that's good that you've faced that hurdle now.'

'I suppose so.'

'Hello, stranger,' the pizza shop owner shouted when he saw Lockhart walking through the door. He then stared at Marnie. 'Hey! Aren't you that girl from the newspaper? What was that called again, Marnie's...'

Marnie turned around, heading for the door. 'I need to go home.'

'Sorry,' Lockhart said to the assistant behind the counter, 'maybe another night.'

She left the shop empty-handed in pursuit of Marnie.

Lockhart caught sight of her across the road just as she turned down a side street. She ran to catch up with her, shouting, 'Marnie, wait!'

Marnie stopped when she heard Lockhart's cry.

'I thought I'd lost you there. Let's go home and open a bottle of red wine. Red wine always makes me feel better.'

On the short walk back to the house, she glanced at Marnie and saw that she was crying.

'It will never end, Lockhart. People will always see me as the bride who became the victim of domestic abuse.'

'Yes, they probably will, but that is not necessarily a bad thing. Who knows how many other women are in your situation. You may have given them the strength to leave, to make a fresh start. I think that you have highlighted this type of abuse by bringing it into the public eye. You have to look for positives, Marnie. Don't let a man like Ashton destroy you.'

When they reached home, Marnie went straight to the bathroom. Pulling her hair back from her face, she studied the damage that had been left from the attack. The swelling had gone down, but the discoloured bruising still remained, as did the scars from where her skin had split. Again, she sobbed for the loss of her looks, her confidence, her new career and even for her family, who had all but disowned her.

Chapter 52

A bottle of red wine sat uncorked beside two large glasses on the breakfast bar. Lockhart took her moment alone to read her precious text message from Aslan.

Hi, L. I am back at the Blue Lagoon for the start of the season. The resort is quiet, so why don't you come out and see me. Let me know if you can book something. No surprises.

She didn't have to think twice about whether she could travel to Turkey. Of course, she was going to make it happen. Leaving Marnie alone did not sit well with her conscience, so she decided she would speak to Bee about stepping in. Oh, and there was Elsie to think about. She couldn't just abandon her at this busy time.
I'll figure it out before I go, so I'm not leaving anyone in the lurch.
Memories of her last trip to Turkey flitted into her mind. The sex on the balcony, the erotic sessions which lasted practically all night long, the day trips filled with anticipation of returning to the bedroom, not forgetting the private touching of each other under the table in pavement cafes. Her thoughts then elevated to the laughs they had together and the nights that they could lie sleeping side-by-side. There was no question in her mind about going. It was something that she simply had to do.
Reaching for her phone, she sent a quick text message to Bee.

Lockhart: Hi Bee, if I booked a week away, would you be able to look after Marnie? I don't want her to be alone.
Bee: Billy and I have booked a cottage in Mull for a week. We'd love her to come. We leave a week tomorrow. Would that be any good?

Lockhart: Perfect! Thanks. The trip is important to me.

Bee: I'll send you the link to the holiday cottage. Show it to Marnie.

When she heard Marnie emerging from the bathroom, she poured two glasses of rich, red Chilean wine. Another text message from Bee came through her phone. It held the link to the cottage. Lockhart clicked on it.
Marnie entered the kitchen; her expression was sombre.
'Here's your wine,' Lockhart said, handing over the glass. 'It's my absolute favourite. Rich, fruity and from Chile.'
'Thanks.'
'I've got news for you. Look at this.' Lockhart showed Marnie the photos of the holiday cottage, which stood proudly overlooking the sea.
Marnie swiped from photo to photo of the interior and exterior of the beautifully bespoke house Bee had booked for the week.
'What a gorgeous place. Where is it?'
'It's on the Island of Mull. Bee and Billy have booked it for a week. They would like you to go with them. It would do you the power of good to get away from here

for a while. There is nothing more healing than being near the ocean. What do you think?'

'I would love to go, but I can't possibly leave you here alone.'

'Oh, Marnie,' Lockhart laughed. 'I will be absolutely fine. In fact, I will take the opportunity to go and visit a friend in Turkey.'

Marnie sipped on her wine, looking again at the photos of Mull.

'Do you want to know something really peculiar?'

'What?'

'I got the strangest feeling of Deja-vu when I looked at these photos, you know, like I'd been there before, yet I know I haven't. Oh, I know that sounds silly.'

'No, Marnie, it doesn't sound silly at all.'

Chapter 53

After the regular embankment walk with Marnie on Monday morning, Lockhart made her way up to Princess Bride. Getting the week off to see Aslan was so important to her, but she owed Elsie a great debt of loyalty. Her job had changed everything for her, it had provided a new focus and purpose in her life, but her beautiful Aslan was hopefully going to be her future. Relationships needed careful tending. If she had learned one thing from her time with George, it was just that. This one needed more than most as there was not only the distance between them but also a significant generational gap.

On entering the shop's front door, she thought of how best to word her request.

Elsie smiled when she saw Lockhart, as she always did.

'Lockhart, I'm glad you're here. I have made a very important, dare I say, life-changing decision, and I want to talk to you about it.'

'I'm all ears, Elsie. Then I would like to talk to you about something.'

'You can go first if you like,' Elsie offered out of politeness.

'No, you're the boss. You go first.'

'I have decided to reschedule the appointments in the diary for next week so that I can go to London. I want to get more dresses from Bartlett, but not only that, I want to have a very serious talk with him. Now, Lockhart, you can come if you wish, but I may have to leave you on your own again because this is not only a business trip. It is a personal mission.'

'No, Elsie, I won't come with you. I think this is something that you need to do alone. I will use that time to maybe go and visit Aslan in Turkey.'

'That's a wonderful idea.'

'So, Elsie, tell me about your mission.'

'I lay awake all night thinking about my future. I am certainly not getting any younger and I no longer want to be alone. Bartlett is the only man that has ever truly made me happy, and although it has never been spoken of, I think we have been in love for over forty years. We have had some wonderful years together, having fun and partying, but we have never talked seriously about our feelings. We have spent the night together many times but never consummated the relationship. I can't say that we've wasted the years that we've had because we have had great times with lots of laughs, but it is time to set things in place. If that means me moving to London, then so be it. I know that my shop will be in good hands.'

'Wow, that is quite a mission! If it is something you want badly, you must get it. Grab life with two hands. If you don't, it will pass you by. Will you be all right on the journey by yourself? Do you want me to book your flights and the same hotel we were in the last time?'

'Yes, I will be fine. I used to make this trip several times a year. I think I just got lazy. I would be delighted if you could make all of my bookings for me, though.'

'Consider it done.' Lockhart could not quite believe how things were falling so neatly into place for her to take the trip to see Aslan.

'Oh, what did you want to tell me about, Lockhart?'

'Just forget it. It's not important.'

Chapter 54

Lockhart: Hi Aslan, I will be arriving on Wednesday, late afternoon. I was going to surprise you, but I know you don't like surprises.

The no surprises comment that Aslan had made in his text had eaten away at Lockhart.

Why had he said no surprises? Maybe he wanted to make sure he could arrange plenty of time off while I was there. On the other hand, he is not entitled to any time off to be with guests. His job is his job. Aslan works long hours, seven days a week because it is seasonal work. So why no surprises? Did he not want me to catch him in the act of something that he shouldn't be doing? Or it is possible that he didn't want to think maybe today is the day she is coming, then I disappoint him by not arriving. Yes, I can understand that.

From the chest of drawers in her bedroom, she gathered together all of her summer clothes to take on holiday. Whilst folding the items carefully into the case, she was proud to notice that there wasn't a flowery blouse or pair of linen trousers among them. It had been almost a year since she packed her case for Turkey the first time. Back then, she had boarded the plane feeling lower than she had ever felt. On the return flight, she had been transformed, filled with hope, desire, and a fresh excitement for her future. Aslan had turned everything around for her. He deserved all the credit. He had filled her with confidence, allowing her to see a side of herself that she would never have known was there.

It would be fair to conclude that George had reduced her life to nothing more than a heap of rubble. Aslan had helped her to build something beautiful from it.

Chapter 55

Bartlett Northcote had been ecstatic when Elsie told him she was flying to London to see him. On hearing the news, he had booked an excellent restaurant in the heart of the city for the second night of her stay. He thought that she could get settled into her hotel on her arrival. Then the following day, they could conduct their business at the shop before going to the restaurant in the early evening. Whatever happened after that, he would not plan. Instead, they would see what the evening had in store for them. He wanted the night to be perfect, as there was an important issue he felt needed to be discussed.

*

When Elsie reached the hotel, she took her two recently purchased outfits from her suitcase. Bartlett had informed her that they would be dining at an exclusive restaurant, so she wanted to look her best. The hyacinth blue suit she bought for the evening had been expensive, possibly the costliest item in which she had ever invested. To her mind, it was worth it. He was worth it. A smile crept across her lips.

Bartlett has always liked me in hyacinth blue.

She allowed a giggle to escape her.

It is absolutely perfect for the occasion.

There was no turning back now. She had decided to lay her cards out neatly on the table. There had to be more in life for her than just the shop. After all these years of being involved in strangers' weddings, it was time to think about planning a special day for herself.

The journey had entirely sapped her energy, so Elsie changed into her nightdress before sliding beneath the

Egyptian cotton sheets. It was not even seven o'clock, but she felt exhausted and, added to that, the heart palpitations she had been experiencing lately had returned with a vengeance. There had obviously been too much excitement for one day, but nothing a good night's sleep wouldn't sort. Bartlett was not expecting to see her until the morning and her batteries would be fully restored by then.

Chapter 56

Marnie was standing watching from the window when Billy pulled up in front of the house. Bee sat in the passenger seat, waving vigorously.

Suitcase in hand, she ran to open the front door. Billy was on the doorstep to meet her.

'All ready and raring to go, Marnie?' Billy asked, reaching for her case.

Marnie despised the shyness with which she was cursed.

'I sure am,' she answered, following him to the car.

'Well, let's crack on then. The sooner we get on the road, the sooner we get there.'

Billy had a way of using stock phrases to take the awkwardness out of a situation.

When they had passed through the main street of town, Billy automatically reached over to take Bee's hand whilst he drove, telling Marnie that it would take them around two and a half hours to get to Oban. From there, they would board the ferry for the Island of Mull.

'Hey, Marnie, can you guess what you call a person who comes from Mull?' Billy asked, turning around while driving.

Bee playfully slapped his arm. 'Try not to kill us before we get there!'

Billy dismissed Bee's comment with a tut. 'Ignore her, Marnie. Can you guess what you call a person who is from Mull?'

'I don't think that I can.'

'Wait for it…a Mulloch.'

Marnie paused momentarily before saying, 'I thought that was a hairstyle that footballers used to have.'

'No, you're mixing that up with a mullet. People from Mull are Mullochs. My grandmother was a Mulloch. When I was a boy, I spent every summer with her in her little cottage in the town of Pennyghael. I never wanted to leave. In fact, I can remember crying the whole way home when my mum picked me up at the end of the holiday.'

'So, you are almost a Mulloch then if you spent so much time there,' Marnie commented. 'I don't know anything about Mull, or any of the other Scottish islands for that matter.'

'Oh, Marnie,' Bee said, shaking her head. 'You are treading on dangerous ground here. You are going to open a door that you will not be able to shut. Once you start Billy talking about Mull, there's no escape.'

'Honestly, I don't mind. I'm interested. I think it's time someone educated me.'

Billy smugly cleared his throat.

'Let me see, where shall I start? The main town in Mull is called Tobermory. Now, the name Tobermory means Mary's Well in Gaelic. It was dedicated in ancient times to the Virgin Mary. Not many people know that.'

Marnie stared out of the window as she listened.

'There's a fascinating story that may or may not be true which happened in the 1500s...'

'Maybe you could just keep the information to more recent times, eh Billy,' Bee suggested.

Billy ignored her and continued. 'As I was saying, back in the 1500s, a member of the defeated Spanish Armada came into the harbour where Tobermory is now in an attempt to evade the English fleet who were hot on his heels. The story goes that the people of the town were frightened by this, so they asked the local witch to cast a spell on the ship, and lo and behold, the ship blew up.'

He paused for effect.

'Really?' Marnie asked.

'Yes, but here is the interesting part. The ship sank in the harbour carrying a cargo of gold bullion. It has never been found and is thought to be embedded in the mud on the seabed. Or so the story goes,' Billy added with intrigue.

'That's so interesting,' Marnie said. 'You must have had a great childhood. I went on my first holiday when I was twenty-two. My boss in the council office where I work, or should I say worked, arranged a team building holiday to a ski resort for the staff. It wasn't abroad or anything. It was up north in Glenshee. That was where I met Ashton. He was there with some boys from his football team. He was such a gentleman back then. Anyway, that's the only holiday I have been on. So, thank you for inviting me to yours.'

'We are delighted that you decided to come,' Bee said. 'I usually have to endure his stories on my own, but now that you're here, we can share the burden!'

'Happy to be of service,' Marnie laughed.

Chapter 57

The driver took Lockhart's suitcase, lifting it into the open boot of the taxi.

'Did you say you were going to the airport, darlin'?'

'Yes, that's right. Thank you.'

Lockhart sat in the back seat for the short journey. It was such a relief for her to leave with a clear conscience regarding Marnie and Elsie. The trip would have been somewhat bittersweet had she left either of them home alone. It almost seemed like the stars had aligned to allow her to go to see Aslan.

She smiled at the idea of this.

Good old Elsie. Boarding a plane to London to ensnare the old boy of her dreams. I hope it works out that way for her.

There was, however, a nagging doubt at the back of her mind, but sometimes nagging doubts could be wrong.

Hopefully, Marnie will come home from Mull refreshed, ready to join the rest of the world. Knowing her background, I don't know how she turned out to be such a sweet, refined girl. She has been dealt a dreadful hand of cards time after time. She deserves so much better. Could this holiday change everything for her? I really hope so.

It was a smooth, uneventful flight, and Lockhart slept through most of it. Life had become so hectic these days at the shop, and added to this was the worry of Marnie's welfare, all of which had left Lockhart feeling drained. A week of sunshine and rampant sex was exactly what she needed. That said, her laptop was packed away in her suitcase to keep her connected to the world. Staying on top of things while she was away meant she wouldn't be overwhelmed when she returned. There would be plenty of spare hours in the day to fill when Aslan was working. Lockhart's case appeared first on the carousel.

See, the stars are definitely aligned!

Outside the terminal building, a row of taxi drivers waited expectantly. Lockhart approached the first one in the line.

Seeing her in his rear-view mirror, the driver exited the car in time to greet her.

'Where you go to?' he asked.

'The Blue Lagoon, please.'

'Ah, nice hotel,' he commented, reaching for her suitcase.

The taxi drove through the makeshift town where she had initially been booked on her holiday with the girls. They travelled along the main street, passing the holiday rep's office. She smiled as she saw Judy Bailey sitting near the door, talking on the phone.

She imagined her saying, 'Hello, my name is Judy Bailey. If you need anything, just call, and ask for Judy Bailey…'

The taxi drove past the pavement café where she had sat alone, feeling wretched.

A hundred yards along from there were the apartments where the girls had stayed. The grounds had since been landscaped, giving a more finished look to the area.

She felt nothing but fondness for this Turkish resort that had been the first rung in the ladder of her happiness. Had she not agreed to go, chances are she would have taken George back when he came calling.

The taxi climbed the meandering driveway that led to The Blue Lagoon. It really was an incredible hotel, and it was so lovely to be back.

Chapter 58

Elsie awakened with a yawn, followed by a stretch. Glancing at the radio clock on the cabinet beside her, she was astonished to see that she had slept right through the night. Usually, she would visit the toilet at least three times before morning. Breakfast would be out of the question; she was already running late.

Throwing back the plump duvet, she made to leap out of bed. Unfortunately, this resulted in a dizzy spell taking her quite by surprise. Dancing stars circled around behind her eyes; a queasiness unsettled her stomach. All she could do was to sit on the edge of the bed and wait until the episode passed.

I've managed to get myself in a big state over this trip. I've known Bartlett nearly all my life, so why am I getting all in a pickle now? He would be cross with me if he knew.

As the giddiness began to subside, Elsie arose shakily to the standing position to retrieve her suit from the wardrobe. *Bartlett is going to adore this outfit. He has always liked me in hyacinth blue.*

After dressing, she tonged a few wayward curls into position before applying her shocking pink lipstick. One last look in the mirror gave her the confidence to walk out onto the busy London streets.

I may be in my seventies, but I could give any woman half my age a run for her money.

Foreign languages and accents could be heard from the passing tourists as Elsie strolled along the short walk to Bartlett's shop. The city looked so wonderfully colourful, and the air around her was seasonably warm. In her opinion, there was nowhere like London. The fashion, the food, the culture, the history. It felt like coming home.

Elsie was greeted at the door by a cheerful young woman who usually sat at a sewing machine in the back of the shop. She was a far cry from torn-faced Norma.

'Hello, Elsie, come on in. Bartlett is waiting for you. I'll put the kettle on.'

The muscles in Elsie's stomach tightened. Nerves began to take over. Her hands became sweaty, and her mouth dry.

What am I doing? I need to stop this silly nonsense. How can I be so fraught over a date with my special Barty? It's ridiculous.

'Just go through to the office. He's in there.'

'Thank you,' Elsie replied, her twig-thin legs trembling beneath her.

Bartlett saw her through the glass on the office door. He rose to his feet with outstretched arms.

'Elsie, my darling! You look knock-out in that shade of blue. It matches your eyes.'

His hands caught hold of hers, drawing her near. She giggled quite uncontrollably.

'Have I ever told you how much you suit blue?'

'You have, Barty. You also say it matches my eyes. That's why I picked this outfit.'

'What do you say we get straight on with business, work through lunch, although I will ask Trudy to bring us some pastries and perhaps a little fruit, then we can go out for drinks until our reservation at the restaurant. It's an early booking, so there won't be time to get sloshed, sadly.'

'Bartlett, that sounds just wonderful. My days of getting sloshed are over now anyway.'

Chapter 59

Billy turned left onto a single-track road which ran alongside the sea. The holiday home they had booked for the week could be seen standing where the road ended. All three of them gasped at the sight of the house. It was a modern structure, mainly glass-fronted, maximising the sea view.

'What do you think, girls?' Billy asked.

Bee kissed him on his lips, grabbing his cheeks with both hands.

'I think you are a very clever boy for booking this wonderful house for us.'

'I've never seen anything like it. It's beautiful,' Marnie told them, feeling quite mesmerised by everything around her.

'We'll go and look around inside before we unpack the car. Come on, now's your chance to pick your bedroom,' Billy told them.

They headed to the front door. Billy was armed with the key at the ready.

Marnie looked at the area of grass across the road. There was a downtrodden path which she hoped led to the beach.

'Do you guys mind if I see the house shortly? I just need to go and look at the sea for a minute. I'll be back in time to help with the bags.'

'Go for it, Marnie. It's your holiday, so please yourself,' Bee told her, as she followed Billy into the house.

Taking the ready-made path, Marnie wandered down towards the sea. It was a calm day with the gentlest of breezes. Tears filled her eyes when she saw the white sands against the emerald-green ocean. Removing her shoes, she ran the remainder of the way.

Over the past few months, she had begun to feel numb towards everything in life, but today, with the cold water splashing over her feet, she felt alive again. Awakened.

She waded in, pulling her dress up around her bare thighs.

'Aarrgh!' she screamed across the ocean. 'Aarrgh!'

When she returned to her friends at the holiday house, she noticed they had brought in all the suitcases and the shopping from the car. There was even a smell of cooking in the air.

I must have been gone for longer than I thought.

'The wanderer returns!' Billy joked.

'I'm so sorry. I just dawdled along the beach, looking for shells.'

She stood holding her dress gathered at the front to hold the seashells. Sand still remained between the toes of her bare feet.

'How's the beach?' Bee asked.

'Unbelievable. I will be down there every morning if you're looking for me.'

The dining table was in the centre of the extensive open-plan living area. Bee had set three places with the cutlery and crockery from the cupboards. They sat down together on their first night in the house. It was blissfully peaceful, making them feel cut off from the outside world.

'Ladies, I found a folder with all the information about things to do while we're here.' Billy left his plate for a moment to collect the literature. Resting the large book on the table beside his plate, he began flicking through the laminated pages as he ate. 'Here's something I didn't know. There is a little bar, and it's walking distance from this house. It's in... let me think,' as he struggled to get his bearings. 'It's in... that direction, no, that direction,' he demonstrated, pointing his finger. 'It says here that there are quiz nights and live music, oh, and there is even karaoke. Anyone interested?'

There was no response from Marnie.

Bee raised her hand. 'I'm very interested, especially in the quiz night.'

I don't want to go out. I don't want to be with people. I like it here where it's quiet. I came on holiday to get away from company. I'll say that I can't go, I'll tell them I'm ill. Why do things always get spoiled?

Chapter 60

As planned, Billy woke Bee and Marnie the following morning at seven a.m. The first full day of their holiday would be spent scaling Ben More, the only Munro on Mull. Billy had conquered it many times, including on his honeymoon with Bee. As far as he was concerned, a trip to Mull was not complete without an early morning climb to the top of the Munro.

In preparation for their holiday, Bee had packed spare climbing boots for Marnie, along with outdoor clothes to suit all weathers. She had been caught out once before, leaving the house in spectacular sunshine only to find heavy snow when they reached the peak. Lunch was made of sandwiches from the previous evening's leftovers, with a few energy bars thrown in.

According to Billy's research, the weather was fine, and the walk should take five hours, including a stop for lunch. He took charge of the heavy backpack which contained their supplies.

'I will administer snacks and drinks as and when required,' he announced officially, slinging the bag over his shoulder.

'That's good to know, dear,' Bee said, with a roll of her eyes behind his back.

Marnie laughed.

Chapter 61

Lockhart checked in at the reception of the hotel. A porter led her to her room, carrying her suitcase. The room was very similar to the one she had stayed in, only with a view of the sea from a different angle. After being tipped, the porter left her alone in the bedroom. She saw that the balcony door was partially open, inviting her to go outside. Standing in the sun's warmth, staring out across the still ocean, Lockhart began to feel aroused by sexual memories of the past and what was yet to come. Her nipples pressed against the fabric of her top. Her underwear began to feel damp. She was ready to embrace anything that Aslan suggested.

The receptionist informed her that there were two available massage appointments for the day. Lockhart chose the earliest, as her need was great.

Her preferred appointment left her only enough time to shower, put on her special underwear and make herself look as presentable as possible. Her hands shook as she slipped on the black lace all-in-one item, designed not to be removed during intercourse. Knowing how sexually excited Aslan would be was an incredible turn-on for her. Her final touch to the outfit was a pair of black stiletto-heeled shoes with open toes, which were, as yet, still in the box. During previous conversations, it had become clear to her that shoes of this type were something he enjoyed.

Leaving the clothes she had arrived in strewn across the bed, she headed toward the spa wearing the white towelling robe. The doors of the lift opened. She entered, pressing the button for the top floor. Standing in the elevator, which was about to take her to paradise, she thought about the state she had left her bedroom in.

I was judgemental of the young girls I came to Turkey with last year. I was appalled by the mess they created in the room. Instead, they were simply happy and excited, just like I am now.

The familiar aroma seduced her senses when the doors opened, triggering an erotic response within her. Lockhart smiled at her own Pavlovian conditioning.

The young woman standing at the reception desk greeted her with a smile. Lockhart blushed.

Does she know what I'm really here for?

The woman asked for her name and room number. Lockhart supplied the information with false composure. The woman smiled again, instructing her to go on in.

She then said, 'Enjoy.'

Lockhart's heart thudded against her ribcage as she nervously turned the handle of the massage room door.

'Calm down, calm down,' she internalised repeatedly.

'Hello!' a booming voice echoed in broken English. 'My name is Beyza. I am your masseuse for today.'

Lockhart spun around, feeling startled. A Turkish lady of very generous proportions stood with her legs astride, her hands on her hips. Her grey, thinning hair had been pulled back severely into a small bun at the nape of her neck.

'Take off your clothes,' she commanded.

From that moment, Lockhart suffered mental and physical agony for a full sixty minutes.

The relief she felt when the session was over was immeasurable. There had been no relaxation involved in the procedure, only pain and humiliation. She scuttled past the young girl at reception and boarded the lift to take her as far away as possible.

Back in the safety of her bedroom, she sent a text to Aslan.

Lockhart: Where are you?

A reply vibrated through almost immediately.

Aslan: I've been waiting on the terrace for you. I've swapped some of my shifts over.

Lockhart: Heading down now.

Lockhart swiftly changed, then ran down the hotel's stairs through the dining room, which housed glass doors leading to the terrace. The first glimpse she caught of Aslan was of him facing the opposite direction. How familiar his lean muscular physique and his broad athletic shoulders were. There was no mistaking him from the back. She knew every part of him so well. A fleeting memory returned to her of seeing Aslan out of the window in a restaurant in London.

I could have sworn it was him, but there again, I could have sworn the man I followed the next day was him. Though justified, she removed the thought from existence... again.

He turned at the moment she approached as though sensing her presence. A gasp was released from both their mouths as they rushed hungrily towards one another. Their embrace was filled not only with passion but with painful yearning. They stood holding on, rubbing their faces together, kissing and inhaling the other's essence.

The feel of Aslan's skin, the sweetness of his breath, and the strength of his caress made Lockhart feel light-headed. This man was her heart's desire, her saviour, her world.

Tears of laughter rolled down Aslan's cheeks when Lockhart explained that she had dressed in erotic underwear for a massage with him but was instead met with the decidedly butch Beyza.

Seeing Aslan laughing pleased her, especially knowing that she had induced it. His crooked smile and the slight twitch that occurred occasionally were the most endearing imperfections to her. She loved his spoken English, which was almost perfect, with barely a trace of an accent. Still, she also adored his mother tongue, which he used when speaking to colleagues.

Lockhart shared the remainder of the bottle of wine between their two glasses.

'You seem so tall tonight, Lockhart,' Aslan observed.

'Perhaps these could have something to do with it,' she said, lifting her leg up to show Aslan her stiletto heels.

A serious, almost dark look appeared on Aslan's face when he saw the shoes.

'Are you still wearing the underwear that you wore for Beyza?'

'Yes, I am,' she told him in a slow drawl.

'What the hell are we waiting for?'

He downed his wine in several gulps, putting the glass down purposefully on the table. Not another word was exchanged as he took Lockhart's hand, leading her up to her room.

They did not switch on the light in the bedroom when they entered. Somehow, they both knew that they wanted things to happen on the balcony. Lockhart gripped the wraparound railing as Aslan stood behind her. She waited to see what he would do. The anticipation began to feel unbearable. Her breathing became heavy, her legs, apart and ready, quivered. All she could feel was his erection pressing against her back and his warm breath on her neck.

Come on, Aslan. Do it now. I can't wait any longer.

Her thoughts were thrown into turmoil as he suddenly lifted her dress from behind. She bent over the railings slightly, allowing him to enter with ease. Letting out a shriek, she felt him penetrate deeply.

He moved slowly in time to the rhythm of the ocean, which stretched out in every direction before them.

This was the first of many sexual experiences during the evening. Aslan could keep going for most of the night and had the skill to keep things excitingly varied.

Lying beside each other with their arms and legs entwined, Aslan gently stroked Lockhart's arm. It was a tender, affectionate gesture which was not sexual but more loving. Whilst he caressed her this way, he spoke softly in the room's darkness.

'Lockhart, I want you to know that I have never felt like this about any woman. You are the only one I have ever had feelings for.'

Lockhart could not answer for fear of him knowing she was crying tears of joy for the words she had longed to hear.

Aslan had agreed to work several weekends in a row for Beyza, to get the following day off to spend with Lockhart. He delivered the good news that he was free for the day, followed by the bad news that they were going out on the motorbike. He was well aware of the major concerns she held about the hairpin bends on the clifftop road and the speed at which he travelled.

'Don't be afraid,' he told her. 'I drive on that road several times a week. I could ride my bike along there blindfolded. That's how well I know it. All you have to do is shut your eyes and think of Scotland.'

She managed to laugh at this useless piece of advice. The very thought of that dangerous road, to say nothing of the sheer drop that lay below, filled her with terror.

I don't want to look like an old fuddy-duddy. This is something that he enjoys. So, I have to go with it. What's the worst that can happen? Oh yes, I could die.

'Okay, but will you promise me you'll slow down a bit.'

'I promise,' he told her, touching his heart.

Like the love-sick fool that she was, she believed him.

After a terrifying journey, resulting in Lockhart keeping her eyes closed for the duration, they arrived at the old market town.

Aslan parked his bike in a designated area beneath a small copse of cypress trees. He laid his arm proudly around Lockhart's shoulder as he led her towards the bustling market stalls and outdoor restaurants, which were set amidst the backdrop of castle ruins. The haze from the intense heat somehow added to the ancient aura of the town, as did the smell of Turkish food cooking to the sound of local music.

As though reading her mind, Aslan asked, 'Do you like this music?'

'Yes, I do,' she said. 'I think I am experiencing the real Turkey for the first time.'

'I know what you mean,' he said. 'When we went to Edinburgh Castle and heard the bagpipes and drums, I got a sense of the culture of Scotland. The music you hear is a baglama, a stringed instrument with frets. It is similar to a lute. There is also the sound of a kanun, a stringed instrument that you lie across your knee and strum. It is apparently one of the most difficult instruments to play. It sounds nice, don't you think?'

'It sounds great,' she said, totally immersed in everything around her.

Hand in hand, they wandered through the market, surrounded by the shouts of the haggling shop owners luring in the tourists. Every once in a while, Aslan stopped to kiss Lockhart passionately on the lips.

'I think I need to stop and get a bottle of water,' Lockhart said, as she neared one of the stalls. 'I am so thirsty.'

The canopy offered them welcome shade while waiting for the customers to be served. From the corner of her eye, Lockhart noticed an old woman sitting on a seat between the stalls. Her black dress was of a heavy fabric, reaching down to her ankles. A black veil concealed a portion of her face. A skeletal hand reached over to take Lockhart's hand as she pleaded something in Turkish.

'Ignore her,' Aslan said, pulling Lockhart's hand free of her.

'Aslan, don't be like that. She is just an old woman.' Lockhart smiled at her. 'What is she saying?'

'She's just an old beggar who wants to tell your fortune. Walk away.'

Aslan's expression turned to one of anger.

Slipping her hand into her handbag, Lockhart took out some lira, handing the notes to the woman.

The elderly lady revealed an almost toothless smile before taking Lockhart's hand, palm upward. For a moment, she said nothing, just staring at something unseen to everyone else. Then, an unnerving droning sound began to vibrate from the lady, which lasted for an uncomfortable length of time.

The humming noise stopped in an instant. The woman looked up fearfully at Aslan. Her gaze flitted from one to the other as though she was making sense of what she

hat followed turned Lockhart's blood cold. The
n, whilst focused on Aslan, let out a screech,
ting, 'Hayir, hayir, hayir, before thrusting
khart's money back into her hand. Unsteadily, she
rose from her stool, lifted it, and left.
'What just happened?' Lockhart asked rather shakenly.
'Oh, forget it,' Aslan told her. 'She's just a crazy old fool.'
'What was she saying?' Lockhart asked.
'She was saying, no, no, no.'
'What do you think she meant by that?'
'Put it out of your head. She is deranged. Don't let it spoil the day.'
It already has.

Chapter 62

With all their business concluded, Bartlett arranged for a taxi to take them to The Cat's Cradle, an intimate bar across the road from the restaurant he had booked.

The bar layout was designed for privacy, with booths around the walls and a few tables in the centre with seating for two. Candles lit every table, and apart from a few spotlights illuminating an unused stage, there was no other light source.

'I love dark, cosy places like this,' Elsie told Bartlett. 'No one can see my wrinkles.'

'What wrinkles? You are beautiful. You are as youthful as the day I first met you.'

'Oh Barty, you make me feel eighteen again. I am having a wonderful night already.'

Bartlett directed Elsie to a booth at the far end of the bar. When they sat down, a waitress wearing a black leotard and dickie bow tie approached them for their order.

'I think we should both get a Manhattan,' Bartlett announced.

'No complaints from me,' Elsie agreed. It was plain to see from her face that she was in her element.

No sooner had the waitress left, but Bartlett reached over to take Elsie's hand.

'Elsie, you are my oldest friend, and I mean that in the nicest possible way. Tonight, I want to tell you about a decision I have made for the future, involving you.'

'Bartlett, I, too, have decided it is time to talk. Life can't be all fun and parties forever. There has to come a day when you take the plunge.'

It was emotionally overwhelming for Bartlett to comprehend that Elsie seemed to be able to mirror his thoughts. A deep, genuine love for this woman enveloped him.

'Tell me what you've been thinking,' Elsie asked, leaning forward on her elbows.

Waving his finger in the air, Bartlett said, 'Not yet. Wait until we get to the restaurant. I want to do this properly.'

Using the menu card, Elsie fanned her hot, flushed cheeks. 'You are too much, Barty. Way too much.'

'Ready for more drinks?' the waitress asked as she passed the booth with an empty tray.

'No, thank you,' Bartlett said, checking his watch. 'We have places to be.' The waitress nodded before moving to the next booth.

Bartlett stood, holding out his arm for Elsie to take. 'Shall we?'

'Yes, we blooming shall,' she giggled.

Elsie gripped tightly to Bartlett's arm as they made a reckless dash across the busy road. Whenever she was in his company, he brought out the fly-by-the-seat-of-your-pants side to her nature. With Bartlett by her side, she was young, carefree, and up for anything. After holding the restaurant door open for Elsie, Bartlett then gave his name to the waiter at the desk.

'Welcome, Mr Northcote. Let me show you to your table.'

They followed the waiter as he strode through to the main eating area, which was quite obviously full. Removing the reserved sign from the table at the window, he pulled the chair out for Elsie to sit down. Bartlett seated himself.

'Can I get you some drinks, Mr Northcote?'

'Yes,' Bartlett announced. 'Champagne. Your finest!'

'Very good, sir.'

Elsie couldn't stop laughing at Bartlett's flamboyant behaviour. She had never seen him quite like this before.

'Elsie, I have a surprise for you.'

'I can't take more excitement. I'm feeling giddy as it is.'

Bartlett stood up. 'I will be back in a moment.'

Left all alone at the table, Elsie's mind raced.

What is going on? I hope he isn't going to do anything public that will embarrass me. I think I feel one of my turns coming on.

She rested her head until the dizziness began to subside.

When she lifted her head, she saw Bartlett standing before her with a young man by his side.

'Elsie, I want you to meet Anton. Anton is an actor. In fact, he is in a play at the theatre around the corner. So perhaps we might find the time to go and see him perform.'

'I'm very pleased to meet you, Anton. What play are you in?' Elsie asked.

'The Importance of Being Earnest. It's running this week and next. I can arrange tickets to be left at the door for you. I play Ernest.'

Bartlett then stepped in by saying, 'You may wonder why Anton is here. Well, Elsie, I want you to be the first to know that he and I are going to be married. I would like you to be my best man, or woman, to be more precise.'

'I have to leave,' Elsie yelped, rising from her seat.

'Oh, my darling, are you unwell?'

'Yes, I'm sick. Sick to my stomach.' Leaving her jacket and handbag behind, she made an undignified exit from the restaurant.

Chapter 63

Having reached the top of Ben More, the three climbers returned to the house exhausted. Bee prepared a simple pasta dish for dinner while Billy took all the boots outside to scrape the mud from the deep grooves in the soles. It had been a tough climb, but they were pleased they had been fit enough to complete it. The view from the top was breath-taking and well worth every tiring step. Marnie had not exercised since the incident, so she appreciated the chance to start the challenge of getting in shape again.

Dragging her feet slightly, she headed upstairs for a shower before dinner. She stood under the steaming hot water, enjoying the powerful jets beating therapeutically down on her shoulders.

What will I do about tonight? They won't go if I say that I don't want to go out. This is their holiday. I'm just a guest. It was so good of them to bring me. I can't spoil it for them. Billy is really keen to go to and hear the music, but I can't face being with people. On the other hand, no one will know me here. Marnie's in a Quandary was a local thing. I'm anonymous here in Mull. What should I do?

The shout of 'dinner' came from downstairs, urging Marnie to get dried and dressed.

Bee gave one last stir to the pot of creamy pasta in a large bowl before taking to the table. She then ran to the oven to retrieve the over-cooked garlic bread with its blackened crusts.

'Don't just stand there doing nothing, Billy, there's a salad to be made.'

Gathering the lettuce, tomatoes and onions from the fridge, Billy then reached for the chopping board.

Bee watched him chopping away at the tomatoes, singing at the top of his voice as he did so.

He really does have the most wonderful singing voice. He is always happy, and he cares about everyone. I'm so lucky to have him.

'I don't think we'll ever talk Marnie into coming out,' Bee said. 'I won't leave her here by herself, so let's just have a nice time together in the house. I've already spotted Trivial Pursuit on the bottom shelf of the bookcase. It'll be fun.'

'Yes, I think you're...'

Billy was interrupted by an introductory cough from Marnie.

They turned to see her dressed in jeans, high-heeled boots, and a black lace top. Her beautiful raven hair lay across her shoulders, her face was tastefully made-up.

'Any of you guys fancy a night out?' she asked in a sassy tone.

Bee and Billy laughed.

'That's ma girl,' Billy said, rushing over to hug her.

'Hey, I'm your girl!' Bee argued, swiping at Billy in jest. 'Marnie, you are full of surprises. Now come, sit down and eat.'

The evening was warm, with a few straggling rays of sunlight still left on the horizon. The three of them followed the road in the direction of the local pub. It was too mild for jackets, but Billy had advised them to take them anyway for the walk home.

'When the sky is clear, with no blanket of clouds, the temperature will drop considerably,' Billy warned them. 'The clear nights in Mull are my favourite because you can see all the stars. There is no light pollution here on the island, so you get a clearer view of everything in the night sky. We will probably see shooting stars, so have your wishes at the ready.'

Wishes. What would be my wish? I think I just want to be happy. I'm not sure that I ever have been, Marnie thought.

Billy did most of the talking on the walk, mainly sharing stories of his childhood on Mull. They continued walking along the road, which was winding, with tall hedgerows growing on either side.

The first one to see the little bar was Bee. 'Hey guys, we're here, look!'

It was a quaint bothy painted white with fern-green shutters. The light from the windows was warmly welcoming, and the sign above the door read The Pub.

'I could murder a pint,' Billy confessed, quickening his pace.

Marnie experienced the grip of fear in her stomach.

I don't know if I can do this. Oh God, please don't let them turn around to stare.

Billy held the door open, allowing the ladies to go in first. Nearly every seat at every table was taken. Even the stools along the curved bar were occupied. When they entered the pub, everyone stopped to look at who had come in.

Marnie's worst nightmare unfolded.

Seeing the terror on her face, Bee took her by the arm, leading her straight over to the bar.

Everyone had lost interest in the new arrivals within seconds, as they continued their conversations.

The young barman appeared through a door next to the optics on the wall. He was carrying a crate of bottled beer. On seeing Marnie, he stopped to stare momentarily before setting the crate down on the floor.

Billy caught the bartender's eye, then leaning over the bar, he shouted, 'A pint of lager and two red wines when you have a minute, mate.'

'No problem,' was his reply.

Marnie lifted her eyes from the floor to sneak a glance at the young man. She decided he looked a bit like Hugh Grant in his early days, with his neat but rather floppy hair at the front. His crisp white shirt also drew her attention. There was something highly appealing about a man in a white shirt, in her opinion.

I wonder if his girlfriend irons his shirts, or maybe he doesn't have a girlfriend. Am I imagining things, or does he keep looking at me? I probably just remind him of someone.

The barman lined up the drinks on the bar before giving Billy the total cost.

'Will you have one yourself?' Billy offered.

'That's very kind of you. I'll get a pint when things quieten down a bit. Are you staying at Strathbeg House along the road?'

'Yes, we are. How did you know?'

The barman smiled. 'My mum and I own that house, so I knew three guests were staying this week. You three are not locals and this pub is off the beaten track, so it wasn't that difficult to work it out. I'm Struan, by the way.'

'Pleased to meet you, Struan. I'm Billy. This is my wife Bee and our friend Marnie. Join us for that pint when you are free.'

'Will do, Billy. Thanks again.'

Billy took the drinks to the girls, who were chatting conspiratorially together. He explained that Struan, the barman, and his mother, owned the bar and the property in which they were staying.

Marnie glanced up at Struan, who was looking over. Reaching for her drink nervously, she turned from his stare.

A section inside the bar had been cleared of tables, and within this area, a stool sat with a microphone beside it. At nine, the bar fell silent as a man in his forties walked onto the makeshift stage. His long grey beard had been pleated neatly into a pigtail. A small tartan fez sat on his head. The room erupted with cheers and claps at his arrival. Giving a short bow to the audience, he sat at the microphone. After a few tuning strums, he broke into Dougie McLean's Caledonia. The crowd went wild, and piercing wolf whistles came from several corners of the room.

Now on her second glass of wine, Marnie could feel herself starting to relax. With yet another furtive look, she saw Struan leaning on his elbows, watching the singer. At that same moment, he looked across at her. Again, she turned swiftly away.

By the singer's third song, a few people came forward to the clearing on the floor to dance. When he struck up the first few notes of Wonderful Tonight by Eric Clapton, Billy grabbed Bee's hand, dragging her onto the tiny dance floor. They danced slowly, holding each other tightly as they shuffled around in a circle.

Marnie watched them dancing.

Will I ever find that kind of love in my life?

A voice from behind her asked, 'Do you mind if I join you for a minute?'

It was Struan.

Marnie shook her head, gesturing for him to take a seat.

'Are you just here for the week?' Struan asked, knowing that she was.

'Yes,' Marnie replied, looking terribly nervous.

'Have you been to Mull before?'

'No,' she answered, looking at her drink.

'Did you do anything nice today?'

'Yes, we climbed Ben More.'

Struan was relieved that it was more than a one-word answer, but he had to concede that the conversation was going nowhere, fast. He sat silently for a moment before saying, 'Good talking to you. Enjoy your holiday.'

He hurried back over to the bar, where no one was waiting to be served.

'Okay, we can stop dancing now,' Bee said. 'She's on her own.'

They returned to the table, where a disappointed Marnie was kicking herself for having the curse of shyness.

The singer finished for the evening, and the bar's people gave him a resounding cheer, clapping above their heads. When he left, so did most of the customers. Billy realised that the majority of the crowd there tonight had come to hear the singer.

They agreed to finish the remainder of their drinks then start back on the long, winding road to the holiday house.

They were about to rise from the table when Struan came over with the pint that Billy had left him the money for earlier. He sat down with them and asked them where they were from. Billy launched into the tales of being in Mull as a boy, staying with his grandmother in the summer holidays. Bee rolled her eyes at Marnie, who smiled.

'Where in Mull did your grandmother live?' Struan asked.

'She lived her whole life, from cradle to the grave, in the same house in Pennyghael.'

'My father came from the town of Pennyghael,' Struan interrupted. 'He must have been a similar age to you, Billy. Perhaps you played with him back then.'

Billy was intrigued. 'What's your father's name?' he asked, excited by the prospect.

'Duncan Anderson,' Struan told him.

'I can't bloody believe it!' Billy said in amazement. 'Duncan Anderson was a very good friend of mine. We had some great laughs together. We built a bogey with some old pram wheels and a crate and took it up a hill near his house. We both got in it and pushed off from the top. We flew down at what felt like a hundred miles an hour. When we reached the bottom, we hit a rock and the bogey turned over twice in the air, hit the ground and smashed into pieces with us still in it.'

He laughed hysterically as he related the events of the story. Bee remembered him telling her they had turned over once in the air. But who was counting?

Then an idea came to Billy. 'Do you think he would like to meet up? Perhaps come over to the holiday house and have dinner with us?'

'My father passed away a year and a half ago.' He paused for a moment to regain his composure. 'It was pancreatic cancer.'

This revelation clearly still affected him as he struggled to say the words.

Marnie felt Struan's sadness when he spoke of his father. Seizing the moment, she asked, 'In that case, would *you* like to come for dinner at the holiday house one night?'

All three at the table turned in disbelief at Marnie for being so bold. No one was more surprised than she was.

Chapter 64

Despite the disconcerting incident at the market, Lockhart enjoyed her day with Aslan. As far as she was concerned, it didn't matter where they went as long as she was by his side. On the way back along the coast road, they paid a visit to Aslan's Uncle Demir in his vineyard. Demir seemed to recognise Lockhart, but he needed reminding of her name. When Aslan told him who she was, he made a joke in Turkish, to which Aslan forced a smile. Lockhart could tell he wasn't pleased.

Demir poured them both a large glass of wine. Lockhart was fearful of Aslan drinking alcohol as they still had the clifftop road to travel, only now it was dark outside.

When Demir asked about their day in the old town, Lockhart mentioned the fortune teller.

'What did she tell you?' he asked.

'Nothing really, she just screamed, no, no, no. She pushed the money I paid her back into my hand, then ran off.'

Demir took this episode a lot more seriously than Aslan had. Shaking his head, he told her, 'This is not good. Really not good.'

Aslan changed the subject from the fortune teller to business, asking Demir about how his current crop of grapes was faring.

Demir explained that his crop had not been as plentiful due to the wet weather conditions.

Lockhart watched as Aslan poured himself another full glass of the rich red wine.

'We had better get back now,' she suggested, feeling ever more concerned by Aslan's alcohol consumption.

Driving fearlessly, Aslan did not slow down when approaching the hairpin bends. The motorbike tilted almost onto its side as it raced around every corner. The sound of the revving motor could be heard on the road's straight sections when Aslan opened up the engine.

Tonight, I am going to die.

She kept her eyes tightly shut and felt like she was clinging on for her life.

Is he showing off? Is he trying to frighten me, or is he just drunk? Oh God, please save me tonight.

The thought of the sheer cliff drop below terrorised her.

As long as I live, I will never go on a motorbike again. I am not young or carefree. I'm fifty. I don't need to look for excitement. My life is exciting enough. Oh, why did I agree to this?

When they finally came to a halt, it was all Lockhart could do to stop herself from getting down on all fours and kissing the ground. It had been the most terrifying experience of her life. The memory of it would live with her forever.

Thank you, God, I owe you for this.

Aslan looked at his watch.

'I drove that road in record time. I told you there was nothing to worry about. I know these roads inside out and back to front.'

With a pleased smile on his face and a cocky spring in his step, he headed through the glass doors of the hotel entrance.

Lockhart decided she would say nothing about his treacherous driving or the broken promise he made about taking it slow.

There's no point in nagging at him. It will only make me feel like his mother.

On the hotel terrace, they sat together with a bottle of wine. Lockhart's nerves still felt frayed from the bike ride. She sipped on her wine to gain her composure. It wasn't possible for her to feel angry with Aslan. She loved him way too much.

'Your uncle made a joke when you told him my name. What was it?' she asked.

'I don't remember. He's always making stupid jokes.'

'I knew by your face that you didn't like what he said. Tell me, I won't be hurt.'

I think he just made fun of your name. It is unusual. I know you probably think my name is unusual, but in Turkey, Aslan is a very common name.'

For now, she was satisfied with his explanation of Demir's comment, but she had heard the phrase *chok fazla* and tomorrow, she would find out what that meant.

'I meant what I said last night that you are the only woman I've ever had feelings for. You are not like anyone I've ever met. I need you to believe that.'

'I do,' she told him. 'The same goes for—'

Aslan's phone, which lay on the table, resounded with his ringtone. His screensaver lit up, displaying a picture of the Tower of London.

Chapter 65

Elsie returned home traumatised. Feeling old and foolish, she headed straight to the safety of her shop, locking the door behind her.

You stupid woman. Was I really hoping to be the oldest virgin to walk down the aisle? Why did I think that Bartlett would want me for his wife? I just can't understand this man marrying a man business. Things like that don't happen here. It's a big city thing. I don't want to see Barty again as long as I live.

Tears of humiliation dripped from her chin as she walked around her precious shop, running her fingers over the satin gowns on the rail.

This is my life. I don't need anything else. I've managed this far on my own.

She was distracted from her thoughts by the phone ringing.

'Good afternoon,' she said. 'Princess Bride, how can I help you?'

The caller on the end of the line wanted to book an appointment for a fitting for her daughter.

'Now let me see, I have Thursday at 3.15pm or Friday morning at 9am … Perfect, I will look forward to seeing you then … I have the most wonderful dresses arriving from London tomorrow morning,' she concluded, replacing the receiver on the cradle.

That's more like it, you silly old goat.

Chapter 66

Billy laughed when he saw Marnie standing ready, waiting to go out to the pub. It was no longer a case of them coaxing her out the door. She looked beautiful, but there was something different about her tonight. He couldn't say she was more like her old self because he didn't know her before the attack. But this evening, she glowed. Bringing her to Mull with them had been the best medicine, that and a certain barman called Struan.

The gentle evening breeze felt mild again as they walked the winding road.

'Haven't we been very fortunate with the weather,' Billy commented, taking deep breaths of the fresh Mull air.

'We really have,' Bee agreed. 'Marnie, when we came here on our honeymoon, it was damp and drizzly every day. I didn't mind that because the fine drizzle is supposed to be good for your skin. What I really objected to were the midges. Those tiny creatures terrorised us and ruined our holiday. We had bites everywhere, even in places I shall not mention.'

Marnie laughed. 'Sounds awful.'

'Oh, it was awful. I was scratching my butt cheeks all day and all night long.'

Butterflies fluttered around Marnie's stomach as they entered the door to the bar. In an attempt not to be too obvious, she looked around the room before fixing her eyes on the bar to check for Struan.

He was there.

'A pint of lager and two red wines, Struan,' Billy said, when it was his turn to be served.

'Aw, Billy, it's good to see you back in tonight.'

Billy detected Struan straining to see if Marnie was behind him.

Marnie was looking in every direction but Struan's.

'Are you taking part in the quiz tonight? The prize is a bottle of champagne.'

'Of course we are. We'll give you Mullochs a run for your money.'

Struan handed him the quiz sheet and a pen. 'Give your team a name and write it here along the top. It starts at nine on the button. Good luck.'

'Thanks, Struan, but we don't need luck. We've got the brains. I'll keep the bubbly for Sunday night when you come over.'

When Marnie passed the bar to get to the table, she gave Struan a small wave.

Damn this cursed shyness. Why can't I just go over and talk to him? He must think I'm a freak.

The music volume dropped at precisely 9pm, just as Struan had told them. The crowd clapped, cheered, letting out ear-splitting wolf whistles. Billy joined in, clapping above his head, and letting out a few whoops.

After a discussion with his teammates, Billy wrote their collective name across the top of the sheet. The Three Non-Locals.

Marnie was an expert on celebrities, movies and soaps, whereas Billy was the sport and current affairs specialist. Bee knew almost everything else, making The Three Non-Locals a dream team.

For an hour, the quizmaster asked general knowledge questions. During this time, the room was quiet as all were completely focused on the task in hand.

When the time was up, team leaders handed in their answer sheets at the bar. Billy used this opportunity to buy more drinks for his table.

'How do you think you got on, Billy?' Struan asked, taking his sheet of answers.

'Pretty good. We were stumped on a couple of questions, but overall, I think we are in with a shout.'

'That's big talk. We'll soon see once they are marked. You'll find out in about twenty minutes.'

'Why don't you join us for a drink when you're finished tonight?' Billy asked, mainly for Marnie's sake.

'Yes, I'll do that, Billy, thanks. You won't believe how quickly this place empties once the winner is announced. People come purely for the quiz.'

Billy took the drinks over to Bee and Marnie.

'You may or may not be interested, Marnie, but Struan is joining us for a drink once he's finished in here.'

Marnie's pretty face broke into a smile.

'What are you telling me for?' she laughed.

'No reason. Absolutely no reason at all.'

The Three Non-Locals did not win the bottle of champagne. They were placed third in the quiz.

Bee had a very competitive nature, so she felt disappointed. However, when the answer sheets were returned to them, she studied every question, counting up the marks for herself.

Billy was a sport, clapping loudly for the winning team.

Only one thing in the room interested Marnie, and it had nothing to do with general knowledge.

The crowd dispersed immediately, just as Struan had predicted. After the top prize was given out, everyone had headed for the door within minutes. Struan made his way over to Billy's table with a pint of lager in his hand.

'I'll take a break now with you guys. The tidying up can wait until later.'

Struan pulled out a chair next to Marnie and sat down.

'Good idea,' Billy told him. 'How long have you had this place?'

'I bought it with my mum several years ago, but it didn't start making us any money until we hosted events like tonight. Now, we are full almost every night. It's a great crowd that come. There's never any trouble.'

Bee asked if he had ever spent any time on the mainland.

'I went to university for four years in Edinburgh. I studied architecture. In fact, I designed the holiday house that you are living in for the week.'

'It's a very beautiful house,' Marnie told him. 'I've never seen anything like it.'

'Aw, thanks,' Struan said. 'I'm quite proud of it.'

When an opportune moment arose, Marnie said quietly to Struan, 'If you don't mind walking me home, I'll stay on to help you get this place in order. I want to give Bee and Billy a bit of time on their own.'

'Are you sure you don't mind helping?' Struan asked, thoroughly excited by the prospect.

'I don't mind at all.'

Billy left with his protective arm around Bee. 'We won't wait up!' he shouted from the door.

Marnie rose to her feet to start the cleaning, and from a storeroom behind the bar, she found a broom. After pulling all the chairs out from the tables, she swept the whole bar area, creating a mound of crisps, paper and mud.

'Struan!' she shouted into the storeroom where Struan was collecting stock for the bar, 'Do you have a dustpan?'

'Cupboard near the sink,' he shouted back.

With two of them working, the place was soon ready for opening the following evening.

Struan locked up the heavy storm door before heading off with Marnie in the direction of the holiday house.

'It normally takes me hours to get the place back in shape. You made it so much easier for me. Thanks, Marnie.'

'It was nothing. You have such a great place there. Mull is the most special place I have ever seen. Honestly, I haven't been to many places, but Mull is still my favourite.'

The road ahead was in pitch darkness. The vast array of stars that could be seen in the sky's dome offered a little light on their path.

Marnie slipped her arm through Struan's, moving closer to him. She wasn't afraid of the darkness around her but didn't mind Struan thinking she was.

Struan stopped when the light from the house was in view.

'Will you be in the pub tomorrow night?' he asked her.

'I don't know,' she said, teasing him. 'It's a toss-up between your place and all the other pubs around here.'

Pulling her close to him, he lingered a kiss on her cheek.

It felt really good.

Chapter 67

Lockhart could not keep it to herself any longer. She had to ask.

'Aslan, why do you have a picture of The Tower of London as a screensaver?'

Phew, I've said it.

'I would really love to travel to many countries. I love all the iconic landmarks of well-known cities. Sometimes I have the Eiffel Tower on my phone. Other times I have the Leaning Tower of Pisa. It is my dream to see them all.'

That's acceptable. Yes, I can live with that explanation.

'Some day,' she told him, feeling a little guilty for being suspicious. 'I will take you to some of the wonderful places I have visited.'

'Where are your favourite places?' he asked.

'I travelled a lot with George in the beginning. We went to Paris, Madrid, the South of France, Tuscany and California but my favourite was Gardone on Lake Garda. You and I will take a tour of all of these places. The only place I will never return to is Madeira. I have miserable memories of the city of Funchal.

The following day, she took up her usual place at the pool, under the shade of the cypress trees. She set up her laptop to complete some financial matters relating to the shop. On impulse, she lifted her phone to call Elsie. There was no point in emailing her because she never checked them. After three rings, the familiar voice answered.

'Good morning, Princess Bride. How can I help you?'

'Well, you can start by telling me how you got on in London,' Lockhart replied.

'Oh, Lockhart, it's you. I got on great business-wise. I have picked up some incredible bridal gowns in larger sizes. Bartlett gave me a very good deal on them. I think they are going to sell well.'

Lockhart detected an edge of sadness in her voice as she delivered all the great business news.

'How did it go with Bartlett?' she asked, suspecting the worst.

'Oh, Lockhart. Don't even ask. Have you ever heard of such a thing as a man marrying another man?' she asked in bewilderment.

Lockhart squirmed for her friend as she imagined the scene in her mind. Of course, it made sense that Bartlett was gay. Elsie would never have suspected in her wildest dreams that Bartlett's flamboyancy and ability to connect with his feminine side were related to homosexuality. She had enjoyed the attention and compliments; in her black-and-white world, men loved ladies, and ladies loved men. Simple.

'Elsie, I am so sorry. You still have a really good friend there, and you have had happy times with him. Don't let go of the friendship. This is more common than you think and is just a normal part of life. We are all made differently and should be allowed to be who we are. I hope you parted friends with him,' she said.

'Actually, I didn't. I just ran away. I may phone him one day when I recover from the shock.'

Lockhart lay back on her sun lounger. A text came through her phone.

Aslan: Meet me at the outdoor bar near the pool. I am on a quick lunch break. I need to ask you a favour.

Lockhart was intrigued. She put on her wrap and walked over to the outdoor bar. Aslan appeared soon after. He took her by the hand, directing her at full speed along a path and into the woodland at the back of the hotel. They kept walking until they reached an area where the trees had been cleared. All that could be heard in the stillness was the sound of crickets coming from the shrubbery all around. The smell of warm earth was in the air, and the humidity was intense. Lockhart waited with eager anticipation to find out why she had been summoned.

Aslan stood with his back against the tree, beckoning her over. He undid the buckle of his belt, then loosened the buttons on his jeans. He slowly pulled them down far enough to reveal the great urgency. Without exchanging a word, he directed her head downward. Within seconds, he was moaning in ecstasy.

A week with Aslan was too short. Before she knew it, the time had passed, and her flight home was due in the morning. It had been a wonderful holiday, but she had used the time wisely. There had been no sitting around waiting for Aslan to finish work. Instead, her days had been spent in the sunshine, working on the shop accounts, and placing orders. An idea for a wedding fair had been cultivating in her mind. Acting on this plan, she sent information to local businesses such as hotels, wedding cars and florists. Her idea was to bring wedding-associated companies together with brides in a suitable venue. Elsie would get to hear all the details when she returned home, and by then, responses may have come in from her emails.

The following morning, carrying her packed suitcase, she headed down to reception. Sad farewells had been exchanged with Aslan the previous night, with an agreed plan that he would come to Scotland as soon as the holiday season was over. For a surprise, she decided she would book a trip for them to go somewhere special.

Handing over the key card for the room, Lockhart asked if she could settle her bill for the week.

'Have you had a pleasant stay with us?' the receptionist asked.

'Yes, it's been fabulous. It's my second time staying at this hotel, and I will be back as soon as possible.'

She carefully scanned the items on the bill before handing over her credit card for payment. As she picked up her case to leave, a sudden thought came to her mind.

'One more thing,' she said to the receptionist, 'Could you tell me what the English translation for an expression that sounds like chok fazla?'

The receptionist thought for a minute, then pronounced it correctly. She then explained that in English, it meant, so many.

Lockhart stared for a moment, her mind digesting the information, trying to put it into context.

'Thank you,' she replied.

So many what?

Demir couldn't remember her name because there were so many.

Perhaps it was so many letters in the name Lockhart. No, that's just stupid. So many what, then?

There was only one explanation. She couldn't bear to think about it.

In the back seat of the taxi, she thought over the wonderful things Aslan had said to her.

You are special. Different from anyone else. Did he mean she was different from the so many*? More special than the* so many*?*

Feeling tearful, she desperately tried to be rational by looking for a positive slant in Demir's comment.

There can't possibly be so many*. His love and actions towards me are real. No one could play-act affection like that to* so many *women.*

In the end, she settled on the explanation that there had been so many women in Aslan's ***past***. For the sake of her sanity, she had to believe that.

Chapter 68

Marnie woke up very early the following morning. The sun shone warmly through her bedroom window, landing on her face. It felt nice. For some time, she just lay there, enjoying the stillness, thinking over the previous night's events.

With the pleasing sound of the birds chirping their morning call, she tossed back the duvet and leapt from her bed. Her jeans and sweatshirt lay draped across the armchair from the previous night. Slipping them on, she crept downstairs without making a sound.

Her trainers lay at the front door. Her feet slipped inside the shoes without undoing the laces. Then, ever so gently, she pulled the bolt back, opening the door to the wonderful, misty morning outside.

The grass in the field across from the house was wet with morning dew drops. She inhaled the fresh sea air into her lungs, feeling thankful for the first time that she was alive.

Removing her trainers, she walked along the chilly water's edge. It felt so good. Whilst walking, she allowed her mind to drift back to her destructive relationship with Ashton. The details of that awful night flooded her thoughts; she did not prevent them from entering. Childhood memories also revisited her. The treatment she received from her parents, who were supposed to love her, the foster homes she was placed in, where she was forever the outsider. Why had her parents always fought to get her back when they didn't want her when she returned? Did they simply see her as their property?

The dark memories she had kept locked away in a vault of misery just kept coming, and she allowed them to do so. Tears for her younger self came spilling out into sobs. These sobs should have been released many years before, but here they were, escaping from her on a beautiful beach in Mull.

It was not until she lifted her eyes from the shoreline that she realised how far she had walked. There were sand dunes on her left with long reedy grasses sprouting. In the distance, she could see hazy cupcake-shaped islands that appeared to float on the sea's surface. Standing still for a moment, she listened to the squawks of the sea birds accompanied by the waves' gentle splashes against the rocks. The Island of Mull had not only offered a rich healing balm to her hurts, but it allowed her to let flee the demons of her past.

On the long walk back, she collected pretty shells that lay like half-buried treasure in the sand. The pockets of her sweatshirt bulged with her collection of sandy finds.

The welcome aroma of sausage, bacon and egg engulfed her nostrils as soon as she opened the front door of the holiday house. Only then did she realise how hungry she was.

Billy had laid out tourist attraction leaflets across the dining room table.

'Right, girls,' he said. 'We have choices to make here. What would you like to do today?'

'Billy, can you move the leaflets away, please? I am about to serve breakfast for everyone,' Bee announced.

Marnie gathered all the literature together, laying it in a little stack beside the tomato sauce bottle. They all sat down at the table, perusing the information as they ate.

It was agreed that they would visit the island of Iona, which was only a short ferry crossing from Mull. Billy told them, in great detail, all about the ancient abbey, which was well worth seeing.

The brochure wrote about the island being a spiritual retreat. Considering Marnie's experience on the beach earlier, she felt it would be a fitting day trip for her.

On the way to the ferry, Billy took them on a slight detour. He wanted to show them Pennyghael, where his grandmother lived. After the sign for Pennyghael, Billy drove along the small main street, then took a left down a dirt track. Unfortunately, the road was full of potholes, wreaking havoc with the car's suspension.

'Billy, is this absolutely necessary? We are going to need a new car after this. It had better be worth it,' Bee said scornfully, just as they hit another pothole.

'Oh yes, dear wife, it is absolutely necessary. You'll see.'

The twisting road finally ended, and they faced an old stately home in the early stages of ruin. Billy switched off the engine, telling the girls to get out.

'This is Pennyghael House. My grandmother was a chambermaid here when she was fourteen years old. The house has a chequered history, many strange stories circulated around it. We used to dare each other to go and knock on the front door or look through the windows. It was terrifying.'

'Who owns it now?' Marnie asked.

'Well, I don't know. The rock band Genesis bought it in the nineties, but I believe they sold it.'

All three stared up at what would once have been a magnificent house. Still, the neglect of the property had encouraged nature to reclaim it, with trees and vines growing up inside its walls.

Bee turned to her husband. 'This really was worth seeing, Billy. Maybe not worth wrecking the car over, but I'm glad you showed it to us.'

'Me too,' Marnie agreed. Another strange feeling of déjà vu passed over her, giving her a sense that the house had significance. But she told herself that it was her imagination.

'I only remembered about it last night. I was dreaming about being here as a boy. I wanted to see if it was still standing.'

He was pleased that, although it was in a precarious state, it was, indeed, still there. It also felt good to tell the girls something new that had appeared to capture their interest.

They drove back along the dirt track, taking a left turn towards Fionnphort, the town where they would catch the ferry that would take them across the sea to the island of Iona.

Chapter 69

Lockhart arrived home in a taxi from the airport. Spending time with Aslan had been great, but she was glad to be home. Elsie needed her in the shop. The appointments had been building up, which meant they needed more than one pair of hands.

Marnie had left the house clean and tidy, which came as a pleasant surprise to Lockhart. When she walked past her bedroom, she saw that Marnie had made her bed with the throw, cushions, the works.

What a difference from a couple of weeks ago. Here's hoping her sunny disposition lasts. I wonder how she got on in Mull? I hope she wasn't bored.

Princess Bride didn't close until six, so Lockhart decided to walk up to see how Elsie was feeling. It was a warm evening, so she left with her cardigan draped loosely over her shoulders. At the end of the road, she took a shortcut through the lane which led up to the main street.

When she reached the foot of the lane, she was stopped in her tracks when she spotted a familiar family across the road. They were laughing and happy. The man pushed the pram whilst smiling in at his baby. It was George, her George, being a proud dad. Lockhart looked at Gemma and for the first time could see why George fell for her. She was youthfully beautiful.

She stood watching until the family were out of sight.

How do I feel? Why am I crying? George, a doting father, who would have thought it.

In her heart, she felt happy for George, just terribly sad for herself. Gemma was around Aslan's age, and seeing this happy scene begged the question of whether she would be depriving him of a family. There was no doubt that she had something special with Aslan, but in the longer term, he may grow to resent her.

George and Gemma had not noticed her. She was glad about that. It gave her a chance to privately come to terms with George's fatherhood. The next time she saw them, she would be properly prepared with heartfelt congratulations.

Life is full of strange twists and turns, she thought. *Just when you think your future is set in stone, life can throw you a curve ball and send you in the opposite direction. It's a blessing that you can't see into the future.*

This thought triggered a memory of the fortune-telling lady dressed in black at the market in Turkey. What a bizarre experience that had been. She didn't want to start overthinking the incident. Still, it had given her a jolt, a sense of foreboding for the future.

Elsie was busy working in the back of the shop when she heard the shop door opening. This brought her running through to see who was there.

'Lockhart!' she shouted. 'I have missed you, don't dare go away again,' she pleaded. 'I didn't realise how much I needed you. I can't do this on my own anymore.'

'You won't need to do it on your own ever. I am in this venture for the long run. Oh, and I've had a few ideas while I've been away. Did you get back in touch with Bartlett?' Lockhart asked.

'Yes, he forgave me for running away. In fact, we had a good laugh about it. He is getting married to Anton, who is an actor. He has invited me to the wedding and asked me to be the best man, er… I mean lady. I'm allowed to bring a partner. Will you come?' she asked.

'Of course. We will make a little holiday of it.'

Elsie's eyes moistened on hearing this comment. She made coffee for them, and together, they sat discussing the idea of a wedding fair. They jotted down ideas and possible venues.

Lockhart agreed to send out details to all the interested businesses. 'Oh, Elsie, what am I thinking?' she announced. 'Let me hear all about the dresses you bought from Bartlett.'

'Well, I got several beautiful gowns. I asked for bigger sizes. Let's face it, brides go up several sizes each decade. Bartlett is sending them by courier, they will be here before the end of the week. He didn't have any photos for me to take away, and as you know, he doesn't have a website, but he did give me some adorable little sketches he drew when he was designing the gowns. I'll get them from my bag.'

Lockhart was impressed that Bartlett still worked from hand-sketched designs, he had not moved with the times at all, yet it hadn't affected his business. Elsie handed the carefully drawn pictures to Lockhart. They had been shaded with pastels of several colours. A layer of tissue paper lay between each drawing.

'Elsie, I want to frame all of these sketches and more if we can get them. They are unique and exclusive. They symbolise the wedding gown's originality.'

'Oh! I agree. Lockhart, you are full of such wisdom,' Elsie gushed.

They were deciding which type of gilt frames would best enhance the sketches when the door opened with a ring of the bell.

It was a father and daughter dropping in to take a look at the dresses. They didn't have an appointment, but as the shop was quiet, Elsie said she would be delighted to offer them a fitting. The girl introduced herself as Susan. Her heart was set on a dress in the style of Marnie's in a Quandary dress number four. Marnie's feature seemed so long ago now. In truth, both Lockhart and Elsie had forgotten the order of the dresses. Elsie told her to take a seat, and she would show her everything she had in her size, or she could choose one and resize it. Susan picked a selection of dresses to take into the fitting room.

Lockhart chatted with Susan's father until his bride-to-be daughter was ready to reveal each dress for his opinion.

'Susan's mum passed away two years ago, so I'm having to do the mum jobs as well as my own. I am going to be honest with you,' he said, 'I think all wedding dresses look the same. I'm not very good at this kind of thing.'

'That's why we are here to help you. Look, it's easy. When she tries them on, pick the dress that makes you feel emotional. I promise you, there will be one that makes you tearful when she comes out wearing it.'

'I'm Lockhart, by the way.'

'Lockhart?' he repeated. 'Not Lockhart Sinclair?' he asked.

'Yes, many, many, years ago, I was Lockhart Sinclair before I became Lockhart Hayes. Do I know you?' she asked, looking into his face to try to see the boy in him.

'I'm David Hill. You started school with me in primary one and left on the same day in fifth year. I wouldn't have known you if you hadn't said your name. I have never known another Lockhart.'

She started to laugh. 'I remember you so well. You were super clever. You always put your hand up in class to answer everything. But I also remember you were never a show-off. I liked that about you,' she added.

The memories flooded into her mind of the boy this man used to be.

They stood reminiscing about their teachers back in their school days, until Elsie shouted, 'May we have the bride's father through, please?'

Lockhart had been wrong about choosing the dress on an emotional reaction. David Hill shed a tear with every dress his daughter tried on.

Father and daughter left the shop happy, carrying a large Princess Bride bag, which contained a gown almost identical to dress number four in Marnie's in a Quandary.

David touched Lockhart's arm as he was leaving. 'Thank you for making this day so special.'

'It was my pleasure.'

Chapter 70

Bee felt terribly sad that the Mull holiday was coming to an end. Another week would still have been too short. Walking along to the pub each night had been a highlight of the trip but seeing Marnie blossoming as each day passed made Bee so happy. Bee knew that she occasionally gave Billy a hard time, but it was always in jest. The truth was that she adored everything about him and his warm-hearted ways.

Marnie stayed behind every night after closing to help Struan set up the bar for the following day.

It had become a pleasant routine, where she cleaned and collected the glasses whilst he stocked the bar and replenished the optics. The walk home was the part Marnie enjoyed the most, when she took his arm as the chatted about nothing in particular. Without fail, he delivered a lingering kiss on her soft cheek.

It was a late finish on Saturday night, but, as usual, he walked her right to the door. Things took an interesting twist on this occasion when instead of his polite kiss to her cheek, he lingered a passionate kiss on her lips, holding her tightly in his arms.

'I'll see you tomorrow night for dinner,' he said. 'What time do you want me?'

All the time.

'Seven o'clock is perfect.'

Bee opened the curtains to allow the view and the brightness of the morning into the bedroom. The glassy sea with its familiar little islands stretched out as far as could be seen. Fanned rays from the early sun bounced off the water and a haze of swirling mist still lingered from the dawn. There really was no sight on earth that could rival it.

'You know, Billy, I will miss getting up to this view every morning. In fact, if you asked me to stay forever, I'd say yes in a heartbeat.'

'One day, we will. We need some cash behind us before we could even consider it.' Billy rose from the bed to join Bee at the window.

'Look! There's Marnie down on the sand. Why does she keep bending over?' Bee asked.

Billy laughed. 'She is collecting shells. I saw her the other day. Watch what she does when she finds a conch shell.'

They stood together at the window, still in their pyjamas, watching Marnie returning from her walk. Before reaching the field, they saw her picking up a shell and holding to her ear.

'Look, isn't that sweet,' Billy remarked. 'She's listening for the sound of the sea.'

'She is such an adorable girl.' Bee smiled at the sight. What a transformation she had noticed in Marnie.

When the sun was ready to return to the horizon, they retired to their rooms to get ready for their visitor.
Marnie had not packed many clothes for the holiday, simply because she didn't care about anything, especially how she looked. If she had only known she was going to meet someone special, her suitcase would have been more plentiful. There was nothing else she could do but return to the jeans and black top she had worn on the first night at the pub.
Billy poured drinks for the girls while they waited for the knock at the door.
'Why don't we play charades, it'll be fun. It's better than sitting here just waiting.'
Billy stood up to take the first turn.
The door knocked.
'Thank goodness for that,' Bee said, 'I thought we were actually going to have to start playing that damned game.'
Opening up the front door, Marnie met Struan with a nervous smile.
He kissed her cheek. 'You look beautiful.'
'I don't,' she said, 'I've nothing fancy to wear.'
'You are fancy enough for me.' He kissed her again.
Marnie led Struan by the hand into the lounge, 'Hey guys, looks who's here.'
'Hey! Struan, great to see you. What can I get you to drink?' Billy asked, patting Struan on the back.

'A can of lager if you have one.' Struan then reached into the plastic bag in his hand, pulling out a bottle of champagne. 'Next week's quiz winner won't be getting a prize,' he joked.

A wonderful dinner was prepared and cooked by Bee, served by Marnie. For much of the evening, they sat around the dining table discussing every topic. Struan discreetly held Marnie's hand under the table, but Bee and Billy had spotted his outstretched arm.

'It's a pity we have to go home tomorrow,' Billy said. 'I saw in the information booklet that Monday night is Karaoke night at the pub.'

'Oh, what a shame we won't get to hear you singing *What's New Pussycat*... again,' Bee said, rolling her eyes.

Struan laughed. 'It's a shame that you have to go home at all.'

He gave Marnie's hand a squeeze.

'I've had a great idea!' Struan said suddenly. 'I may have put a quiz book on the bookshelf somewhere. How about you two against Marnie and me?'

'You're on,' Billy told him, heading over to search for the book.

'Struan, I will apologise for myself in advance. I'm hopeless,' Marnie told him.

'Hopeless? Struan repeated. 'You're very near perfect.'

Chapter 71

Using the wooden pole with the hook on the end, Lockhart pulled the set of step ladders down from the loft. Her curiosity would not be stifled.

The attic space was filled with reminders of George, a set of skis and his golf clubs. A box of his law books from university sat in the corner, collecting dusty cobwebs. Under the eaves was the old wooden chest which had belonged to his grandfather. She did not know what was inside, nor did she care.

After rooting around behind the rafters, she saw what she had been looking for. It was a sealed box with her name written in felt tip pen across the top. She successfully dragged it across the floor to the open hatch. Getting it down would not be easy.

There was only one thing for it. 'Bombs away!' she shouted, pushing it over the edge.

With a pair of sharp kitchen scissors, she sliced the parcel tape that sealed it shut. And then, she rummaged.

I'm sure that all my class photos are down at the bottom, along with my school report cards. They have to be in here somewhere. It's the only box of childhood I own.

The photographs were exactly where she remembered them, under everything else. She pulled them out and took them to the kitchen for a proper inspection.

What was my mum thinking about cutting my fringe like that? Surely she could have afforded to take me to a hairdresser. It's all lopsided. I look terrible.

Her friend Elspeth was sitting next to her in the primary seven photo.

I wonder where Elspeth is now. Did she stay in Australia, or did she ever come home? Maybe I'll try to look her up one day. Oh, what am I saying? Of course, I won't look her up. I haven't seen her for about thirty-eight years.

It was not Elspeth she was interested in. It was the boy in the back row at the end.

David Hill.

So, there you are, David Hill.

He stood tall with his tie straight and his collar sharp. A stifled smile was fixed on his face. Yes, that was exactly how she remembered him to be.

You haven't really changed at all.

A sharp stab of guilt came over her when she began looking for David Hill in the primary six photo. Reaching into her pocket for her phone, she sent a text message to ease her conscience.

Hi Aslan, I miss you.

There would be no reply for hours or even days, but it didn't matter anymore. By now, she had grown used to his ways.

The sound of the key in the front door disturbed the silence and her thoughts.

'I'm home!' Marnie shouted.

Lockhart whooped with delight as she ran to the door to greet her.

'How was your holiday?'

Marnie smiled, 'Unbelievable. I've fallen in love with Mull.'

'I was just heading out to Get Fit With Mags. Why don't you come with me. You can tell me all about your trip on the way.'

'I don't think I can do that yet, Lockhart. People might still recognise me.'

'Oh, so what. Hold your head up high. None of this is your fault. This is your hometown. You should be able to walk down the street.'

'You're right, Lockhart. I have to face this sooner or later. Give me a minute to go and get changed.'

On the walk to the class, Lockhart heard all about Marnie's holiday. In great detail, she described the house and its location, the places they visited on day trips and of course, Struan and his pub.

'Do you think you'll see Struan again?' Lockhart asked.

'I hope so. We've exchanged phone numbers; he has sent a few texts already.'

Lockhart knew all about long-distance relationships. The worst part was the long wait for text messages. She was reminded of the early days with Aslan when she mentally willed the phone to vibrate with a text.

Fortunately, things become less manic. I have accepted the situation now. Otherwise, I would have gone completely out of my mind.

'So, we've made a few possible plans to meet up. We'll see how it goes,' Marnie added.

'If he is the one, then it will all work out for you. Nothing stands in the way of love.'

'Excuse me,' a breathless voice from behind shouted. 'Are you Marnie?'

Neither Marnie nor Lockhart answered. They simply kept walking.

The stranger persisted. 'I wanted to tell you how sorry I was that you had such a terrible experience. There is a lot of support out there for you. I hope you don't mind me intruding.'

'No, I don't mind, thank you.'

Marnie walked on. The stranger left them to cross the road. She had dealt with it, and it had been easy.

'Well done,' Lockhart told her. 'That wasn't so bad, was it?'

Bee had initially thought that she wouldn't make it to the class, but to Lockhart's surprise, there she was, waiting for them at the door of the hall.

'Good holiday?'

'Brilliant holiday.' That was all she managed to say before the door lady in her leopard print ushered them in.

Mags, as usual, worked them all into a sweat. It had been a tough routine, but there had been a few laughs along the way.

'Anyone for prosecco at Decanters?' Bee asked, as they gathered their belongings together.

Marnie nodded. 'Why not?' She knew that she needed to get her life back into a routine. Hiding away was not the answer.

Decanters was busier than usual for a weekday, but the crowd were transfixed to a Scotland football game on the big screen. Bee headed over to the spare seats at the window, while Marnie and Lockhart waited at the bar to be served.

In the corner of the room, Lockhart could see a group of girls sitting together, discussing Marnie. She cringed as she noticed one of them pointing over.

I'll keep asking Marnie questions about Mull to distract her from the unwanted attention.

Lockhart saw one of the girls heading over in their direction.

I'm not sure how to avoid this situation. I think we'll smile, thank her for her concern, and then walk away.

Marnie had just begun describing the ancient abbey on the island of Iona when she felt a tap on her shoulder.

Turning around, she saw the hardened face of a girl in her early twenties.

'Have you any idea what you've done to Ashton?' she said in a raised voice to Marnie. 'He has been charged by the police, his career is over, and the abuse he's had to put up with is ridiculous! I hope you're pleased with yourself.'

Lockhart turned to meet the girl's wrath. 'I really hope to God that you never find out what it feels like to suffer a brutal attack. Now go away and wait until your life is perfect before you spout forth your nasty little judgements on others!'

The girl returned to where her friends were sitting; they were hungry to hear the details.

'Are you okay, Marnie?' Lockhart asked.

'Not really. I'm just going to head home now. It was a mistake to come out. Thanks for sticking up for me, though. No one has ever done anything like that for me before.'

She left the bar.

Lockhart didn't order drinks. There was no way she could enjoy herself while her friend was suffering.

'Bee, I'm going to head home. Marnie had an upsetting experience with one of those girls over there, and now she's going home. I can't leave her.'

Lockhart and Bee left the bar in pursuit of Marnie.

Chapter 72

Aslan: Me too.

What does he mean? Lockhart wondered, staring at the words. It had been so long since they had been in contact. Scrolling through her messages, she saw she had sent him a text some time ago saying she had missed him. She had long since accepted that his schedule at The Blue Lagoon was full on in the summer months, so she didn't expect much contact from him. However, they would hopefully spend plenty of time together once the holiday season was over.

When autumn arrives, I will have him all to myself. Perhaps I could book us the holiday house in Mull that Marnie keeps raving about.

Lockhart had been thinking about her wonderful friends when she hatched an idea. After checking suitable dates with Elsie, Marnie and Bee, Lockhart booked a restaurant in the neighbouring town. It was an elegant establishment, overlooking the boats in the marina.

She wanted to take her friends out for dinner to tell them how grateful she was to have them. In a way, it was also a celebration to mark the day George walked out and left her. One year ago, her old life ended, and the new one began. Surely that was a day worth marking on the calendar.

Discussions had taken place between her and Elsie about offering Marnie a full-time post in the bridal shop. Elsie had admitted it was time to shorten her own working hours or at least take a day off midweek. She had to look ahead to a time when she may be unable to work. The dizzy turns were becoming more common, to say nothing of the extreme tiredness she was experiencing at the end of each day.

The dinner at the restaurant would be the perfect time to announce to Marnie that they wanted her to become a part of Princess Bride. Lockhart also decided that it was time she told Marnie and Bee all about Aslan. Elsie had already been filled in on this relationship when they went to London. If Aslan were going to become a permanent fixture in her life, her friends should not only know about it, but they should have the chance to meet him on his next trip to Scotland.

Lockhart sent out a text message to her three friends.

Friday 8th June at 6.45pm, a taxi will pick you all up for our dinner date at The Boat House. Dress – formal.

Chapter 73

Lockhart tapped the knife against her glass to gain the attention of her friends.

'Ladies, the first thing I would like to say is that I asked for the dress to be formal tonight, and you have not disappointed me. Elsie, you look beautiful in that lilac suit. Bee, green suits you so well and Marnie, you've turned every head in the restaurant, so thanks for that.'

'You're not too shabby yourself, Lockhart.'

'Thanks, Bee. I'll take that as a compliment. One of the reasons I invited you all here tonight was to thank you for your friendship. You all mean more to me than I can say. One year ago this week, my husband walked out and left me for a younger woman. I thought that was the end of my existence. How wrong I was. I hadn't banked on meeting you, and someone else I want to tell you about shortly. I have had the best time of my fifty years, I mean, soon-to-be fifty-one-year life, so thank you for that too.'

'You are more than welcome,' Elsie shouted, giving a little clap.

'There are several reasons for us being here tonight, and one of them is to ask Marnie something from both Elsie and me.'

Lockhart looked across the table at Marnie.

'I'm listening,' Marnie said expectantly.

'We would like you to come and work full-time at Princess Bride with us. Elsie will teach you the business, and I think you would be a valuable asset to the shop.'

The proverbial spotlight turned on Marnie. After a short bashful pause, she said, 'I'm so touched that you would want me in the business, but I have an announcement to make to everyone myself.' She became nervous for some reason. 'I will be moving to Mull in a couple of weeks. Struan and his mum have asked me to help in the bar because they have a new venture.' She looked specifically at Bee to announce this development because she knew she would understand what she was talking about. 'Struan and his mum have bought the old, ruined Pennyghael House. They plan to renovate it and turn it into a hotel.'

Bee was dumbfounded. 'That is so exciting, Marnie. I am thrilled for you. Do you have somewhere to live?'

'Yes, they are giving me the flat above the pub for the time being. It's been empty for a couple of years. It just needs some furniture and a bit of paint. It overlooks the sea,' she added. 'You know how much that will please me.'

Lockhart stood up to make the remainder of her toast and drink to Marnie's exciting future plans. Everyone fell silent. During this period of quiet, Lockhart heard her phone ring. Excusing herself, she took her phone from her bag. It was Aslan. There were seven missed calls. She walked away from the table to phone him back. *This is odd,* she thought. *He has never called me before.*

'Hi, Aslan,' she said. 'Are you okay?'

'Hello?' an unfamiliar voice replied. 'Is this Lockhart?'

'Yes, I'm Lockhart.'

Her hands began to tremble.

'I have been searching through the mobile phone of Aslan Cerci, and your name and number are there. Unfortunately, I'm afraid I am giving out bad news to the people listed in his contacts.'

Lockhart's body tightened rigid as she braced herself for what was coming.

'You are a friend of Aslan Cerci?' he asked.

'Yes, we are close,' she managed to say.

'I am afraid to tell you that Aslan has been tragically killed in a motorbike accident.'

'When and how?' she babbled.

'It happened last night. He hit a patch of oil on a sharp bend on the coast road. His bike skidded out of control. It was instant. There will be a funeral for him next Tuesday if you wish to attend,' he announced.

Lockhart managed to thank him before ending the call. She dropped down to her knees as her legs gave way.

She didn't remember much more about the evening. Her friends had sprung into action by getting her home. Marnie helped her to bed, sitting with her, holding her hand until she slept.

Chapter 74

Lockhart sat in the window seat on the busy flight to Turkey. She would arrive the day before the funeral for her beloved Aslan. There had been no shedding of tears. She had to stay strong. A cold numbness covered her skin.

How could my beautiful and vibrant man be dead? Where is he now? Is he lying on a cold slab in the hospital? How bad are his injuries?

How could she ever have foreseen that her return to Turkey would be to see Aslan lowered into the ground in a box, never to walk on the earth again. A shiver moved across her scalp, travelling down her spine. She pinched the skin on her arm with her index finger and thumb. There was no feeling. Reaching into her bag, which sat under the seat in front, she took out her cardigan, wrapping it around her shoulders. Her body trembled, making her teeth chatter together. She had no control over this.

The taxi drove through the town that she had originally booked on that holiday so long ago. She looked at the young people walking along the street, laughing and chatting.

How can they be so happy? Why is the world just running along as normal? Does no one feel this terrible emptiness?

A feeling of abandonment engulfed her.

How could you leave me, Aslan? We could have had a wonderful future together. I told you not to speed on that clifftop road. I bet you had been drinking Demir's wine before you got on your bike.

Anger towards him rose up within her, but it didn't last long. The heartache was too intense.

How long did he lie there, alone, before anyone found him?

There were so many questions that were too painful to think about.

Walking through the doors of The Blue Lagoon, everything looked the same but felt completely different.

Aslan would not be coming to meet her on the terrace tonight, they would not be spending the night together in her room. Those days were over for good.

The pretty girl on the reception desk was new, or at least Lockhart had never met her before.

As she approached, the girl welcomed her to The Blue Lagoon, then began to tell her of all the restaurant details before explaining the spa treatments on offer.

'I'm not here for a holiday,' Lockhart told her. 'I'm here for the funeral of Aslan Cerci, an employee here.'

'Oh, I'm so sorry. I have all the details here.' She reached under the counter, pulling out a map of the cemetery. 'This is where the service and burial will take place at two o'clock,' she explained, pointing at the south gate. 'Afterwards, there will be refreshments at his uncle's vineyard. Would you like me to organise a taxi for you?'

'That would be very helpful,' Lockhart told her. 'Is there still a market nearby?' she asked.

'Yes, the market is open until late every night.' The girl could see the grief on Lockhart's face; it was difficult to know what to say. 'Were you a good friend of Aslan's?'

'Yes, we were very close,' Lockhart said, holding back a sob.

'I felt sorry for the woman with him,' the girl added. 'It was the first day of her holiday.'

'What woman?' Lockhart asked in disbelief.

'The woman who was on the back of his bike. She was an older woman. I checked her in here at the hotel. She was very nice. It is terribly sad because she told me they were going out to celebrate Aslan's special birthday. She was also killed.'

Lockhart couldn't speak. Mechanically, she reached out her hand without looking, grabbing the key card in front of her. Without exchanging another word, Lockhart walked away. Her brain tried frantically to digest the information she had been given. The facts were not computing with her. She wanted to laugh hysterically for no reason. Perhaps it was the shock.

Of course, it's not true. Aslan doesn't have a special birthday this year. That stupid girl is getting mixed up with the events. I went on his motorbike for his special birthday. What was she talking about?

All the rooms with an ocean view were fully booked. The only available room was on the ground floor, at the back of the hotel. The window faced the bins in the courtyard outside the kitchens. What did it matter? Would the sea view have really eased her grief? Not in the slightest.

The small holdall she had brought contained only her black dress and stilettos. The shoes were for Aslan; he loved her in high heels. Nowadays, it was commonplace for people to wear bright colours to funerals to celebrate the life of the loved one, but there were no celebrations for her. How could she celebrate a life cut so short? Black was the only thing that would reflect the grief, heartache and misery that had consumed her. At the sink in the shower room, she splashed water on her face; her skin did not feel the sensation. The mini bar in the bedroom caught her eye. She raced towards it in a hope of finding an anaesthetic for her pain. The miniature of whisky would do nicely. She downed it from the bottle. Still wincing from the after kick of the first whisky, she reached for another little bottle containing the soothing elixir. Down it went. The sharp edges of her pain slowly smoothed out a little. There was something she now had to do. After calling reception to organise a taxi for her, she headed downstairs to wait in the foyer.

The last time she had visited this market, she had been looking for a dress for her day out with Aslan, for his special birthday. The red dress she bought had made her feel youthful, a little bit sexy. It had become symbolic of her new Georgeless image.

A stall holder shouted, beckoning her over to look at his silver jewellery.

That's where I bought the bracelet for Aslan's birthday. He had liked it, I could tell.

Shaking her head at the man, she walked further into the heart of the market. Somewhere around the corner, she remembered seeing a stall that sold flowers. That was what she had come for.

'Could I have six of these lilies and six pink roses,' she said, pointing at the blooms which rested in buckets of water. 'And I'll take some of this.' A sprig of gypsophila sat next to the lilies. 'Could you arrange it into a small wreath for me?' she asked the vendor.

He nodded, handing all the flowers over to the woman beside him.

'You pay, then come back for wreath,' he said gruffly.

While she waited for her flowers to be arranged, she wandered around looking for a suitable card to buy. Shouts came from every stall as she passed, everyone desperately trying to earn a living.

An older woman served on a stall comprising everything from dream catchers to stainless steel pots and pans. A shoe box at the front of her table contained an assortment of cards. Lockhart began to rummage for something appropriate. Halfway through her search, she found the perfect card. On a white background, a magnificent lion had been delicately painted in the centre. Aslan was her lion, her precious, majestic lion.

The wreath had been packed in a cardboard box, when she returned to the stall to collect it. Lifting the lid slightly, she stole a peek in. It was perfect.

Chapter 75

Back in her hotel room, she took the pen from the bedside cabinet. It didn't take her long to think of what she would write in the card.

> *Vacant heart and hand and eye,*
> *Easy live and quiet die.*
> Lockhart xx

The words were taken from the Walter Scott poem that Aslan had *written* for her. The truth was, she wasn't sure of the poem's meaning, but somehow, it suited perfectly. Her heart was now vacant, as was her hand and eye. No longer would she touch his beautiful brown skin. Never again would she admire him from afar. The grief of his death was more powerful than the possibility of his betrayal; that hurt would be dealt with later. One hurt at a time.

Reception phoned to inform her that the taxi had arrived to take her to the cemetery. Zipping her black dress up to the nape, she then slipped on her black, stiletto shoes. She picked up the shoe box that held the wreath and the card depicting Aslan, the lion, and left the room.

The taxi drove across the countryside to a vast cemetery enclosed by cypress trees. They pulled up at the south gate, where Lockhart could see black clad mourners making their way to the service.

'Could you wait for me?' she asked the driver.

'Yes, cost more money.'

'That's okay. If you wait, I'll pay.'

Aslan's resting place was at the top of the hill, a beautiful spot with panoramic views all around, not that it would have mattered to him.

Lockhart's crippling shoes, coupled with the intense heat, made her last farewell to him even more difficult. In addition, the trees surrounding the cemetery offered no shade at the graveside.

When she reached the group of moaning sorrowers, she recognised Demir, which assured her that she was at the right funeral.

Demir stood next to an older woman. Within the woman's features, Lockhart could see Aslan's face. From this, she deduced it was his mother. Loud wailing came from a woman on Lockhart's left. It was obvious that the lady was completely heartbroken by the death of Aslan, as were many of the women that stood at his grave. Lockhart lifted her eyes from the ground, looking around the circle of people who had come to pay their respects. The small crowd was made up mainly of women in their fifties, weeping softly. She counted twelve lone, bereaved females.

After Aslan had been lowered into the ground, Demir brought the elderly lady forward to the sunken coffin. Her loud cries filled the air as she grabbed a handful of soil to throw over where her son lay below.

The wailing from the bereft women intensified when they witnessed this final act in the tragic story of Aslan Cerci.

Lockhart watched the mourners lay flowers with cards beside the grave. She took her pretty wreath from the box to lay as a tribute to her Aslan. There was a suitable space for it next to a single red rose. Lockhart could not avoid reading the words on the card resting with the rose. 'I will always love you, Aslan. You changed my life.' Rita xx

Lockhart wondered which of the bereft women was Rita.

Sweat dripped from her forehead on the walk back down the hill on her swollen feet. A woman in her late fifties, wearing, in Lockhart's opinion, an inappropriately short black dress, walked alongside her. As if to torture herself further, Lockhart asked, 'Were you a friend of Aslan's?'

In her London accent, she explained that they were due to be getting married after the summer holiday season.

'I met him five years ago at The Blue Lagoon, where he worked. I had gone on holiday with a friend after my husband passed away. The attraction between Aslan and I was instant. We've been together ever since. He comes to London to see me, or I fly out to The Blue Lagoon to be with him.'

The woman broke down sobbing. 'Why did this have to happen? I know that he drove too fast on his bike, but he knew that road so well.' Through her tears, she gave an ironic sigh. 'He used to tell me that he could drive that clifftop road with his eyes shut.'

Lockhart did something instinctively when she witnessed how vexed the woman was. She wrapped an arm around her shoulder, offering kind words of comfort.

'I can't live without him,' she whispered. 'He is the only man I have ever truly loved.'

At the foot of the hill, the driver stood against his cab awaiting her return. He moved to open the back door when he saw her leaving the gates of the cemetery.

Before climbing into the car, Lockhart felt a gentle tap on her shoulder.

'It is nice to see you, Lockhart!' Demir said, making a show of knowing her name.

'You remembered. Well done,' she complimented him.

'There is small reception at the vineyard if you would like to come,' he told her.

'No, thank you, Demir. I don't want to be around when all these ladies put two and two together.'

His English was not perfect, but he knew what she meant.

'Would it feel better if I said that you were different?'

'Thanks, but no,' she replied.

There was nothing that anyone could say to make things better.

He nodded his understanding of this situation, then kissed her on both cheeks before making his way back to the funeral procession.

Lockhart was booked on the evening flight back to Scotland. An overwhelming feeling of urgency to leave The Blue Lagoon came over her. She grabbed her things, paid the bill, and set off to the airport several hours too early. It was preferable, in her opinion, to sit among strangers than to be surrounded by reminders of her naivety. No wonder the staff sniggered when they saw her with Aslan. It had nothing to do with the age difference. It all came down to *choc fazla*; so many. There had been thirteen lone women, including her, at the funeral, but she wondered how many couldn't attend at such short notice.

Demir's words returned to her.

Would it feel better if I told you were different? Of course, it wouldn't.

When all those women discover they are one of many, they will all believe that they were different. None of them were different. They were all strung along and used as meal tickets, just like she was.

Several hours later, she boarded the flight, her mind still dissecting the revelations of the trip.

Wait a minute. What if I look at things from a different angle? Instead of Aslan being a Casanova, what if he was like a guardian angel to women like me who had reached rock bottom. What did he actually get from me financially? A jacket, shoes, a phone, and an airline ticket. Did he ask for these things? No. Did I enjoy giving them? Yes. What did I get from Aslan... my life back, my self-worth, a sexual awakening, and the strength to rise up from the rubble of a broken marriage. Who was the winner in this relationship? Definitely me. Would I pay out again for Aslan? Hell yes!

Lockhart could feel the pressure of the descent on her eardrums.

Nearly home.

The past year, for Lockhart, had been filled with sadness and joy in almost equal measure. A future with Aslan would never have worked, her clear-thinking head always knew that. But she gave him full credit for picking her up off the ground, brushing her down and setting her back on her feet. For that, she would always love him.

Unclicking her seatbelt, she reached for her bag from under the seat in front of her. She took her place in the aisle behind the long line of suntanned holidaymakers waiting for the doors to open.

Walking through the airport, she felt great sorrow for the love she thought she had. Thinking positively, she reminded herself that she had only ever spent a matter of weeks with Aslan. The majority of the relationship had been lived in her head.

When the electronic doors opened, she was faced with a most wonderful sight. It was Marnie, Bee and Elsie with their arms outstretched towards her. Running straight over to them, she accepted their embraces gratefully.

In the airport car park, Bee asked, 'Do you want to talk about it?'

'One day, I will tell you the whole story but it's too raw right now. I will keep it for Decanters.'

Elsie reached into her handbag. 'David Hill came into the shop looking for you. He has invited us to his daughter's wedding. That's two weddings we have now. Bartlett's is next week.'

Lockhart looked at Marnie. 'I almost forgot, Marnie, you will be leaving soon for Mull. I thought we could all book a cottage in October and come see you.'

Lockhart then turned to Bee, 'I was thinking about having an option for customers to book appointments online. Can you add this to the website?'

Bee laughed. 'No problem. By the way, Billy says hi.'

'Tell him I say hi back. Elsie, accept David Hill's invitation. That is a wedding I would really like to go to. Oh, and I will book us a nice hotel in London for Bartlett's wedding. We will make a jolly holiday out of it.'

She added this, knowing how much it would please Elsie.

'Now, about this wedding fair...'

Find out more about Marnie's life in Mull in the novel:

Summer Led to Autumn

Available from June 2024 on Amazon

Also by this author and available on Amazon:

Exitum: A Classic Disappearance